A SONG FOR
LONELY WOLVES

A Joseon Detective Novel

LEE EVIE

INTERSTICE
PRESS

Also by Lee Evie

Lee Evie has the following current and upcoming historical fiction titles set in old Korea.

Visit **www.leeevie.com** to learn more.

PROMISE SERIES:

Promise Season

Promise Thief

Promise Dream

JOSEON DETECTIVE SERIES

A Song for Lonely Wolves

An Ode to Hungry Ghosts

A Hymn of Soldiers Lost

VERSE NOVELS

Barley Fields: A Joseon Love story

For you

Author's Note

This novel is set during the Joseon dynasty of old Korea.

At this time there were women known as *damo*, indentured tea servants of Joseon's police bureau, who cooked and cleaned for their superiors. There is also evidence that *damo* were sometimes used for undercover operations or to question witnesses that normal police officers could not approach, due to the strict barriers placed between men and women in Joseon society.

PLEASE NOTE: This novel is written in British English, and some spellings may differ from those used in American English.

A SONG FOR
LONELY WOLVES

A Beginning

Joseon Korea, winter, 1590

THE DOOR SLAMS and outside we hear screaming, words barely audible. I keep my head low and concentrate on pouring tea as the minister's personal guard crouches by his side, whispering into his ear. I cannot hear the words but the minister's face changes, brows drawn tight. Hands clenched.

"The establishment is under attack," he spits abruptly, throwing his gambling sticks onto the pile of fine jewellery before him.

I say nothing, for it is not me the minister wishes to warn, but the man who sits opposite, his head shaved, wearing old worn clothes. That man, Poong Yi, is already on his feet, only stopping to gather the fine goods he was well on his way to losing, pushing jewelled hair ornaments and elaborate pins deep within his *hanbok* robes.

Such fine things for a lowborn man to gamble away so carelessly.

More shouts ring from the yard and the thick scent of smoke begins to fill the room. Something is burning.

Coughing, the men gather their belongings, the minister shouting orders at his bodyguard. I slide out of their way, kneeling with my side pressed against the wall, trying to remain invisible. Yet the man Poong Yi crouches to take my chin roughly in his hand, forcing me to meet his hard eyes.

"Girl! When the police come you say we left by the north gate, you hear me?"

His fingers dig painfully into my skin but I manage to nod. Poong Yi lets go and I cower on the floor at his feet, arms wrapped over my head protectively, quivering with fear and obedience in the dim candlelight.

The minister is already being pulled away through the inner door by his personal guard, not glancing my way once, lowly servant that I am. It is only the bald man that still hovers above me with one last look. But then the minister's guard shouts that the whole compound will soon be crawling with police officers and Poong Yi follows quickly after them. They disappear into the inner hallways of the compound.

I am alone.

It does not take long before the doors swing open again. Four big men, warriors with swords and wide leather belts, enter the room, bending low beneath the doorframe.

But they are not police officers.

They are Poong Yi's men. Mean-looking private soldiers and mercenaries employed to protect this place, to protect Poong Yi and the illegal business he conducts here.

Their bulk fills the tiny private gambling room and I push back hard against the wall, my shaking hands clasped over my mouth, my tea tray discarded at my side. I've seen them before, hanging around the inn, guarding important patrons who do not wish to be interrupted. The oldest of them scowls when he sees it is only me remaining, his mouth pulling tight.

"Where is the minister? Did he escape?" I am silent and he roars, "Answer me, girl!"

Flinching, I gesture wildly to the doors leading back outside into the courtyard. "They went north." My lips tremble and I begin to cry. "I overheard. They said they would escape through the north gate."

It is enough. The men move past as I push myself to my feet, back still pressed against the wall. As the last and youngest of the men comes near, I dart my hand out to take a hard hold of his arm, slowing him. Swiping the tears from my cheeks, I reach high to press my mouth close beside his ear. "Man Seok, they've gone to the south gate. I heard talk of a boat waiting at the river for the minister."

"And the other one?" Man Seok breathes. "Poong Yi?"

"Still with them. Not for much longer. He'll run."

He nods curtly, then hesitates. "Someone must open the main gates."

Shouts echo from beyond the room, the other guards swearing at him to hurry. I point at my chest to indicate I will do it. Man Seok doesn't look pleased, jaw tightening and hands clenching, but he says nothing. Within moments he is gone and I am left alone, candlelight flickering wildly across the walls, yellow against the black.

My hands move quickly, well-practised under pressure. The inside door was hurriedly bolted; the scene of the gambling exchange left untouched, flat cushions still strewn across the floor, gambling sticks lying discarded in piles. I take only one remaining treasure that the criminal Poong Yi has missed, half hidden beneath a mat. A string of jewels unlike any I have seen before, opaque and shimmering in the darkness.

With both doors bolted shut from the inside, I step onto a low cabinet and launch myself high to reach a tiny window, slamming against the shutters to squeeze my body through the narrow space. I vault head first out into the cold night. My hands hit the wooden *maru* terrace outside and I curl my body into a roll, taking the brunt of my fall on my right shoulder, twisting until I am standing again. Only my long skirts cause me to falter.

The frost of deep night burns my skin, cutting through the thin maidservant uniform I wear as if it was not there at all. I have only my indoor slippers but leap into a run across the stony courtyard anyway, melting into the shadows clinging against thick stone walls and overhanging bare winter branches. No moon shines tonight, only low clouds heavy with snow, frost biting at my bare hands. Beyond the courtyard the front gates of the inn are ablaze with light; the burning torches within small and paltry compared to the flames that lick the outer walls. The police must be burning the storage sheds beyond the gates, trying to force their way inside.

There is nowhere to hide; the entire entrance courtyard is awash in yellow light. Men scurry across the open space, their footsteps burning pathways in the slushed snow. Bracing the heavy courtyard doors with their broad bodies, they check that the iron bolts are secure. Beyond the main gates rages the sounds of battle, metal ringing through the cold air, men screaming and shouting.

Dying.

Poong Yi's men are out there, I know, defending the compound, fighting off the police officers, holding them back—giving Poong Yi the time he needs to escape. With the gates at their back, the guards of this place have a defendable position, two men with bows above, the police outside funnelled close together by the road and wildwood.

Even so Poong Yi's men will not last long against the full might of the Kingdom's police and military—just long enough to help their leader escape. And the minister too, the nobleman Poong Yi is bribing.

There is no time left to hesitate. Man Seok said the gates must open, and so they will open.

Breathing on my stiff fingers, I step from the shadows, walk calmly across the stony courtyard straight to the gate, running my hand over the bolt. A man runs past, a warrior holding a wide heavy sword. He does not stop. Does not even glance at me.

He will though. The moment I move the heavy latch they all will. I lean away from the door, my fingers still exploring the lock, arching my back as I peer into the darkness at the bowmen above. Only one of them now, the other must be dead, hit by an arrow from outside.

Another guard runs desperately by, veering close. I ignore him, ignore the shouts ringing from behind the bolted gates. It must be done now. I lean against the door and begin to scream hysterically, pointing back toward the nearest building. My legs give way, sliding heavily toward the ground, only for my elbow to be caught by one of the passing guards, his face alive with panic.

"I saw police officers," I babble at him, tears streaming. "Up there, on the roof! They're already inside! Do something! *Do* something!"

He leaves me sobbing against the gates, three nearby men joining him to storm the places my pointed finger has led them.

Nowhere.

The moment they reach the building and disappear into its depths I twist back toward the gate, leaving my cheeks wet as I work. The first bolt slides easily but the second is stiff and I must push my whole weight against it. It barely moves.

A shout from behind me. A man's voice, gruff and commanding of my attention. I ignore him until he says my name.

"Dan Ji *ssi?*"

I turn slowly. It is a man I know, a man I have seen many times before working within the compound, one of the guards here. He is much older than I, much bigger too, his sword sharp and gleaming in the torchlight.

"What are you doing? It's dangerous here. The soldiers are outside. You can't open…" He trails off into silence as his expression changes, light dawning in his eyes.

He hesitates a long time before advancing, before lifting his sword. And I hesitate too, staring back at him, slowly shaking my head. I know him. But the guard advances anyway, pushing loose black hair from shining skin. I turn back to the bolt desperately, numb fingers scrambling to loosen it, to drag it open. The gates beneath my hands are thumping now, something slamming heavily into the wood from the other side.

The bolt moves just as the guard lunges. His sword slashes through the air, hitting nothing but the gates themselves as they open, pushed from the other side. I twist to avoid being crushed by the heavy swinging doors, three men bursting through the open space, two of them dressed in police uniforms and the last, a criminal fighting for his life. The police officers are quick and efficient. The criminal dies loudly and savagely just as the guard's hand closes over my collarbone, fingers digging into bone as he manoeuvres his sword in the confined space behind the moving gate. He knows me. Yet he will kill me. My back slams hard against the stone wall and I fight the wail that rises on my lips for he will impale me, gleaming metal breaking skin and bone. Instead his life-blood sprays across my face, an errant arrowhead emerging through the soft flesh of his throat, shocking us both. The tip is visible through the parted skin, awash in wet red.

The man's mouth widens and our gazes lock for a heavy thick moment before he falls, both of us in shared surprise, both of us expecting a different ending to our struggle. He is dead before he hits the ground.

The battle has spilled into the torch-lit courtyard now, arrows flying haphazardly, chaos and screaming and fire all around. I huddle behind the heavy gates with the dead man, dirty snow seeping wet into his clothes as more and more police officers plunge through the opening I have made for them.

Taking one last look at the body huddled at my feet, I wipe his blood from my face. It smears across my skin as I breathe heavily, chest heaving. I cannot remember his name. But I knew him. No one special. No one in particular. Just a guard. And now a wayward arrow misfired has saved my life and ended his. But I remember a moment in the depth of winter, sitting on the terrace wrapped warmly against the snow, this man offering me a ginger taffee he bought for his own young daughter.

A kindness.

I stare down at him. And then I slide quietly from behind the thick doors and leave him behind, creeping alongside the stone walls and scanning the warring men who fight bloody across the stony ground. There is no way out of the compound now, police officers stopping everyone they see, maidservants and guards, not letting anyone through. They will not listen if I try to explain. I slip into the shadows and climb up toward the battlement. It is empty now of archers, both of them lying huddled and lifeless in the darkness, shadows of hollow flesh. I climb over one body to the railing, peering down carefully onto the road outside, scanning the men who mill beyond the gates.

At the back, an older man sits tall on a war horse, beard wiry and streaked with grey, plumes of long feathers bound to his wide-brimmed hat. A swinging string of heavy beads hangs from the brim, affixed above each ear.

I watch, calculating and assessing.

Man Seok will follow Poong Yi and the minister to the river. Yet he is only one man.

It will not be enough.

I glance at the buildings behind me, watch as the fighting ebbs and the police officers herd prisoners into the courtyard, forcing them to kneel grouped together in the cold. I look back at the man in uniform, sitting straight and imposing on his war horse. He is the man I must speak with, the man who has authorised this raid. And he is the one who must authorise reinforcements to be sent to the river to find the minister and to stop Poong Yi from disappearing into the night.

To cut the head off the snake.

Man Seok cannot arrest these criminals on his own.

I take a deep breath and climb over the railing, into the blackness below.

2

The Request

I STAND before the grand desk in silence, my head bowed. Imposing shelves rise against the walls, filled to the brim with manuals and scrolls. The heavy office doors remain closed tight, the room dim with only muted sunlight filtering through a latticed window.

Man Seok stands beside me, in uniform, as am I. He's dressed only as a minor police lieutenant since his recent demotion. Mine is the uniform of a *damo*, a lowly government office servant, expected to serve tea and whatever else my superiors might request. Together, we wait unmoving, all outward patience and jittery nerves as the police chief sits before us, assessing with narrowed eyes. He is flanked by a secretary, a younger man with a shrewd cold expression, who acts as an official office scribe.

The silence deepens, filling the room. Tension rises, filling my body.

I do not know why we are here.

It has been many days since the raid, quiet slow days spent inside the *podocheong*, the police bureau. I have given my statements, I have provided the evidence of corruption

I gathered at the gambling compound, and passed over the string of shimmering jewels left behind by the criminal, Poong Yi. And Poong Yi himself, he will never run an illegal organisation like it again; he is long gone.

Wiped from this earth.

The silence draws out, almost stifling, and I steal a glance at Man Seok beside me. He looks different now, clean shaven and young with his hair pulled high into a topknot beneath the brim of his uniform hat. His face is impassive. If the silent presence of the police chief makes him nervous, he does not show it. And if he is angered by his sudden demotion, it is hidden just as deep. But I am used to it now, the way his expression never changes. Man Seok never speaks unless there's something to say. Silence does not make him uncomfortable. Silence is his natural state.

I peer back down at the floor, clearly alone in my fear of this meeting, unable to understand why a great man like the police chief would call someone as lowly as myself into his private offices. It's true that Man Seok and I were instrumental in gathering intelligence against this recent case of deep corruption. Without our actions on the night of the raid, that criminal organisation would still be skimming goods from the people's tax tributes. They would still be selling them and bribing officials to turn a blind eye.

And the criminal Poong Yi would still be alive.

I shift uncomfortably from foot to foot. I do not believe we've been summoned here for thanks. The room is too cold, the silence too long.

The secretary clears his throat loudly and I startle. Have I done something wrong? Or has Man Seok? Perhaps his demotion is only the first of many punishments he'll receive for his transgression during the raid. The way our two superiors stare prickles my skin despite the deep chill of winter.

Finally, the police chief speaks. "State your names."

"Damo Dan Ji, *Yeonggam*," I say, addressing him respectfully.

He raises his brows at Man Seok.

"Lieutenant Jo Man Seok, *Yeonggam*."

"And how long were you each embedded at the gambling establishment prior to the night of the raid?"

I hesitate, expecting Man Seok to answer, for he outranks me.

He does not.

Finally, I say, "One year and one month, *Yeonggam*."

Man Seok clears his throat and answers in his quiet slow way. "I was there six months, *Yeonggam*."

The police chief considers us carefully.

"And are you well rested since returning to the offices?"

I am not sure what to make of that, glancing once again at Man Seok, whose expression only remains the same. Finally, I venture, "*Yeonggam*?"

The police chief exhales slowly. "It seems we have need of your services again. There is a district magistrate in a county far to the north. He has requested assistance from the capital with a rather … complex case. After careful consideration, I have recommended you both. I trust you will be capable of aiding this regional magistrate in solving his particular problem."

The police chief gestures impatiently at his secretary, and the younger man departs the room briefly, leaving us in uncomfortable silence. When the doors swing open again the secretary ushers in another *damo*, dressed in the same uniform as me, her gaze lowered to the ground.

"This is Damo Choon Shim, she will accompany you both to the north, reporting directly to Lieutenant Jo."

I peer across at Choon Shim but she does not look back at me. Her hair is smoothed from her face, tight and neat, but her expression has a softness to it, round and sweet despite her down-turned mouth.

I am unable to hold my questions back, though it should be Man Seok who asks them. Yet I cannot rely on him to fulfil my curiosity, as he has none of his own.

"*Yeonggam*," I venture. "Two *damo* have been requested for this case?"

The secretary is affronted by my audacity, speaking without being spoken to, yet the police chief holds up his hand to silence the younger man before he can berate me.

"Indeed, the magistrate has need of two *damo*. One for undercover work," he motions toward Choon Shim, "and the other to aid in the investigation, to question the people that his own men cannot."

I nod, satisfied. A delicate balance exists within this world, so it's not always possible for men to directly question noble daughters or even lowly women. I can pass through doorways that men cannot. I glance back at Choon Shim.

Her role in this, however, is still shrouded in mystery.

"The magistrate has no *damo* of his own? At his office in the north?" I ask my question boldly, for when I find a thread I must pull it, always I must pull it.

Once again, the secretary narrows his eyes but the police chief silences him. "The magistrate did," he says. "But no more."

No further explanation is given and a thick heavy silence slowly fills the room. I am forced to push down my curiosity, and turn my mind to my next question, asking quietly, "*Yeonggam*, this case, what does it involve that the magistrate has sent for aid from the capital?"

The police chief ignores me. "Lieutenant Jo, do you not have any questions? Only this *damo* speaks for you?"

Man Seok's face does not change. "No, sir," he says. "I have no questions at this time."

I curl my lip, annoyed, but the police chief only says, "I see."

His gaze runs over Man Seok's hard blank face and new minor lieutenant uniform, assessing and calculating. Finally, his eyes seem to rest on the younger man's hands, which tightly clutch a thin lacquered sword scabbard, his skin scarred and knuckles scabbed. Man Seok is no stranger to violence. And it shows across his marred skin. The police chief's brows draw close together, with … disapproval? Disgust? I cannot say.

The moment passes and still the police chief says nothing, finally waving a hand at his secretary, who quickly steps forward to take over the briefing.

"This should not be a difficult case," the secretary informs us. "Yet it is a delicate one. A young woman has disappeared from her village home. There is great pressure on the district magistrate to recover her quickly."

The police chief clears his throat. "The girl is the daughter of a nobleman with connections to the royal family."

"Correct, sir," agrees the secretary. "The nobleman's uncle was a close friend of the prince when they were younger, and he has called in a favour, asking this situation to be resolved quickly."

I push my luck. "Which prince?"

The secretary's lips tighten. "*Which* prince does not matter, *damo*. That the royal family is involved at all should be your main concern." He does not like me; it is clear. He believes I do not know my place.

Perhaps he is right.

"The royal family has a vested interest in the outcome of this case." The secretary looks at us pointedly, and I understand this to mean that pressure directly from the royal family is being applied not only to the district magistrate, but to the entire *podocheong*.

A knock raps on the door and an older officer enters. It is like a candle being snuffed out; the police chief's attention shifts from us completely and we are dismissed without another glance—albeit for the secretary taking a further few moments to brief us on travel arrangements before we are hurriedly ushered away.

Emerging outside into the wide-open courtyard, I stand blinking in the pale sunlight, wrapping my arms around my body to combat the sharp wind. The yards are busy; police officers' bustle about their business, weaving in and out of the official buildings lining the wide stark courtyard. Man Seok stands beside me, arms crossed. Nothing in his expression sheds light on what he thinks of our assignment.

"It could not be so very important," Choon Shim says suddenly, reminding me she is there.

She is a little taller than me, her body shapely yet strong beneath her uniform. I frown at her. "What do you mean?"

She hesitates, glancing up at Man Seok, eyes darting to his face and then away. I realise she is afraid of him. And perhaps she is right to be. Yet because she does not wish to speak while he is here, I grow impatient.

"What do you mean?"

"Well, the police chief … he said there is pressure to close the case, yet they do not send their senior investigators. They send only a minor lieutenant and two *damo*. Is that not … strange?"

I shrug. "The pressure is only from a slight connection

in youth to the royal family. It's not as if the missing girl or her uncle are direct relatives of the prince."

"True…" Yet Choon Shim does not seem satisfied. "But surely if the girl cannot be located it means the district magistrate will lose his position. It means the stakes are high."

"For the district magistrate, perhaps," I mutter. "I doubt the police chief will care what happens. Sending us is simply a formality. Whether we recover the missing girl or not."

I turn to Man Seok for his opinion and he nods in quiet agreement. "It is simply a regional matter. The news of it will not travel."

Choon Shim raises her brows. "Not travel … sir?" I notice she does not meet Man Seok's eye.

"It means there will be no public dissent here in the capital," I explain. "Even if the case is not resolved, so the worst possible outcome is the district magistrate being demoted. Even with pressure from the royal family, it will make no difference to the police chief."

"I see … It is why he only bothers to send us." Choon Shim bites her lip. "I feel sorry for the girl."

"Why?" I ask, my tone sharper than I mean it to be. "Because it is only us being sent to help her?"

Choon Shim tilts her head to the side, assessing me. Finally, she smiles. "I've heard about you, Damo Dan Ji." She leans close to whisper. "The other girls call you the battle axe."

I cough. "They call me what?" I am offended.

"Because of your temper."

Choon Shim begins to walk across the courtyard and I hesitate a moment before following her, still annoyed. When I glance back there is something different about Man Seok's face, as if he might smile if he knew how.

When I reach her side, Choon Shim chimes a low laugh, as if to soften her words. "Dan Ji, it is a compliment. You are the battle axe who never backs down. All the girls know about the taxation corruption case." She shrugs. "I haven't done work like you. I stay here in the office mostly, doing chores."

I nod. Although *damo* can be used for undercover operations or for questioning women, it is not a regular assignment. Essentially, we are only lowly servants. We cook and clean and bring the high-ranking officials their tea and meals. We do as we are asked. It is the kind of life I've lived until I made something more for myself—until it became clear I could be relied on during real cases. That I would not break or bend.

I will never go back to how it was.

I peer at Choon Shim closely, wondering if she feels the same.

"And when you are not here in the offices?" I ask her. "What do you do?"

Choon Shim makes a list on her fingers. "I questioned a noblewoman about a family dispute she witnessed. I eavesdropped at a *gibang* entertainment house while a murder suspect visited his favourite *gisaeng* there. And I investigated adultery charges … three times."

She looks at me, as if waiting for my approval. Her eyes shine and I do not know what to say. I blink. "That is … very good."

Choon Shim beams. I have said the right thing.

The three of us walk slowly toward the men's and women's quarters where we are housed—Man Seok trailing behind, our footsteps crunching across the stony yard. The sunlight is waning, the air turning crisper and cooler by the moment. When we reach the high stone wall

Choon Shim speaks again, louder now, braver. I wonder if perhaps she has forgotten Man Seok is still here.

"Damo Dan Ji, what do you think about this missing girl? Could she have been kidnapped?"

Already I can feel myself reaching for the answers, pulling at the threads, trying to discover the truth behind this new case.

It is how I felt when I was first embedded at the gambling inn, when I first realised my assignment was not a petty illegal merchant ring; it went far deeper, reaching into political corruption and bribery.

And now again I am curious, already it chafes at my mind to understand more.

We stop outside the gated building of the *damo* quarters, and I turn back to face Man Seok. "How long do you suspect the girl has been missing?"

I wait while he calculates how long it might have taken for a message to arrive at the capital requesting our aid. Man Seok has travelled far more widely than I.

"At least half a moon," he says eventually. He is grim now, gripping his sword in one hand, the other tucked behind his back. "More by the time we arrive into the magistrate's county. That village lies deep within the mountains. Far to the north."

I nod, turning back to Choon Shim.

"Whether she has been kidnapped or not, after so long I think we must prepare ourselves to find a body."

Choon Shim is taken aback, but I prefer she does not operate under false assumptions.

A buried body is much easier to hide than a living breathing girl. It does not take a royal investigator to understand that much.

3

An Arrival

THE MOUNTAINS RISE higher and higher. They close in around us, peaks lost in heavy mist. I crane my neck to peer at their disappearing slopes, the sky above close and thick with cloud.

As the winding road draws nearer our destination, the barren winter woods recede. Farmland emerges along the foothills, low fields painstakingly carved into sloping ridges, their edges crowded with thick spindly trees. Small thatched-roofed dwellings dot the sharp rises, trails of thin smoke rising high into the sky.

The valley is deep and long, and we ride onwards on pack horses, the snowy peaks drawing closer and closer. Here in the mountains the air smells like rain.

At the edge of the village we are greeted by a cluster of spindly wooden totems. Tall wooden deities carved from pine trees.

Jangseung. Each has a human face. Their fierce eyes follow us as we pass the boundary they protect, the spaces between the outside world of demons and the small clustered village they keep safe.

The community is larger than I expect, sprawling across the rolling hills along the length of the far-reaching mountain valley. The dwellings cluster closer together the further toward the main streets we venture. Here, the thick smell of cooking meat and steaming tea fills the spaces between a chaotic mass of market stalls. A small rundown inn spills wooden stools and platforms across the road. A few peasant commoner men already drinking bowls of cloudy white liquor, peer up at us with red flushed cheeks as we ride pass.

We are without our uniforms, wrapped tightly in worn commoner clothes instead, threadbare and frayed. Man Seok rides with his gaze fixed ahead, never wavering at the scents and sights of the bustling streets. Choon Shim is less disciplined, taken by the smell of simmering stew, the frying wheat-flour cakes on a wide black pan hissing thick steam into freezing winter skies. We pass baskets of salted fish and my attention lingers on soft rice cakes, coloured green and white and laid out in small towers on a merchant's table.

The market bustles with peddlers laying out their wares —rolls of hemp fabric and rabbit pelts, even mulberry paper and calligraphy brushes. Soft flower scents waft from a stall selling women's accoutrements. I turn back as that merchant calls out his wares: camellia oil and ribbon, carved wooden combs, and soft winter hats stitched with black silk lined with rabbit fur.

Beautiful things.

Man Seok catches my lingering look and I turn forward again quickly.

Beautiful things not meant for a *damo* like me.

The horses provided by the police chief have lent us speed, and we arrive days ahead of schedule to this isolated place. Despite our appearance as outsiders, the people on the streets do not pay us much attention, as if used to outside interference. I imagine they get many traders here, a centre of commerce between the wild sea and the main road from the mountains back toward Joseon's capital city of Hanseong.

Beyond the marketplace we ride through a maze of low slung *hanok* houses, small dwellings with curving thatched rooves of plaited rice straw. Wooden *maru* terraces rise from yards of dirt and mud, and chickens squawk beneath stiff woven cages. The sound draws a child outside. Stepping onto the road, he stares at us, his feet sinking deep into the black mud. Like Choon Shim and myself, he has a roughly woven cloth wrapped around the top of his head, secured beneath his chin for warmth. Unlike us, his face is smeared with dirt.

Choon Shim smiles at him but he does not smile back.

It is late in the day when we reach the high gates of the government office. The sun slants through the bare trees, the sky already a dusky blue. Here in the deep mountains the days are short. The peaks block the setting sun and it grows dark all at once; one moment we are bathed in weak light and the next it is as if a shadow has fallen across the whole valley, the air growing chill and sharp.

Guards wait outside the office gates on night watch, flickering torches flaring from brackets fixed to the entrance way. Man Seok agilely lowers himself from his saddle to speak with the guards. I do the same, only much slower and more awkwardly, my body stiff and sore from our long journey. My feet sink into the black wet ground, moisture soaking into my white *beoseon*, the socks beneath my travelling shoes. Clutching the reigns of my weary horse, I stand waiting as Man Seok calmly explains who we are, watching as one guard disappears inside the gates.

Choon Shim hovers by my side, looking much how I

feel, dark shadows beneath her eyes with her long, braided hair hanging limp and undone about her face. It seems she will drop where she stands. I place one hand upon her shoulder and squeeze reassuringly, though the truth reveals a different story. I also have never been so far from home.

Soon enough, Man Seok gestures for us to follow him inside. We enter the inner courtyard, a wide space not unlike the *podocheong* offices back in Hanseong, only in miniature. And in this place a forest of evergreen pine and bare-branched hawthorn rises like a wall beyond the stone enclosure, black and filled with shadows of deep night. Strange sounds creep between the trees. Harsh bird calls. Snapping branches. And I am sure, the soft distant howl of wolves.

Our horses are taken away by the guard and all three of us are ushered into the main long building that sits in the centre of this outer courtyard. This is the magistrate's quarters, an open *maru* terrace in the middle, his private room to the right and office to the left. Despite my exhaustion I am aware enough to feel pleased when Choon Shim and I are not immediately dismissed from this initial meeting. And even more pleased when we enter the magistrate's office to find steaming bowls of hot tea, rice, and *jiggae* stew laid waiting on the long wooden table, lit with flickering candles. Even a few small side dishes of brightly coloured fermented vegetable have been placed around the three settings.

The magistrate himself stands to greet us, attention only on Man Seok whom he addresses as Lieutenant Jo. He explains how appreciative he is of our fast arrival, how hopeful he is that we can help him. The words leave him in one fast flush of air, and then he stands deflated, hands gripping the back of a chair as if the wooden frame will keep his wiry body from the floor. He gestures uncertainly at Man Seok.

"Please, Lieutenant Jo. Sit."

Choon Shim and I immediately drop to our knees in front of the low table and begin to ravenously eat. I glance at Man Seok between spoonfuls of thick boiling *jiggae* but he remains sitting straight-backed, as if the meal laid before him is not at all tempting. Right now, Lieutenant Jo Man Seok is no weary traveller, he is an investigator sent by the capital to resolve this magistrate's problem. I can almost see the weight of it settling across his shoulders, though his expression never changes.

Despite what he did at the end of our last case, despite the quiet whispers that now follow him wherever he goes, and the demotion he received for that one act of brutality, I realise Man Seok is still a man of the *podocheong*, through and through. And he will represent the police bureau as he should.

As I eat, I discreetly scan the deep creases in the magistrate's cheeks by the flame light, the scraggly grey beard and thin hands. He resolutely ignores Choon Shim and I, so my attention is free to roam the bright loose layers of his office uniform, material dyed blood red and sun yellow. His hair is bound high into a tight grey topknot and a wide black *manggeon* band is strapped across his forehead. A quick glance around the near empty room finds his large uniform hat on a side table, carefully placed to protect the long bright feathers that adorn it.

My attention flicks back to the magistrate as I lift a cup of tea to my lips.

This man looks old, worn out and tired.

I want to ask how long he has held this office, if it was a position hard fought for or something he had yearned for, which now threatens to slip between his fingers all because of one missing girl.

But I do not.

The heavy worry etched into his creased brow fills me with pity, for I am sure the girl must be dead. There will be no happy ending here.

Despite the heated floor beneath me and the warm *jiggae* in my belly, the room remains cold.

"I am grateful you have arrived so quickly," the magistrate is saying to Man Seok. Despite Lieutenant Jo's lower ranking, the magistrate still treats him with respect, like a saviour. Perhaps because the whispers surrounding Man Seok have not yet breached the walls of Hanseong, or perhaps because the older man is very lost. He may still lose his job over this case, and if the missing girl's family is really as connected as they say, the magistrate may suffer even worse—exile to some forgotten part of Joseon perhaps, serving out the rest of his days in utter disgrace.

Or death.

Depending on how far this goes. Or how incompetent they decide he's been.

Again, that surge of pity in my belly. I shake it off, uncertain why it should matter what happens to this old man who sits before me, this man who steadfastly ignores me.

"Magistrate Hong." Man Seok clears his throat, candlelight flickering across his skin. "Please tell us the series of events in order, so we can fully understand your situation."

"Of course, of course." The magistrate straightens, running a hand across his brow. "Please eat, I will tell you as you eat. Please, Lieutenant Jo. Eat."

It is only now that Man Seok finally relents, taking the hot tea into his hands to warm his fingers. Only now that I have already scooped my bowl clean. I look at the empty side dishes, glancing at Choon Shim though she does not notice my guilt, her face still bent low to her bowl.

"It began at the dawn of winter." The magistrate's deep voice draws my attention. "Lord Song is a local nobleman. He reported his daughter had gone missing overnight. He came here in the morning to request our hel—"

"Were any of her belongings missing?"

Magistrate Hong gapes at my interruption. He turns to Man Seok expectantly, awaiting a reprimand, yet Man Seok says nothing, only continues to eat.

The magistrate clears his throat awkwardly, gritting his teeth, gaze locked on Man Seok's face. "I am not certain. Lord Song did not clarify whether anything was..."

"She disappeared alone then?" I bite my lip. "No one heard anything? No witnesses?"

Choon Shim watches me, her eyes shining. But I do not care if she is thinking again about the battle axe. I know how to do my job. It is why I no longer have to attend to the officers; no longer must I bring tea and meals at their beck and call.

Now I am … *more*.

The magistrate draws a deep calming breath. "Lieutenant Jo, I expect you will agree it is time for these *damo* to retire for the evening. I will have one of my men escort…"

"They may stay."

Magistrate Hong shakes his head uncertainly. "Lieutenant Jo?"

"We have come to help you resolve this complex issue, Magistrate Hong, before it is your career and your head that must face the consequences." Man Seok's dark eyes are hard and flat. "Do you not wish to accept our aid?"

The magistrate flinches at Man Seok's blunt words, for he is not yet used to the younger man's direct ways. I do not mean to smile quite so widely when the magistrate finally nods in stunned defeat. Quickly, I wipe the curl from my lips and turn my expression back to stone.

Man Seok gestures for me to continue but I say nothing, still waiting for the magistrate to answer my questions.

He does eventually, though it is still Lieutenant Jo that he addresses, not me, despite it now being clear he is no longer sure he likes the younger man quite as much as he did before.

"No witnesses," the magistrate admits. "Yet it was difficult to interview the servants within Lord Song's estate. He would not allow us to take statements from them; my men could only speak with selected servants in Lord Song's presence."

Interesting.

I lean closer across the table. "Lord Song requested you locate his missing daughter, yet did not allow you to speak to any potential witnesses? And did not tell you whether the girl had taken belongings with her, as if planning a journey, or if her room was askew, as if there had been a struggle?"

Slowly the magistrate nods, overwhelmed and blinking rapidly.

"And do you have any theories, Magistrate Hong?" I press. "Or any suspects?"

The magistrate clenches his fists on the table, though this time I suspect his anger is not directed at me. "No, I am blocked at every turn. Lord Song asks me to find his daughter, yet he forbade the people in the valley to speak with me, threatening those who live on his land with higher tributes and taxes if they do. Lord Song owns much of the land here in this valley. Many of the people who farm it or trade here belong to him. He owns much of the market as well. He is very powerful, very influential, and he is making it very difficult for us to investigate anything."

I tilt my head, thoughtful. "Yet he has ordered you to find his daughter urgently?"

Magistrate Hong's attention flicks back to me, uncertain whether he should answer. "Indeed … he … he urges me to send men into the mountains to search for the girl. He asked me to request more men from the capital, for larger search parties. And he applies pressure on our offices to find her, pressure all the way from the capital, yet he will answer none of my questions and forbids the people beneath him to aid in the investigation."

"Strange," says Man Seok quietly.

"Yes, Lieutenant Jo, strange indeed. I cannot understand what he wants from me."

"How old is Lord Song's daughter?" I ask.

"She is of sixteen years."

I nod. Not so very different than I. "But is not yet married?"

"No … She was soon to be married to a powerful clan from a nearby province."

I press further. "And what does her family hope to gain from such a union?"

The magistrate pauses, assessing me again. "I … I have heard the marriage will secure a better trade route from the ocean for Lord Song, an alliance that will make him a very rich man." Magistrate Hong corrects himself. "An even richer man than he currently is."

"What is her name?"

We all turn to Choon Shim, quiet as she has been. She seems small and young sitting at the end of the table, her face blurred by shadow.

"Song Seorim," answers the magistrate finally. "Her name is Song Seorim."

Heavy silence hangs within the room as I taste the girl's name on my tongue, as I begin to picture her as a person instead of a story. I rub my chilled hands together to warm them.

"Magistrate Hong," I say. "The police chief told us you specifically requested us as *damo*, is that true?"

He clears his throat. "Yes. It's true I did." He glances from me to Choon Shim and then back again. "I requested two."

We wait expectantly and I notice the way he sweats despite the cool air, despite the cold inside his room. He curls his fingers into fists again.

Something is wrong.

"I need one of you to help me question the villagers," he says. "So they will not know they are being questioned. I need you to visit the *gisaeng* house and find out what rumours have sprung up since the young woman's disappearance."

"And the other *damo*?" It is Man Seok who asks this. He sits back, arms folded across his chest and face falling into shadow.

"The other must gain work at the Song residence, as a servant."

"At Lord Song's house?" I turn to Choon Shim. Her cheeks are ashen.

"Yes. Heavily armed guards stand at his gates both day and night."

"Is that unusual?"

"Of course. This village is safe. There is no need. It used to only be one man, a gatekeeper. But now ... Lord Song hired new guards, private soldiers. I must know why."

I bite my lip. "With one of us inside, we will also have

the opportunity to discreetly question Lord Song's servants about the night his daughter disappeared."

Magistrate Hong nods, clearly relieved I am not fighting him. Yet I am still not quite ready to let him off completely.

"The chief of police said there were *damo* here before, yet now there are none." I pause, staring at him steadily. "Where did your *damo* go, Magistrate Hong?"

Man Seok shifts his position, waiting, but saying nothing.

The magistrate wipes one hand across his damp forehead, touching his scraggly grey beard, twisting it between his fingers. "Yes. We had one *damo* here."

"What happened to her?" Choon Shim's small voice shakes.

"I placed her within Lord Song's household six days after Song Seorim's disappearance. When I first realised that Lord Song was blocking my investigation. I was ... furious, and she had recently been sent to my office from a nearby town, a girl no one in the valley knew, just newly arrived. I sent her to work for Lord Song, and at first, she reported back as arranged. Every day without fail."

He stops speaking.

"Until...?" I prompt.

"Until she stopped." Magistrate Hong will not meet my gaze. "My men no longer heard from her. No one could find her. No one could find anyone who had spoken to her. Like Lord Song's daughter, she simply ... disappeared."

Preparation

"IT IS MUCH TOO DANGEROUS," I say. "You shouldn't go."

"Yet, *you* will? The police chief assigned this task to me!"

"Choon Shim! It doesn't matter which of us enters Lord Song's house, as long as one of us does."

"Then it should be me. You know it's true. It's *my* task. It was assigned to *me*." Choon Shim will not be moved.

We sit huddled together in the tiny room we've been assigned, tucked away at the very back of the government office compound. Only one stone wall separates our quarters from the black trees beyond. A long drawn out howl breaks the silent night, as if the wolves are calling to each other, as if they are moving closer—as if the forest will spill into our courtyard and swallow us up.

"I saw you at dinner," I say quietly, ignoring the creeping forest sounds. "You were afraid."

Choon Shim shakes her head, only a murky shadow within our dark room. "I was not."

"You are right to be afraid. This is dangerous." I lean

forward to grasp her hands in the darkness. "I have more experience than you, let me do this."

Choon Shim yanks her hands from my grip, and I know immediately I've made a mistake.

"You are so sure I will fail," she hisses. "Dan Ji the battle axe, ready to do anything if it gets you some recognition!"

Her words sting, and I sink back, wounded.

Silence fills the room.

"You know that is not true."

Choon Shim says nothing.

"We are friends, aren't we?" I whisper. The long nights on the road had felt like friendship, playing rhyming games in the darkness, laughter to keep me warm against the freezing wind. Singing and wordplay as Man Seok watched quietly from across the flickering fire. "Friends look out for friends."

"I hardly know you," Choon Shim says, and I slide further from her and her harsh words in the darkness. I stand to pull my bedding out of the wardrobe, throwing hers to her a little harder than I mean to.

I lower myself onto the blanket, pulling it high around my shoulders. And we are quiet, the night deepening around us. It is late now, well past midnight.

Eventually, I hear Choon Shim slide closer, her bedroll stirring.

"I am sorry, *Unni*," she says, calling me older sister for the first time.

I roll away, placing my back to her.

"*Unni*, I just ... I need to prove I can do this."

I am silent a long time. "Why?"

"Because no one ever believed I could."

I turn slightly, yet it is too dark to see her face, no

starlight seeps through our shutters. We are closed in and alone. "Who? Who didn't believe?"

Choon Shim doesn't answer my question. "Let me do this, *Unni*."

I pull myself until I'm seated, shivering against the cold. "Are you sure it's what you want? Pretending to be someone else?"

Her outline nods.

"It's not easy, Choon Shim. I mean to say … it's not that I don't believe you can do it, it's only … during the corruption case I was surrounded by people the whole time, but every moment is unreal. Do you understand?"

Choon Shim says nothing.

"Every interaction is fabricated, filled with lies. At times it was … difficult. To remember who I was. Like losing yourself."

I think of laughter in the snow, a ginger taffee freely given by a man who loves his daughter, a man who tried to kill me but was killed in turn. Blood on the snow. Senseless. None of it was real. In that place only Man Seok was real.

Or perhaps everyone around us was real, and it was only Man Seok and I who were not. We were the ones pretending.

"I do not know how to explain," I breathe.

Choon Shim shifts in the darkness, her body stretching beneath her blanket, settling beside me. "I can handle this, *Unni*."

She does not understand what I try to tell her.

I hesitate a very long time.

"If you do this, Choon Shim, under these circumstances, then you will have to do it my way. Agreed?"

She giggles nervously in the darkness. "Yes. And?"

"Mmmh?"

"We are friends."

I smile, then roll over in the darkness, climbing to my feet.

"Where are you going?"

I squint down at her huddled form. "To speak with Jo Man Seok."

"Now?"

"Mmmh." Stepping clumsily over Choon Shim I reach the doors, wrapping my arms around my body to fight the chill. "Go to sleep."

Outside it is even worse. The air bites, sharp like the blade of a sword. And everything is wet. I push my numb feet into woven sandals and walk across the yard, the black earth squelching as I step, other times crunching and stony. Clumps of snow shine pale in the almost black of night, built up around the corners of the buildings, gathering on the curving roof tile.

I move quickly, the raw cold biting my skin as I hurry from the *damo* quarters into the main courtyard.

Man Seok is housed at the back of the compound too, though on the far side. To reach his room I must creep past the guard quarters, soundless like a thief in the night. Light spills from the magistrate's own private room, flickering behind the paper lattice of his shutters. So late at night, yet still he does not sleep. Until this case is solved perhaps he will not.

When I reach my destination, I kneel on the sheltered wooden *maru* outside his door, pushing off my shoes as I knock quietly.

I call his name softly. Once. Twice.

Sounds of movement stir inside and I settle back, huddling close as the shutters slowly creak open. He pads out quietly, a giant in the darkness, shutting the doors behind him to keep whatever heat there is inside. He does not ask why I am here, only lowers himself to sit across from me on the wooden terrace. If he is cold in his light sleeping clothes, he does not show it. "What have you both decided?"

Straight to the point, as always.

"She wants to go," I tell him.

Man Seok nods, as if that was to be expected. Perhaps already he knows Choon Shim better than I, for all my claims of friendship.

Irritation flares within my chest, though I know I'm not being fair. After all, it is something Man Seok is good at. Noticing things others do not. It's why I so often relied on his judgement during the corruption case. Why I trust him now, even after everything he has done.

Yet my voice is still harsher than I mean it to be when I speak. "It is keeping her safe that worries me." I take a deep calming breath. "Please, Man Seok *ssi*."

I shouldn't use his name like that, I should address him only as Lieutenant Jo, yet our time working undercover together has long since stripped us bare of decorum and barriers. Now we are what we are. Unusual and strange. But he allows me to talk straight with him, and so I do. "I don't want anyone here at the government office to know about her. It must be kept quiet that she's gone into the Song residence."

"Magistrate Hong believes his men are trustworthy."

I snort. "Do you?"

Man Seok inclines his head, just a silhouette in the black. He says nothing.

"What about the guards who greeted us tonight?" I press. "I remember three of them at the gates."

"Magistrate Hong sent two south to Hanseong."

"Already?"

"He was prepared."

I shiver, dragging my feet beneath my skirts, pulling the material tighter across my knees, burrowing down. "And the third?"

"He vouches for the third man."

I remain uncertain. "And what do *you* think?"

Man Seok shifts on the hardwood floor. "I think we need the help."

I sigh. "Then who else knows Choon Shim is here?"

"No one. Just Magistrate Hong and the guard he vouches for. Until dawn at least."

"So, we have until first light to move her elsewhere, somewhere safe. She can wait out of sight until Magistrate Hong makes his final arrangements for her entry."

Man Seok nods.

I rub a hand across my face in the darkness, suddenly weary. It is so very late and the day begins anew in the morning. I sigh. "Do you trust him?"

"Magistrate Hong?"

"Mmmh."

He is silent, thinking. I can almost see the magistrate being picked apart and put back together behind his black eyes. Finally, he nods.

It is enough for me. Man Seok watches and he listens.

I shiver, the chill air biting sharp at my skin. "And how does Magistrate Hong plan on getting Choon Shim into Lord Song's house? It will not be easy."

"He tells me there's a contact in the next town over." Man Seok's voice is pitched low. "A man he bribes that works at a *gisaeng* house."

I wrinkle my nose. It sounds shady.

Man Seok shrugs. "The man who works at the *gisaeng* house says Lord Song's servants came asking for extra help. He thinks he can recommend Choon Shim."

"And last time? How did he do it with the missing *damo*?"

"Differently." Man Seok sounds certain. "That girl was new in town. But there was an aunt in the village. The woman recommended the girl to Lord Song's head servant. The aunt didn't even know the girl was a *damo*."

I nod, as satisfied as I can be.

A missing *damo* and a missing noble daughter.

A quiet country estate guarded day and night by heavily armed men. And a father who requests an investigation but then blocks it at every turn.

I feel the pieces tug at me as the wind picks up, the threads, digging deep beneath my skin. In the distance, howls ring out, carried down the mountain on the whistling wind. I suck in my breath, rubbing my hands together vigorously.

"Return to your quarters," Man Seok says firmly. "I'll tell the magistrate what we need to do. You get warm."

The trees beyond the enclosure rustle with the rising gale, wind rushing through the bare branches. I rise and slip back into my shoes, stepping lightly onto the crunching earth of the yard. Man Seok stands too, moving to the edge of the *maru* until he towers above me.

"Get some sleep, Dan Ji *ssi*," he says quietly.

I hesitate, shifting from foot to foot to keep warm, guilty to leave him.

"Go."

I relent. "You will wake us when it's time to leave?"

"Yes. Before first light."

I nod, grateful for the opportunity of rest, something Man Seok will now get little of. I turn from his small room and trudge through the mud, glancing back only once to see him slip inside his room like a ghost.

Tomorrow it begins.

5

A Rumour

IT IS MID-MORNING. Man Seok and I trudge between market stalls toward the main road, following as it winds through the outskirts of the village. The ground here is covered in black ice, dirty puddles half frozen over with thin frosted crusts. We pass men with hard faces and women with leathery cheeks ravaged by windburn. Gaunt children with black matted hair.

No one looks at us. No one is curious. Their focus remains on the pockmarked road, carefully picking their way over the slush puddles just as we do, weighed down beneath their heavy loads.

I am deeply exhausted, my feet numb, my eyes sliding shut. I struggle to carry my own heavy burden, a wooden box with thick cloth straps bound across my shoulders. My clothes, just like the villagers we pass, are threadbare and worn, a disguise of sorts, and I've wrapped a frayed strip of cloth over my ears and knotted the loose ends beneath my chin for warmth. Mist spills into the air with every laboured breath.

I would ask Man Seok to carry my load if he did not

have one of his own. He strides ahead of me, back straight, sword case in hand, his own wooden box strapped tight to his shoulders. Occasionally he returns to help me when the path grows too steep or slippery, saying nothing as he grasps my elbow in his hand, guiding my steps over the sliding wet earth.

He reminds me now of when I first met him, dressed again in a rough tunic with leather buckles strapped tight across his chest, weapons in place and hair left loose and hanging into black eyes. Lines of his jaw unshaven with the beginnings of a beard.

He had arrived just in time.

Months alone within the sprawling compound of the gambling inn, passing messages and whispers back to the *podocheong*, lying and conspiring against the people all around me. I had become like a ghost. Faded and thin. Empty and disappearing. Until Man Seok came.

Like now, he said nothing, but he was solid and alive and he would sit beside me whenever he could, and it was enough. To not be alone.

The pale sun is high by the time we reach the *gibang*, the *gisaeng* entertainment house nestled high on the side of the valley. A wide view reveals misting bare forests and squalid *hanok* dwellings below, trails of cooking fire smoke rising to mix with the hazy sky above the valley.

We stop just outside the enclosure's main gates and I crouch on the roadside to catch my breath, not yet recovered from the late night and early morning. Yet the sacrifice of sleep was well rewarded, with Choon Shim safely removed well before dawn, long before the guards and officials arrived at the government offices to begin their day of work. Just as it had to be.

We part ways once inside the gates of the *gibang*, Man Seok heading round the back to beg food from the kitchens after a murmured reminder to be careful. Alone, I walk slowly toward the main building, speaking with the guards and then passing beneath a string of unlit lanterns swaying in the chill breeze. The *gibang* is formed of painted wooden pillars and open terraces, stone stairways leading into long dark hallways within. A wide curving roof shimmers in the hazy winter sunlight, black tiles gleaming like fire. It is a stark contrast to the surrounding woods of soft grey, colour all but leached from gnarled branches.

I am ushered into a large room at the side of the building, shutters left open to the winter forest despite the cold. The room is decorated with brightly painted screens, scenes of idyllic countryside and lush coloured flowers, with intricate wooden lattices covering the walls. The wide space feels warm despite the weather, crowded with women in brightly coloured silk, peals of laughter and glossy piles of cushions.

The *gisaeng* all ignore me as I set my box in the corner, yet when I crack open the lid a young girl approaches shyly. She watches with unhidden wonder as I arrange the pins and trinkets inside. Her lips are red and her black hair shining, piled high on her head and adorned with expensive jade pins. Her carefully arranged silk skirts couldn't be more different to my ragged threadbare one. Her soft hands and blushed cheeks, too.

By the time I have finished laying out my wares I have attracted a small crowd, and I cannot help but wonder about the lives that stretch before these women. Young *gisaeng* who sell their bodies and their conversation, living on the sloping valley walls through the dead of winter. Isolated and bored. Hungry for news.

Alive with gossip.

A girl reaches for a *norigae* pendant made from deep green jade and pink woven tassels. She holds the ornamental pin against her chest where it would tie onto the shimmering material of her jacket, tassels hanging down to match the colour of her deep pink skirts. The robes she wears are made from silk. Only men and women of the noble *yangban* ranking are permitted to wear silk.

Only *yangban* and lowly entertainer girls.

"Where did you travel from?"

The young girl's pretty voice breaks the silence and I spread my hands wide, ready to spin my tales.

"All through Joseon I have travelled, from the south to the north and across, ocean to ocean."

Already the girls are captivated, but I add an even greater hook. "Most recently, my brother and I travelled through the very heart of Joseon."

"Hanseong. The capital," breathes one *gisaeng*, the shy girl who first approached me. Her eyes are shining.

I nod. "Would you like to hear the stories that are most popular in Hanseong these days?"

She bites her lip and nods. The *gisaeng* holding the *norigae* places it back in my box, only to pick up a long *binyeo* pin to admire against another friend's piled hair. Five young girls crowd around me now, all of them painted and perfumed and lovely, two hanging rapturously on my words and the others only pretending not to care.

They do not fool me. I see how they shift closer every time I lower my voice.

"Yet you see," I continue. "I only deal in pretty jewellery, and I must earn a living. I cannot share my news with you."

One of the girls whines. "Why not? Please, tell us about Hanseong."

"But if I trade my stories for nothing, what will I live on?"

The same girl whimpers. "What do you want to trade?"

I pretend to think.

"A story for a story. Is that fair?"

The girls all glance at each other and smile, the *norigae gisaeng* even pleased enough with the arrangement to share a cup of hot tea with me for free. I let them play with the box of trinkets as I begin my story, one that truly is popular in the capital.

"Let me see … Tell me, here in the valley, what do the people do with their old folk?"

The girls all look at each other blankly.

I smile. "In the capital there is a rumour of a man who carried his elderly mother to the mountains on an A-frame *jige*. He could not afford to keep her, you see. And so, he planned to leave her there, alone in the mountains. To die."

I pause for a beat and the girls gasp. Just as they should.

"Now, the man's young son followed secretly, and when the man turned to leave the young son asked his father, 'Will you not bring the *jige* home with you, father?' The man looked back at his old mother still sitting on the *jige* and did not have the heart to move her. He shook his head and told his son he no longer had need of the carrier.

"However, his young son spoke again. 'But father, if you leave the cart here, how will I carry you into the mountains when you become old?' And the man was so very shamed by his son's words that he took both the *jige* and his mother back home.'"

I pause at the end of my story. The girls roll their eyes, two even falling into each other in a great show of boredom.

Clearly pious life lessons are not what they are hoping for.

I laugh despite myself. "Perhaps you might prefer something a little more ... scandalous?"

Now they are interested.

I lean closer. "Perhaps you have already heard whispers from other travellers? About the biggest scandal to occur in Hanseong all year?"

The girls shake their heads and I lean forward. "You haven't yet heard about the richest man in the city? A man who had everything in the world and lost it all?"

"Yes! Tell us that one." The *norigae gisaeng*'s dark eyes drink me in.

I sip my tea, taking my time. The room is warming up after all, and the journey from the office was long. I take respite where I can.

I smile.

And nowhere is as fruitful as a *gibang*—always the very epicentre of every community, the place where all news and rumours come and go, where any story can be found.

And the true reason they haven't already heard my tale is only because it is not real.

I wave them closer. "The story begins many years ago, with a young man lost during a storm. There he meets a traveller, a stranger who offers him riches. A title and an estate in the countryside. Everything he ever wanted. All the young man must offer in return is his most precious possession."

The girls nod, hanging on my words like small children.

"Now, the young man came from a destitute noble clan, and had no home and no prospects. His most precious possession was a beautiful sword his father had given him before he died. Even so, the young man vowed to part with it if he could regain his clan's lost riches and ranking. So, he made a pact with the stranger."

"Who was the stranger?" breathes a girl who hasn't spoken before.

I shrug. "Some say he was a demon. Others say he was a king." I shake my head to let them know this doesn't matter. "Whatever he was, the stranger was true to his word. The young man received all he was promised. He lived in a sprawling estate, rich and content. He took a wife, a lovely girl with red lips and pink blushing cheeks."

The girls glance at each other, almost nervous. "And the stranger?"

"The stranger disappears. And the young man's beautiful sword hangs in his home for years and years, waiting to be claimed. Yet no one ever comes."

I pause to take another long sip of my cooling tea. None of the girls is interested in my trinket box now, all their attention focused solely on me.

"Many, many years after their first meeting, the stranger returns. The young man is old now. The richest man in all Hanseong." I pause. "I saw him once, walking through the marketplace where my brother had laid out our wares. It was just before it happened. Before tragedy struck."

"He lost his riches," guesses the *norigae gisaeng*, but I shake my head.

"A much worse fate fell upon his household." I glance around as if to check for eavesdroppers, then whisper beneath my breath, "His lovely daughter disappeared. Without a trace."

The girls turn to each other, whispering, faces filling with uncertainty.

I hold back my smile.

"What happened to her?" asks the shy girl finally. The others remain silent.

I shake my head. "No one knows. The young woman

disappeared from her bed in the middle of the night; one moment she was there, and the next she was simply ... gone."

I am silent, drinking in their reactions, examining their faces for the slightest change in expression.

"Even worse," I add. "The girl was to be married to a young man of a powerful family. He was the most handsome young man in the capital, and was heartbroken his future bride was taken away."

I pause. "What do you all suppose happened to her?"

"It was the stranger," announces the *norigae gisaeng* boldly. "After so many years, of course the sword was no longer the nobleman's most prized possession, instead it was his daughter that he loved the most. So, the stranger took her."

"No," interrupts another girl, one sitting behind who has barely spoken. She squeezes into the inner circle. "The girl probably ran away."

"What makes you think so?" I ask lightly.

The young *gisaeng* flicks her head. "If she was soon to be married, perhaps she was afraid. Perhaps she didn't like her betrothed as much as everyone thought she did."

I nod, staying silent, listening to their chatter.

Waiting.

"Perhaps the stranger visited our valley too," says the *norigae gisaeng*. She glances sidelong at another girl who nods in agreement.

The shy *gisaeng* shakes her head. "You do not truly think... "

"I do. Perhaps Lord Song made a deal with a demon too." The *norigae gisaeng*'s shining eyes suddenly go wide, and her voice drops low. "On the north side of the mountain ... could that be the stranger, come back to collect his debt from Lord Song?"

I interrupt quickly, before they can get too carried away, before they forget they owe me a story.

"What is it you speak of?"

"The north face of the mountain. They say a ghost lives up there. My mother told me it steals little girls who disobey."

"I have heard so too," interjects another girl. "A human ghost!"

The shy *gisaeng's* expression clouds over. "But it's not true. A demon couldn't have taken Lord Song's daughter."

I raise my brows, "Why not?"

"Because she ran away."

Another girl pushes closer. "Yes, I heard it too." She smiles wide and slow. "The girl had a lover."

The shy girl nods. "Yet she could not marry him."

I keep my face carefully blank. "And why is that?"

"He was poor. Only the son of a servant."

Two of the girls begin to giggle but I ignore them. "Do you know who he is?"

The *gisaeng* all shake their heads.

"Then how are you so sure Lord Song's daughter eloped with her lover?" I smile to lessen the urgency within my words.

"I heard the story from a traveller," says the shy *gisaeng*. "He helped the girl's nurse make the arrangements."

"Her nurse?" I am surprised. "And what happened to the nurse?"

One of the older *gisaeng* waves her hand dismissively. "She is gone now too, of course. Both of them. Disappeared in the dead of night to meet the girl's lover."

The *norigae gisaeng* sighs as if it is romantic. "He must have taken her away over the mountains to marry her." She smiles wistfully. "Perhaps they caught a boat north, perhaps he smuggled her out of Joseon."

Perhaps.

Perhaps not.

Yet I latch onto one thread, feeling it tugging at my insides. A truth within a story.

"And the nurse," I ask quietly. "You say she has disappeared too? On the same night?"

The girls nod.

"How can you be so sure?"

One of the girls shrugs. "I heard it from the cousin of a girl who works here. He overheard it from Lord Song's head servant. They both disappeared on the same night. That's what he said."

Another girl chimes in. "It's true. I heard that story as well."

I think of Choon Shim as the *gisaeng* talk, their scattered conversation filled with ghosts and demons threaded through by romantic half-truths and obvious rumour.

By tomorrow Choon Shim will be embedded into the Song residence. None of us knows for sure when she will be able to make her first report. I only hope it is soon, I only hope that she arrives there safely and without suspicion. For it will be Choon Shim who separates truth from whispers.

I file away the threads I have gathered. A missing girl. And a sympathetic nurse. A demon that lives on the north mountain. A human ghost. And a lowly lover, far beneath Song Seorim's station. A lover who may have wished to smuggle his woman north beyond Joseon's border.

A love story.

Or a ghost story.

The threads tug at my chest, becoming stronger.

6

She Smiles

MAN SEOK HAS LESS luck at the *gibang* than I do, and by the time we arrive back at the government office it is late, the sky dark and the rising mountains casting shadow over the narrow pathways.

Torches are left flickering at the gates and two new guards wait outside, swords gripped tight in frozen hands. Man Seok nods at them as we enter, and immediately Magistrate Hong approaches us, his boots crunching as he crosses the wide courtyard.

"Lieutenant Jo. Please, step inside my office."

Man Seok says nothing, just inclines his head to show I should follow. Magistrate Hong does not protest despite a tightening in his jaw, so I trail behind the men as we are ushered toward the magistrate's office. The door opens and a man I do not recognise nods politely at us from the open room, light pooling outside on the wooden *maru*.

I am almost dropping with exhaustion but force myself to focus, standing close behind Man Seok as we are introduced to the room's three occupants. One is the man who nodded at us from the doorway. In his mid-thirties, he is introduced as Secretary Baek and sits at the long wooden table. He wears a wide-brimmed black *gat* on his head, his hair pushed back from his face and tucked beneath a *manggeon* headband, neat everywhere Man Seok and I are not. When the shadow of his *gat* brim lifts, I notice his face holds the same weary shadows as Magistrate Hong's. The case is clearly taking its toll.

The other two men are younger, early to mid-twenties, both of them guards of the office and dressed in uniforms of dark blue layered over white, weapons clutched tightly in hands. The first man, Guard Yu, smiles at me and I recognise him from our first night in the valley, one of the men who let us inside the gates when we first arrived.

I assess his easy smile carefully, for clearly this is the man Magistrate Hong trusts with Choon Shim's true location. An ally perhaps? I am uncertain.

The other man, Guard Kim, seems exhausted and keeps stifling his yawns. Whatever he's been doing all day, I wonder whether it was as taxing as my own walk through the valley. I am glad when Magistrate Hong invites us all to take a seat.

"I wish to know how your investigation fared." A sharp knock sounds at the door and the magistrate turns his head. "Come inside!"

An older woman enters slowly, manoeuvring her large frame through the doorway with a tray in her hands. Simmering bowls of thick *jiggae* send plumes of wisping steam into the cool air and I salivate at the scent of spices.

The woman places a bowl before me and I smile at her gratefully, accepting the scented tea she pours into a small cup. I wrap my hands around the hot porcelain as she sets *jiggae*, bowls of rice, and tea in front of Man Seok and the two guardsmen as well, before bustling from the room.

Silence stretches as we begin to eat, until finally

Secretary Baek clears his throat. He glances quickly at the magistrate before asking uncertainly, "Lieutenant Jo, have you learned anything new since your arrival?"

Man Seok nods curtly, laying aside his wooden spoon, making me frown at Secretary Baek. They should allow him to eat before interrogating him. Though as always, if Man Seok agrees with me he does not show it. Instead he calmly asks, "Is it true that Song Seorim's nurse has also disappeared?"

The men all look at each other uncertainly. It is the magistrate who answers, "Not to my knowledge ... Secretary Baek?"

The secretary glances at the two guards, both of whom slowly shake their heads.

The magistrate's voice rises like a sudden crack of thunder. "Well, can someone not find out? Surely someone in the damn village is willing to confirm it!"

Guard Yu stops eating and carefully replaces his own spoon on the table. Guard Kim peers at his hands and says nothing.

The magistrate sighs in frustration. "What else?"

"A rumour the girl eloped with a lover," answers Man Seok. "A commoner."

Silence in the room, thick with tension. Until Secretary Baek breaks it, his voice wavering and low. "A commoner? That's impossible. How could she have met such a man?"

Guard Kim rubs his temples as if to force himself awake. "In the marketplace perhaps? I heard she used to walk in the marketplace, so it's possible."

Man Seok focuses in on Guard Kim. "And who accompanied Song Seorim on her walks in the marketplace?"

No one answers so Man Seok adds brusquely, "A nurse, perhaps?"

Guard Kim shifts uncomfortably. "I can find out."

Man Seok nods. "Do. And if there was a nurse, find out when she was last sighted."

"Yes, sir."

Man Seok glances at me, but I only shrug, leaving him to organise everyone. He is good at it, and already the others listen intently to every word that falls from his mouth. Not that he gives them a choice. Man Seok has always treated everyone the same, in the past and here again with these men. He does not tolerate mistakes, he does not tolerate insubordinate behaviour. He is hard and cold and efficient. And he cuts to the core of things with no time for soft feelings.

I continue eating my *jjigae*, watching as Man Seok turns to Secretary Baek.

"I want to see all witness statements on record regarding Song Seorim's disappearance, including a written account of her father's initial request to investigate her whereabouts. And Guard Yu?"

"Yes, sir?"

"I believe Magistrate Hong has already given *you* instructions?"

"Yes, sir."

I watch the young man's face as he answers, hoping the others have made the right judgement in trusting him with Choon Shim's care. But Man Seok simply nods, satisfied, and then turns to Magistrate Hong. "Send whatever men you have into the mountains. If Song Seorim is dead and her body dumped, I want to know."

"How many… men?"

"As many as you have, Magistrate Hong. If you need more, request them from down the valley. Do what you have to do."

"It will be difficult in this weather … but I will

49

personally oversee it." The magistrate's face sets hard in determination and I nod. When Man Seok is like this, people wish to please him. Or they are afraid to not please him. Either way he gets the result he wants.

Man Seok does not reply, turning back to his cooling meal. He has nothing more to say and so will not waste his breath. Silence falls across the room.

I take a sip of tea, and just as the others begin to become comfortable, sinking deep into their cushions, and in the case of Guard Kim, eyes fluttering shut, I speak. "Have there ever been any similar cases? Any similar disappearances in the valley before?"

An uncomfortable silence follows, the men glancing uncertainly at the magistrate whose face hardens. He says nothing though, and finally Secretary Baek focuses on Man Seok as he stammers an answer, "Well there was a ... a death last year, but in the end, after the investigation took place, well, it was determined by everyone to have clearly been a ... a suicide. And, of course we have had some land disputes, some issues with adultery and runaway slaves ... which were all successfully ... resolved." He pauses uncertainly.

I wrinkle my nose, understanding what has been left unsaid.

They are inexperienced. The valley is quiet.

Man Seok says nothing, though his eyes never leave Magistrate Hong's face. After an awkward silence the magistrate is compelled to comment.

"It's true. Here in the valley we have been ... lucky. There have been no similar cases. Not during my term." He peers around the table. "I do not believe any of us have experienced a case ... quite like this."

Deep frown lines crease his forehead and his fingers twist endlessly at his wiry grey beard. He already knows the future. I can see it in his lined face. He foresees a demotion. And an exile. An unsolved case and a scapegoat.

Despite his inexperience, it is clear Magistrate Hong is no fool.

Once again, I feel a pang of pity. They are all so utterly out of their depth.

We eat in silence and afterwards I excuse myself from the office, Guard Kim using the opportunity to make his own escape as well. Man Seok nods at me as I leave, black eyes holding mine as I return the gesture.

The winter night hits me like a wave of ice water as I step heavily down the stairs to the courtyard, watching as Guard Kim steals away into the night toward the guard quarters, finally able to enjoy a night's rest.

My body curls inwards, arms folded across my chest against the raw wind. The trinket box waits for me and I slowly heave it to my shoulders, making my own way back toward the *damo* quarters, empty now except for me. Before I reach the gate, the crunch of footsteps sounds from behind. I turn to find Guard Yu breathing heavily as if he has hurried to catch me.

"Damo Dan Ji, I thought you would be glad to know Damo Choon Shim reached her destination safely. Magistrate Hong entrusted me with her travel arrangements. Our contacts will bring her into the Song residence early tomorrow morning."

I am surprised he has thought to tell me, long grown used to being overlooked by the men I work with.

"Thank you," I stammer.

I attempt a smile, for Man Seok believes the magistrate can be trusted, and in turn Magistrate Hong has made it clear he trusts Guard Yu. It is good if there are people here we can rely on.

"Damo Choon Shim asked me to pass on the message

that she is faring well," Guard Yu continues, standing at a respectful distance, half hidden by the shadows.

I nod, dropping my trinket box to the ground beside my feet. "Thank you, Guard Yu. How will she get in contact with us when she is ready to report?"

"I have been assigned to watch the residence. There is a window of time each evening where she will signal to me if she is ready."

"How?"

"A code using candlelight. When she is able to meet, she will let us know." Guard Yu pauses. "Magistrate Hong has not told the others. He wishes to keep the arrangements a secret."

"He must trust you a great deal."

I make the statement sound like a question, inviting him to tell me more, curious because that is how I always am, reaching for my threads, tugging at the pieces.

"Indeed," Guard Yu agrees easily. "My father was Magistrate Hong's head servant."

"Then he is your benefactor," I press.

"Yes. It was the magistrate who enabled me to take the examinations to work here. He knows I am loyal to him." Guard Yu steps from the shadows and smiles, his expression open and his eyes clear. "Without Magistrate Hong I would be nothing but a servant, just as my father was."

I nod. Guard Yu is simple and straightforward. He does not understand the layers within my words. He tells me all, even when I do not ask.

He is too trusting for this line of work, yet I find myself warming to him all the same. His respect for Magistrate Hong is obvious, shining clearly within his face.

Distant animal howls drift from the mountains, echoes carried on the wind. My skin prickles and both Guard Yu and I turn to the source of the sound. Of course, nothing can be seen beyond the high stone walls, deep blackness enveloping the world beyond the courtyard's torches.

"Are they wolves?" I ask Guard Yu.

"Yes. They live on the north mountain, though I have heard packs may even venture to the edges of the valley if the winter draws on too long. If they are starving enough."

I gaze into the blackness, listening to the whistling wind. "The north mountain is up there? The north face of the mountain?"

Guard Yu steps closer and points over the compound wall into the night. "Yes, over there."

"I heard a human ghost lives on that mountain."

Guard Yu laughs. "And where did you hear that?"

Now it is my turn to smile. "At the *gibang*," I admit. I shiver, shifting from foot to foot to keep warm.

"Mmmh, if you ask my *halmeoni*, my grandmother, she will tell you the mountain is home to many demons. She says it's the centre of all evil here in the valley. But she would also tell you that ungrateful children will be gobbled up by ghosts."

I laugh lightly, frosted breath escaping my lips. "And has your *halmeoni* lived here all her life?"

Guard Yu shakes his head. "No, both of us came when Magistrate Hong began his term here. Yet my *halmeoni* is superstitious. In our old home there was also a mountain she quite disliked." He grins.

After a moment of silence, I say, "I am glad of any further news of Damo Choon Shim." I lift my heavy trinket box from the ground, indicating I will retire. "Goodnight, Guard Yu."

I am already walking away when he calls after me. "What do you think happened to her? To Song Seorim?"

I turn back to peer at him through the night. Torches

flare alongside the stone wall as the wind rises. "Did you know her, Guard Yu?"

Guard Yu only shakes his head, almost wistful. "Of course not." The look on his face reminds me he is a lowly man, with no reason to interact with a woman of Song Seorim's standing. A low person without recognition in his own community.

The same as me.

Except sometimes, when I am following the threads of a story, when they are unfolding before me, it becomes possible to forget it.

"I saw her once," Guard Yu admits. "In the marketplace."

"What was she like?"

He shrugs. "Pretty. And young."

I cannot help myself, the easy comradery I felt with him mere moments ago abruptly gone. I begin pulling threads. "How did you know it was her?"

"I was with my *halmeoni*. She knew who Song Seorim was."

"And who was walking beside Song Seorim?"

Guard Yu is taken aback, only now realising he is being interrogated. He stammers, "I am not sure. It was only a moment ... I think ... perhaps ... an older servant woman?"

He is suddenly embarrassed, gaze flicking to the ground, cheeks flushed. "Aaah ... you think it was Song Seorim's nurse?"

"Perhaps."

I pause, for a moment even entertaining the idea that Guard Yu could be the rumoured commoner lover, if such a man even exists. Yet immediately I dismiss it. Guard Yu's words ring true, the wistfulness within his voice tells of a distant admiration only.

"Thank you for your time, Guard Yu." I make sure to

smile as I bid him goodnight, hoping to lessen his embarrassment, thanking him again for his news of Choon Shim, for the time he has given me.

He has given me something else too.

A picture.

An image. Running through my mind.

It is dark and cold within my small room. And empty. I light a candle and the wind outside howls. Or perhaps it is the hungry wolves, starvation driving them ever closer down the mountainside. I do not know.

As I ready myself for sleep, lighting a single flickering candle and untying my tangled hair to smooth and then re-braid it, I imagine Song Seorim.

I imagine her walking through the marketplace in warm sunlight. I imagine her face. Pretty. And so young. Thin soft hands sliding over trinkets and carved *norigae* placed across the market stalls.

I imagine her smiling.

7

The Body

SHARP TAPPING BREAKS into my dreams. I stir, shifting beneath my heavy blanket, blinking. It is night, my room still shrouded in darkness. Five days have passed since we arrived into the valley, yet I am still unused to the sounds of the dark, the howls and the wind, the way the trees creak. I sleep fitfully, half awake and half dreaming.

The rapping begins again and I sit up now, startled fully awake as my shutters swing open, a hulking giant filling my doorway. For a moment I am afraid, small and alone in the darkness without a weapon in reach. Yet the shadow comes no further. Instead I hear Man Seok's deep voice, quiet in the darkness.

"Dan Ji *ssi*, they found a body."

"A body? Who is…?" The words die on my lips as I push the blanket back, untangling myself from sleep. "Where?"

"In the mountains. Get dressed. I'll wait outside."

With that my shutters close again, enveloping me in thick darkness. I fumble for my day clothes, changing from my underthings into a threadbare commoner *chima*, a high-waisted skirt, and padded jacket. Wrapping a scarf around my neck, I place another tight over my head and ears, letting my tangled hair fall in a long loose braid down my back. I am breathing heavily by the time I emerge onto the *maru*, momentarily unfocused and blinking in the bright torchlight that flares across the courtyard. The night air invades every part of my body and sucks my breath away.

Snow falls from the black. Wet. Almost sleet. It settles into my hair and head scarf as I struggle with my shoes, ice seeping against skin as I call, "Is it close to morning?"

"Not yet. It's still late."

Man Seok stands on the muddy ground, back to me and arms crossed over his chest, facing toward the north mountain. Or where the mountain would be if the sky was not so heavy. Shouting erupts from the main yards of the office and burning lights bounce over the stone walls surrounding the *damo* quarters. Every now and then a bobbing head runs past, men in the blue uniform of the magistrate's guard. They have been busy, as have we. And it seems after days of searching the mountains and forest, they have found what they were looking for.

The body of Song Seorim.

I fall into step beside Man Seok.

"Tell me," I say. We hurry toward the main courtyard, passing blinking guards and burning torches.

Man Seok clears his throat, bending low so I can hear. "Three guards didn't return at the end of the day. Apparently, they located a body half buried and were trying to excavate it. They sent a man back to inform the magistrate half an hour past. He and Guard Yu have already gone up."

I am breathless, blood tingling beneath my skin. I cannot help myself and grasp hard at Man Seok's arm, fingers digging deep. "Is it her?"

He hesitates, then nods. "Most likely. It has been confirmed by one of the guards who found her."

I am unexpectedly hurt by his words, falling behind as we stride toward the main gates of the compound. I shake my head, feeling foolish.

I had always understood Song Seorim would be dead.

Yet somehow, I had still wished ... something. I do not know what. Just something else.

I should have known better.

Horses wait at the gates alongside Guard Kim, who says he will bring us to the edge of the forest. The rest of the way will have to be on foot, the trees much too dense for horses.

Once we are riding none of us speak further, only the crunch of the animals' hooves on the stony road breaking the deep night, the huffs and snorts of their breath, white plumes in the darkness. Their footfalls are steady on the uneven ground.

I cannot help but feel bitter. Angry even. I pull the worn material around my neck higher, wrapping it over my mouth and nose, frost melting in my eyelashes. Perhaps the bitterness stems from the past few days spent huddled in the marketplace, Man Seok and I taking turns exposed in the cold. We sold our trinkets and gathered rumours from anyone who cared to speak with us.

We gained nothing. Nothing we did not already know.

Song Seorim's nurse is indeed missing.

And the village is alive with the undisputed certainty that Song Seorim is nothing but a whore, a girl who allowed herself to be seduced by a peasant. They spit when they say her name. She is not pious, she is unfilial and wanton. Her father must be filled with shame.

They say with scorn that her lover has carried her over

the mountains and sea, beyond the far-flung borders of Joseon.

Untrue.

Song Seorim has spent almost a moon lying dead on the mountainside, frozen and alone.

Somehow it hurts far more than I expected.

The way to the forest edge is dark and water falls relentless from the sky, somewhere between rain and snow. We travel on the quiet roads, threading through the deserted pathways down toward the river. There is silence there too.

It now seems Choon Shim's successful placement into Lord Song's residence will be for nothing. Perhaps Lord Song truly has nothing to hide, perhaps he hired those private soldiers simply to find his daughter. Perhaps those men guard his gate to keep the villagers out, so Lord Song need not listen to the awful rumours running rampant through this community.

I shiver.

Except the story cannot truly end with Song Seorim's body found in the mountains. For there are other pieces to this tapestry, pieces that do not fit. A *damo* disappeared from the face of the earth. A nurse. And Lord Song's wish to block every channel of investigation, while calling in favours from the royal family to push it ahead.

I feel the threads within my body stir, feel them unfurl and spread. I am not ready to let go yet. This case may end with Song Seorim's death, but mystery still stirs within these hills.

We follow the curve of the river in silence. I am transfixed by the black ice bobbing in chunks across its surface, by the glow of pale tree trunks creeping alongside the far bank. A grey beech forest, thick and ghostly. The snow falls harder and my hair grows wet with sleet. When we reach the mountain base Man Seok must help me from the saddle for my hands and feet have numbed, becoming clumsy and slow. His breath clouds hot and misted beside my cheek, bristles sharp against my skin as he lifts me down and then it is cold again as he steps away. I flex my fingers, letting the blood flow again as Guard Kim shows us the way.

"Is it the north mountain?" I ask him.

He only blinks at me blankly, then shakes his head. "No, the north mountain lies behind the government offices." He points away, back where we have come. "Why do you ask, Damo Dan Ji?"

I say nothing, just following him into the silent forest, Man Seok close and reassuring behind me. The ground crunches beneath our feet, and it is like stepping into another place, another world. Guard Kim lights a thick torch of dancing flames, casting strange moving shapes across the snow-covered earth, across the bare branches that reach for the sky as if they were fingers. Oaks and hawthorns. Ghostly grey beech trees. And hidden in the depths, yew trees, blood red and glowing in the firelight. I touch cold fingers against their trunks in reverence. Thousand-year-old yew trees that live on even after they die, leaves growing in the summer even when their roots are severed. Immortal.

There is no path here, but Guard Kim moves purposefully, and we trudge forwards in a steep incline, breaching the mountainside, moving deeper and higher into the winter forest as the wet snow grows heavier.

As we walk, I find myself imagining it differently. Imagining that the guards had never found her. Instead they walked right by Song Seorim's body. And when darkness fell the snow crept over, settling across her skin for the whole of the winter. Nothing to find until the thaw of spring. It is a miracle that she has been found. We have been lucky. I focus on it as we walk, as the exhaustion and cold set in.

We are lucky.

We stop and rest twice on the steep hike through the snow, and I catch Man Seok's black eyes following me through the dark, watching with tightened jaw. I forcibly calm my laboured breathing and heaving chest, for I do not want him to think I'm not strong enough, that I shouldn't have come. Despite my trust in him, I would not wish him to see my weakness. Or at least not any more than he already has, when he first entered the corruption case and found me fading within the gambling inn walls.

For the rest of the hike I avoid his stare, thinking dark thoughts of hungry wolves and vicious tigers, until finally lights twinkle ahead through the trees, torches burning in the vast still night. As we draw near, a group of men emerges from the shadow, crowded within the smallest of clearings. Trees pen them in as a few guards attempt to break the hard ground with thick branches, others standing exhausted further back, huddled together.

Guard Yu sees us as we approach, and there is a strange look in his eyes as he slides quickly down the incline to meet us, clapping Guard Kim on the shoulder in greeting. As he passes me he leans close, breath warm against my cheek and voice low. "It isn't her. The body is not Song Seorim."

Then he has moved on to speak with Man Seok, leaving me staring after him.

Magistrate Hong calls for Lieutenant Jo then, and because Man Seok is busy I rouse myself to struggle those last few steps to the magistrate's side instead. I am unable yet to see inside the gaping wound within the black earth where the body must surely lie.

The magistrate's attention keeps flicking down the mountainside the way we have come. His mouth is twisted and tight, his distress even more obvious in the way he speaks to me directly, meeting my eyes for the first time since I arrived into his valley.

"Lord Song is on his way," he informs me. "One of my damn fool guards must have gone straight to him as soon as we identified the body!"

"What do you mean? He's coming here? Now?"

Magistrate Hong confirms it with a curt nod, his skin flushed dark. "My man watching his house came ahead of him. He must have passed you on the mountainside. He believes Lord Song could arrive at any moment."

Man Seok reaches us then, towering over us both, and I listen again as the magistrate tells him too that one of his men is on Lord Song's payroll. Yet I am still fixated on his earlier words.

It is inconceivable, a man like Lord Song venturing to a place like this. He is more powerful than any man in the valley, richer, more influential. And a man like that waits in his warm house for others to climb the frozen mountain and return his daughter's body to his side.

I glance across at Man Seok, watch the firelight on his face as Magistrate Hong speaks with him, as his frown deepens.

An important marriage ruined and our investigation blocked at every turn. I had not thought Lord Song the kind of man to brave a wet winter night and climb a mountain in the dark. I had not expected him to let common lowly men see him dishevelled in the snow, soaked through with sleet and dirt.

It can mean only one thing.

It is so simple yet I never expected it.

Man Seok moves close to my side, lowering his head to whisper in hushed tones. "What do you think of this?"

I stare up at him, hands numb, chest numb too. "I think … I think Lord Song loves his daughter." As simple as that. "He loves her."

Man Seok says nothing and I do not know if he agrees with me, for right then the other guards call harshly for attention, all of them gathering around the gaping hole in the ground. Some lean down to light the way with their flaming torches, letting the light seep into the dark places where it has not previously reached.

It reveals her body.

Flickering flames across blue-tinged skin. Black dirt caked inside her open mouth, hair frozen stiff and her eyes wide open, staring up, up, up at the sky, glassy and unmoving.

Yet it is her hands that do it.

Her frozen fingers curl in on themselves like claws and I am thrown by the sight of them in a way I cannot quite explain, left blinking in the sudden light.

I have seen bodies before. I have seen young dead girls before. In the capital I often help examine the victims brought into our morgue. Often. I have grown used to it.

Yet I have never seen hands like hers before.

The sheen of her skin reminds me of the jewels I collected from the corruption case, the discarded string of opaque shining beads left beneath a cushion. And the shape of her hands reminds me of a man's fingers, reaching out in the snow to offer me ginger taffee, pink and flushed with pumping blood and life.

Now curling and blue with cold.

I take a step back. I do not mean to.

My body meets someone else's, Man Seok, and his hands come down firmly on my shoulders to steady me. I would break away except his fingers grip me tight, digging in and holding me in place. So I stay there, pressed back against his chest as they pull the girl from her shallow grave, her body stiff and hard like she's carved from wood.

I imagine her living. Breathing.

Like Man Seok is. His breath warm against the top of my head.

She is dressed as a commoner, like a village girl, and Guard Yu's words ring inside my head.

It isn't her. The body is not Song Seorim.

8

A Father

NO ONE KNOWS who the dead girl is.

She is an enigma. A mystery. A body alone in the dark forest.

Guard Yu remains adamant she is not Song Seorim. He tells us over and over how he saw her in the marketplace, how her features then were different, that she was taller and fuller. Older. The other men are not so certain. I ask about the missing *damo* but Guard Kim says this one is too young.

No one knows anything for sure.

So, she lies before us unnamed. And Man Seok, when he has crouched close in the torchlight to examine her body, announces there are no signs of rot, no decay. Her flesh has frozen blue and white, preserved and whole.

"The only missing person report filed this winter has been for Song Seorim," stammers Secretary Baek. It is clear who he believes the body belongs to. "There has been no one else."

The men gather around in silence as Man Seok works, staring as he carefully checks her skin for wounds, examines her for signs of struggle. I look at the scene around us, but find nothing to explain who left her here, half-buried in the dirt. If there were signs of a struggle they are long gone now. The snow is churned into mud from guardsmen boots, the earth opened up with tools and the girl's body pulled from her grave.

A small stained pack has been buried with her, a bamboo bottle filled with water long since turned into chunks of ice, four frozen wheat-flour cakes and a threadbare change of clothes.

This girl was going somewhere.

But it is all that I find. Nothing is left that was not hers to begin with. Nothing that may have belonged to the person who left her here. No evidence to reveal whether she climbed this mountain by herself, or was brought here against her will.

Snow falls heavy from the thick sky. Soon, everything will be swallowed up.

When Man Seok is done it is my turn.

My breath comes sharp and fast as I crouch in the gathering snowfall to examine her body. I remind myself I have done this before. Many times. Though it is strange how this time feels so very different. I cannot explain it. The thought worms its way inside my chest as I lean closer, pressing my fingers against her ice skin, ignoring her clawed hands.

Perhaps it is because she is so young, at my guess only fourteen years of age. It is such a sad thing, for one so young to be here alone.

Lifting the worn sleeves of her *jeogori* I find bruises staining her arms, thick and black. The marks have set in deep, clearly spread beneath her skin long before her flesh has frozen. I raise my eyebrows at Man Seok who stands above me.

The bruises were made prior to her death.

Man Seok's expression does not change, but shadows dig deep across his skin, his mouth grown tight and hard, confirming what I already know.

There was a struggle.

The girl's clothes beneath the clinging dirt are brightly coloured, her worn skirt burning red like fire, dimmed behind a layer of grit and seeping snow. Her outfit is not fine, but it seems to me she must have cared for it greatly. She has been careful to repair the worn material so the stitching remains always hidden beneath the hem, careful to present her best.

Yet no ribbon is tied to the end of her long braid.

It is the way young unmarried women dress, a matching ribbon to bind their hair. I scan the mud surrounding us but there is nothing. It is gone, lost on the journey here. Or never worn at all. I cannot be certain.

A thread cut loose.

I do not let the men watch, forcing them to turn and face the silent twisting hawthorns. I lift the hard, stiff material of the girl's skirt to inspect her legs beneath her underclothes. I find no bruises on her inner thighs, no evidence left behind of sexual violence. Only the wounds on her arms.

And, of course, on her neck, for it is twisted and broken, bone pressing against her throat where it should not. It is what killed her. Perhaps from a fall. Perhaps not. I glance into the darkness. Though the mountain side is sloped, there are no rocks or cliff to fall from, no steep loose earth to slide across. Only thick trees and this small clearing. And this shallow grave someone has dug for her.

When I am finished the magistrate takes Man Seok aside. I trail behind to listen and he glances at me but does not tell me to leave. A kind of progress I suppose.

"Well, what do you think?"

Man Seok remains quiet, so I answer for him. "The girl was buried here sometime within the last moon at least, she cannot have been here prior to the deep cold setting in."

"How can you be so sure?"

"No decay," interjects Man Seok.

I nod.

"What else?"

"Well, it depends," I continue. "If she truly is not Song Seorim, that means it's feasible her death may have occurred around the same time as Song Seorim's disappearance. These instances could possibly be connected. Or they could not. We cannot know for certain. Yet I do believe there are signs here of a struggle, so this was certainly no accident."

"How can you be sure? She carried a pack. She must have been travelling through these mountains, perhaps even running away."

I glance back at the lonely grave. "True … yet the bruises on her arms suggest another person was present. And it was not the dead girl who dug that grave, Magistrate Hong. So, it is murder then, perhaps. Magistrate Hong, what will you do about your men in the mountains? I hope you will not call off the search?"

He blinks at me, as if seeing me now for the first time, his skin flickering with torchlight. "No … There is still a possibility that Song Seorim … is out here. Somewhere. We will wait. We cannot ignore that chance."

I nod. "Good. Please, Magistrate Hong, when you send your men out again, will you check something for me? Will you send your men over the north face of the mountain behind your enclosure? I want to know what is out there."

The magistrate narrows his eyes. "What have you heard?"

"Only rumours. People in the village do not like the mountain, it seems. I doubt it means anything at all, but it's worth looking into."

The magistrate glances at Man Seok who gives the smallest nod, authorising the change.

We stay after that, waiting in the dark and in the cold. Magistrate Hong suggests that I should leave, but I will not. I will wait for Lord Song. I want to watch him arrive, to see what kind of man he is.

Someone makes a small fire far away from the body, but it spits and steams and will not flare, thick grey smoke filling the clearing.

When he comes he is heaving and wet, out of breath and soaked through with sleet, just like the rest of us. Yet unlike the rest of us he wears a fur-lined hat, a thick padded jacket folded across his wide stomach, and he is followed by three servants bearing sparking torches, one of them supporting his heavy frame.

When Magistrate Hong approaches, Lord Song abruptly holds up his hand. He does not even glance our way. There will be no conversation. Not yet. He waits, just out of reach within the trees, his body filled with tension as his manservant crouches beside the dead girl, touches her face, hands trailing down her shoulder to the crook of her elbow. The man rubs dirt from her skin and then shakes his head. "The mark is not here, my lord. This is some other girl."

Lord Song seems uncertain. "Are you positive? Check again."

"It is not her, my lord. I am certain. There is no birthmark."

I study Lord Song's face as he staggers closer through the shadows, watch as he is confronted by the sight of the girl's body laid out across the frozen earth, her skin burning blue in the dancing torchlight.

Relief, utter exposed relief floods his face when he sees the dead girl's twisted hands, when he drinks in the sight of her curled frozen body and sees it is not his own daughter —that it is someone else's. There is no pity for the girl before him, but I do not blame him for it. He is a nobleman, a *yangban* lord. And the dead girl is surely a lowly villager. Or a servant. Someone who doesn't belong to him, not his own flesh and blood. No one.

Lord Song runs his hands through his wiry grey beard, which hangs heavy and wet, whispering beneath his steaming breath. I wonder if he is praying. He doesn't bother speaking with the magistrate, such an insult that it is not lost on any of us.

And when he leaves, Lord Song places his hand in gratitude on the shoulder of one of Magistrate Hong's guards, a man who hovers behind our party. The nobleman is so very relieved that it is not *his* daughter lying in the shallow grave, that he does not realise he has just given himself away. Now he's lost his chance of ever being alerted in such a way again.

Lord Song and his retainers begin their struggle down the mountainside and, as grey dawn breaks across the mountainside, Magistrate Hong dismisses a guard for the first time since his term as magistrate began. In the same breath he organises the dead girl's transportation back to the office.

We depart ahead of the procession, leaving the guards and Secretary Baek trailing down the mountainside behind us. Guard Kim never speaks, focused only on his feet as he leads us through the dim morning light, winding through the trees with Man Seok and I a few steps behind.

Struggling through the snow, I speak in hushed whispers, so Guard Kim cannot hear.

"Man Seok. What do you make of it?"

He hesitates, face only shadows and sharp lines in the dawn darkness. "I am not certain. You?"

I draw closer to his side. "I think if the dead girl was attempting to flee the valley on foot, to head north out of Joseon, it's very possible she may have chosen to come this way herself. No one would see her." I gesture back into the thick forest. "And from here she could have travelled straight across to the north face of that mountain, out of the valley, toward the coast. It is surely the quickest route out of the valley. It could be managed on foot."

Man Seok nods. "She had supplies."

"Yes."

"Perhaps her killer escaped out of the valley that same way after burying her."

"Most likely," I agree. "Which means he is long gone. It leaves us where we started."

"Worse than when we started. Song Seorim is still missing, and now there is a murder, connected or otherwise."

I don't know what to say at the bitterness lacing his words. It seems this night has taken a toll even on Man Seok. I do not know why I'm so surprised. He is human after all.

The frozen girl's curled fingers stab into my mind, digging deep and raw.

"Man Seok *ssi*," I breathe. "Have you ever seen anything like that before? Something so … sad, I mean."

He is quiet and only when I reach for his arm with numb fingers does he curtly nod his head. His brows draw close together, mouth tight and hard. "Yes," he says finally. He will not meet my eyes. "And worse."

I blink. The heaviness in his voice has me examining him anew, stealing glances as we trudge through the snow. There is much to Man Seok I do not know.

I breathe out softly, finally admitting, "I haven't. Not like that."

Silence settles across the rest of our journey down the slopes, and we remain quiet as we emerge from the thick trees onto the valley floor, dawning sunlight creeping over the range. The sky hangs low and the black iced river almost glows in a small window of light. As we mount our stamping horses, brought again to meet us, I glance back at the mountain behind, shrouded now in heavy mist. The peaks are hidden from view, the window of light long gone.

BACK AT THE enclosure I leave Man Seok alone at the office gates. He will wait there for the procession of men who bring the dead girl's body. I do not wait with him. Instead I creep into the kitchen behind the magistrate's main office building, where I crouch to warm my numb hands against the flaming hearth beneath the cooking cauldrons. I do not know where the cook is, the large older woman who's been preparing all our meals, a job often left for *damo* back in the capital.

When my stiff fingers once again move and bend as they should, one by one I open the dark brown earthenware pots lining the shelves, peering beneath the lids of the woven baskets piled in a corner, searching for something to eat. One is filled with wheat flour, so I fry small mung bean cakes on the wide metal pan above the hearth, squishing the small mounds with my fingers when they need turning. The cakes sizzle and pop on the hot metal.

Slowly the heat from the fire seeps within my bones, and I almost forget the grave on the mountainside. Almost.

I turn and peer about the tiny kitchen, at the dirt floor and the black wood of the inner beams holding up the roof. Behind the hearth lies a tunnel, only small, lined with wide flat river stones and baked clay. It runs from my cooking fire to spread beneath the magistrate's quarters, seeping warmth through the *ondol* flooring until the oiled paper surface becomes a heater to hold the winter at bay. Magistrate Hong is a lucky man. When he returns from the mountains his room will be like fire after the sleet of the night just gone.

The house where I was born had a kitchen much like this one, also connected by a pathway of river stones to the bedrooms of a noble family. That kitchen was small and heavy with heat. Summers in the capital are blistering hot, and the kitchen was always heavy with damp and sweat. I worked there beside the others, my small child hands just as quick as theirs, chopping and cutting and fanning just as skilfully. Working to earn my place in the house I was born into. The house I belonged to. After all, slaves cannot stay if they do not work.

I peer at my own hands now, no longer small and thin as a child's. My flesh is chapped from the cold, nails ragged and bitten. No longer the hands of a lowly servant. These hands belong to a *damo*.

I push the images from the mountainside deep down. I am focused and sharp. I will not forget my duty, will not be lost within nightmares and dreams.

I will finish this job and finish it well.

Taking deep breaths of the cold morning air, I carry the steaming *nokdujeon* to Man Seok at the enclosure gates. We stand close together eating in silence as dawn breaks over the mountain ranges, light spilling across the river and the valley far below.

Until Guard Yu arrives.

He sags with exhaustion yet still seems relieved to see us, taking me aside, clearly not wishing the guardsmen charged with protecting our gates to overhear.

"Last night ... I did not have a chance to tell you. Damo Choon Shim has lit her candle. She is ready to meet you, Damo Dan Ji."

I blink, my mouth full with mung bean cake. "When?"

"Now. We must leave now if we are to reach her in time."

9

Reunion

CHOON SHIM PEERS over the wide stone wall. Only her eyes are visible, dark and nervous in the early morning light.

We meet at the very back of Lord Song's residence, where his stone walls press into the mountains, cold layered rock reaching deep into the ancient trees. A small crumbling shack lies collapsed and leaning against Lord Song's stone enclosure. Abandoned. I imagine no one has walked here for a long time.

Trunks rise thick and twisted from generations of bleak winters, heavy wood lopsided or fallen against the garden walls. It is the perfect place for a meeting, hidden from the main buildings of Lord Song's house and deserted. I huddle against the cold rock of the thick wall, shifting my balance on a twisted juniper trunk growing sloped against the enclosure. My fingers dig deep into the rough crevices within the rock, my body leaning half-hidden beneath the evergreen juniper branches.

Choon Shim peers above the wall. "Have you been well, *Unni*?"

"I have. And you?" I reach my fingers over the cold stone and she grasps my hands within her own, gripping tightly. I do not tell her the truth, that my lids grow heavy enough to sleep where I stand, that my body beats with exhaustion.

Choon Shim's eyes crinkle. A smile. Yet hurriedly she glances over her shoulder, the expression fading. "I do not know how long we can speak."

I nod. "Let us be quick. Tell me."

She smiles again, different this time, proud and fierce. Her words are a rush of urgent whispers. "I have learned much, Dan Ji, the servants here have loose tongues. It seems Song Seorim disappeared in the dead of night alongside an old servant, a woman who has cared for her since birth. Neither have been seen here since."

I nod. "The nurse. I have heard so as well, but no villager is brave enough to confirm it."

"Yes, our Master puts pressure on them. He threatens to raise their taxes if they speak with the police."

"Why? What can Lord Song gain from stalling our investigation?" I shift my position on the fallen log. It is damp with snow and my legs shake. "I saw his face, Choon Shim. Lord Song loves his daughter. He truly wishes to find her. I cannot understand it."

Choon Shim only shrugs. It seems she does not care to guess. "There is more. Everyone here is certain that Song Seorim ran away to meet a lover." Choon Shim tries to pull herself closer against the wall, eyes shining with pride like she has won some kind of game, though I think it was only her that was playing. "Dan Ji, there was no sign of a struggle in her room on the night she disappeared, and three maidservants reported items from their clothing going missing. What does that tell you?"

She does not wait for me to answer.

"*Unni*, it means she was wearing a disguise that night! Song Seorim was dressed as a commoner."

"That is good news," I tell her. I cannot help but smile. "Now that is something new."

"It is not all. I overheard our Master speaking with his head servant, the leader of his private soldiers. I found out why the Master has guards posted at his gate all day and night. It is because he is afraid for his life. He fears someone will kill him!"

I pause. "Who does he fear?"

"Now that I do not know. Except it is so strange, because I also heard that when the Master found out only two investigators were sent from the capital he was furious. Apparently, he had wanted more. Many more. Supposedly he said … the mountains should be crawling with police officers. Strange, is it not?"

"Mmmh."

"One last thing, though I cannot believe it could be real. One of the servants swears he saw a crying ghost at our gates the night after Song Seorim disappeared. He said she was wearing a flowing dress but he could not see her face."

I hesitate, letting it seep in. "A ghost?"

"He says it was an omen. He said the ghost came to warn us."

Choon Shim half laughs, as if she thinks the man is foolish, but I see the fear flaring in her eyes. She is superstitious, and the sighting of a ghost has made her nervous.

We lapse into silence, and I am half expecting to be interrupted or discovered at any moment, my body filled with tension. Choon Shim keeps glancing behind her.

Yet nothing happens. The garden remains quiet.

No sounds at all except the wind whistling through the

pines, the creaking of the tree trunks, the falling needles. Choon Shim suddenly giggles softly, an outpouring of nervous energy finally overflowing. I take her hand again over the wall, the cold stone biting against my bare wrist as she squeezes my fingers.

"You look tired, *Unni*," she whispers.

"I am. So very tired. We had a difficult night."

"I know. I've heard the rumours."

When I raise my brows at her questioningly, Choon Shim only shrugs. "It's a small valley, word spreads fast. By mid-morning everyone will know what you found up there."

I am not overly surprised. Even in Hanseong news travels fast. There is nothing else for the people to do. So, they talk.

I shrug. "Well, perhaps it will aid us. We have not yet identified the girl, though we do know she is not Song Seorim."

"Perhaps someone in the village will hear the rumour and come to claim the body."

"Perhaps." I pause. "And you, Choon Shim, how have you found it? Have you been safe?"

"Not safe from work." She pulls away from my hand and holds her fingers up where I can see. They are red and raw, blisters and cracked skin around her nails and red swollen knuckles. "It is from washing clothes in ice water. It is a terrible job."

"I am sorry."

She shrugs, and then flashes me a hopeful smile. "Did you have to work like this during the corruption case?"

I nod. "My back ached from carrying water from the river. It was so far away."

Choon Shim's smile grows wider. "That is my job, too!

Yet they never bothered to prepare us for that during the *damo* examinations."

I cannot help but laugh, memories stirred of those long-ago trials. I passed for I am over 150 centimetres, fast, agile, and able to lift a bag of rice weighing more than 40 kilograms. And I can drink three bowls of *makgeolli*, a potent and sour fermented liquor. And so, where other girls failed, I did not. I became what I am now. A *damo*. As Choon Shim did after me.

"I could do with some *makgeolli* right now," Choon Shim whispers seriously, before erupting into giggles. I do not join her laughter this time, for honestly, I agree with her. *Makgeolli* would warm my frozen body from the inside out, thawing my bones.

I sigh. "What is Lord Song's house like?"

"Large. And filled with people. Servants everywhere, but he has his own personal soldiers too. It is so busy. Always bustling, even with the young lady gone."

"And Song Seorim's mother?"

Choon Shim shakes her head. "A sickness passed through the valley last year."

I nod and sigh again, rubbing my temple with the heel of my palm. "Choon Shim, I am so sorry, but I must go."

"I know." She is almost wistful, as if she doesn't want to let me. She abruptly asks, "And Lieutenant Jo? How is he?"

"Man Seok? Good." I hesitate and then add, "Tired."

Choon Shim frowns. "Do the people at the office know about … what he did during the arrests? For the corruption case?"

I cannot meet her gaze. "I do not know. I don't think so."

"Good. It will be easier if they don't. Be careful, *Unni*."

I hesitate, hoping she will not say what I think she will. "Careful of what?"

"Of Lieutenant Jo, of course."

My gaze drops to my hands. "He isn't … there's nothing to be careful of, Choon Shim. You remember how he was when we travelled here together, on the road. There was nothing to be careful of. Only rumours."

"What happened was not some rumour. But yes, of course I remember. He was … not unkind while we travelled."

I nod, somehow grateful to hear her say it. "You also must be careful, Choon Shim. While you stay in this house. Be very careful. And trust no one else, only myself and Man Seok. Only Guard Yu." I smile encouragingly at her.

She is just about to leave when I change my mind and call her back. "You have done a good job, Choon Shim. You should be very proud of it. And whoever didn't believe in you at home … well, you have already proved them wrong."

My final view of her face is a good one, eyes shining and mouth curved into a pleased smile, until she disappears deep into the undergrowth of Lord Song's grounds.

Choon Shim is right.

By the time I have returned to the government office, word has spread like wildfire and the whole valley knows about the girl we found lying frozen in the mountain.

10

A Mother

I STAND OUTSIDE the little house, feet planted in the muddy ground of the courtyard. A low crumbling wall of piled rocks surrounds the small yard, separating it from the winding mud pathways of the village. The black ice river creeps at the edges of the squalid dwellings, mountains rising into heavy cloud beyond the snow-covered banks.

It is an old place, the wooden doors to the *hanok*'s kitchen practically rotted through, dampness infecting the hardened clay and dark stains clinging to the walls. I swing open the doors and peer into the dingy shadowed depths, find an old woman crouched in front of the low furnace, poking at it with a stick. Her back is bent deeply, head lowered, and a heavy sadness fills the musty space, mixing with the thick smoky smell of wet wood burning. Black stains cover the walls above the hearth from years of cooking fires.

"Jeok Gong Hwa *ssi*," I call her name softly.

She glances at me, and I see she is not so old after all. Young eyes shine through a face aged well before her time, skin weathered from the cold, cheeks gaunt from too many bitter winters and too much physical work. And too many days of starvation. This woman is not old. She is poor.

"Yes." Her voice is empty of all emotion. "I am Jeok Gong Hwa."

I step inside the damp kitchen. My boot sinks into the soft earth as I crouch beside her to warm my hands in the thick heat of her furnace.

"They tell me the girl we found in the mountains is your daughter."

She turns away. "I already told the magistrate everything. I identified her. What is there left to say?" She pokes at the fire, her movements slow, as if she is underwater.

As I watch her reach for more damp firewood I imagine she is drowning in the black frozen river beside the forest, imagine her body sinking below a thick crust of bobbing broken ice.

"I want to find out who did it." I reach firmly for her arm, stopping her laboured movements, forcing her to cease the incessant *doing* of things. "There is much left to say. For I want to help you."

She stares at me, eyes big and black. Empty.

"Tell me, why did you not report your daughter missing all that time ago?"

The woman goes back to poking her fire. "My daughter ran away. She always told me she would. She hates this house. She says it is rotted to the core."

"She did not like living here?"

The dead girl's mother blinks at me. "Would you?"

I say nothing.

The woman clears her throat and just for a moment I see her hard face crumple, as if she will fall into pieces, as if she will begin to scream and wail and cry. But then it is gone. "I could not give her enough. Of course, she wants to go."

"Can you tell me when you first knew she was gone? What day was it?"

"A moon ago … Or less than that. My daughter works in the marketplace, serving at the inn there. She did not come home. She always used to come home. But I knew what she wanted so I imagined … and … I did not search for her."

The woman begins to choke and I reach for her again, hands hard on her face to force her mind to focus on me, force her to look only at me. I have no time for her nightmares. I am cold and harsh for I have a job to do.

"I was sent here to your village for a reason," I tell her. "I am here to find Lord Song's daughter, Song Seorim. She disappeared. Did you know?"

The woman nods, confusion leaking into her strained expression.

"Tell me, the evening your daughter disappeared, was it close to the time Song Seorim went missing? Think carefully now, I need to know."

Her gaze flickers back and forth across my face.

"I do not … I do not know … perhaps … I think, yes, I think so. In the marketplace, when I went to find my daughter at the inn the next morning, I heard … rumours something had happened to Lord Song's daughter … she ran away too."

"Perhaps," I tell her, still holding firmly onto her face. "Perhaps not. Tell me, why is it you did not fear for your girl's life if she had run away? The road is long for a young woman travelling alone. Why did you not send someone after her?"

Tears fill the woman's eyes. "Her older brother … my

son. His name is Shin Yonggae. I thought ... I was so certain..."

"Tell me about your son."

"He is a travelling merchant, a peddler. My daughter, she adores him, idolises him. He was here recently, he stayed months longer than usual. So much longer. And she said that when he went away, this time she would go with him. That is what she told me. I said no, but ... but I was so sure..."

"How often does your son return home from his travels?"

"Once a year. My son comes home to see me. To see his ... sister."

"And what does your son sell when he travels across Joseon?" I let the woman go because she is swaying now, slumping onto the packed earth, hands to her face.

"He sells women's things," she whispers. "Pretty things. Face powder and perfumes. *Norigae*. *Binyeo*. Things I could never buy for my daughter. But Shin Yonggae would bring his sister things. Expensive trinkets. Pretty gifts. She loved him so very much."

The woman begins to cry.

"Where is your son now? Tell me where he is."

Sobs wrack her body and she folds into herself, becoming smaller and frailer until there is almost nothing left.

"I do not know," she breathes. "He left for Hanseong the night my daughter went missing. I do not know where my son is."

I let her cry, hand on her shoulder. Muffled sounds echo from beyond the kitchen, the heavy wooden doors creaking open as Guard Yu peers inside. The woman does not even look up, lost within her nightmare, and I wave him away impatiently, not yet finished. Only when the missing girl's mother has cried herself dry, when she is gazing blankly at the flames dancing inside the furnace, do I ask her the route her son travels. And only then do I leave her alone to grieve in that dark stained room within her crumbling house, both her children long gone.

Guard Yu waits in the courtyard, boots sinking deep into the mud. I emerge blinking into the weak light and he turns around, expression questioning as he blows warm air onto his fingers.

"Did she tell you anything, Damo Dan Ji?"

I nod. Bone-deep weariness creeps inside my body now, gnawing like the cold. I gaze around at the winding pathways of the village, at the crumbling stone walls beside the road and the destitute homes. At the people who walk by and glance at Guard Yu suspiciously, their hair matted and their fingers blue with cold. And I think of the woman I have just left alone inside that stained kitchen. Remember her daughter's blue fingers curled like claws in the night forest, left there beneath the dirt all alone.

I walk straight past Guard Yu, leaving him peering back uncertainly at the little *hanok* behind us. "Is she alright?" he asks as he catches up outside the gate, falling into step beside me, mist escaping his lips in clouds.

"I doubt it."

Guard Yu frowns. He must hear something more than I like to reveal in my shaking voice, for next he says, "It will be fine, Damo Dan Ji, we will unravel it. We will find the people responsible for her daughter's murder. And we will find Song Seorim."

I peer across at him. "You sound so certain, Guard Yu."

"I *am* certain. Magistrate Hong has faith in your abilities."

"Magistrate Hong has faith in Lieutenant Jo Man Seok," I correct.

Guard Yu smiles, unembarrassed. "Yes, that is true. The magistrate believes Lieutenant Jo is not the kind of man to give up."

This makes me smile. "The magistrate is right. Lieutenant Jo does not give up."

Guard Yu hesitates and then says, "Lieutenant Jo, he is clearly a good investigator, but he is a little ... difficult, do you not agree? I mean ... it must be difficult for you to work with him."

I stop walking. "What do you mean?"

Guard Yu shrugs. "Well, he's not an easy man, is he? Many of the other guards are a little ... nervous of him already. It seems to me he is a hard man."

I begin to move again, slowly, almost losing my footing on the wet pathway. "They are afraid of him?"

Guard Yu nods, oblivious to my discomfort. "Of course. Isn't that obvious?"

I keep frowning.

"Surely you have heard the ... rumours?"

"You should not listen to rumours, Guard Yu. It is beneath you."

"Yet he was demoted. Does it not seem then that the rumours could be true?"

I shake my head, skin prickling beneath my clothes. "I do not know what he has done to the other guards, but if Man Seok has frightened them there was good reason. I trust him. As should you."

Guard Yu shrugs easily. "I do trust him."

He is unaware how his words have twisted inside my gut, for now he seems almost disinterested by the very conversation he has started. He walks away, as if he does not really mind at all what Man Seok has or hasn't done.

I stare daggers into his back as he struggles ahead up the sloping hill toward the government office, muttering beneath my breath. "Man Seok is not a hard man. He is a good man."

But Guard Yu is too far ahead and he does not hear.

11

The Threads

IN THE EVENING the world grows dark and still I cannot sleep. I toss and turn in my little room, listening to the wailing wolves as their howls drift from the mountain peaks. I cannot imagine why a young girl would travel alone with her small pack into those forests by choice. Even tigers might walk those mountains, hunting and stalking, though it was not a tiger that killed her.

I sit up in the darkness, shivering with cold. On nights like this, my mind moves too quickly, facts and ideas and memories tearing my insides like the storms that envelop Hanseong in the spring. Yellow dust smothering Joseon, blown all the way from the deserts beyond our borders. I clutch at threads but cannot tie them together, the loose ends raging inside my head. My cold stiff fingers will not uncurl from the fists they have become. I sigh, facing the truth. Sleep will not come. Lying here is a waste of time.

I climb to my feet and drag my worn padded jacket across my sleeping clothes, smoothing back my hair as I step outside into the sharp night air, shivers slipping beneath my clothes and spreading across my skin. Pulling on my shoes, I walk slowly through the deserted *damo* quarters and into the larger outer compound, slipping past the guards on duty. They stand huddled around wide metal bowls filled with raging fire, crackling and popping with sparks flying upwards into the night sky. Flickering light dances across the stone walls.

I drift toward the magistrate's office, for light still filters from behind the closed shutters. I am not the only one who cannot sleep it seems.

I peek inside to find Secretary Baek and Man Seok poring over piles of thick dusty annals, books strewn across every space available on the long wooden table. Secretary Baek is pale in the candlelight, sweat shimmering across his clammy skin. When I open the door, he is whispering furiously to Man Seok, voice low and hands fluttering in front of his face.

Neither man seems to notice I have entered until I clear my throat. "What are you both looking at? It is so late."

Secretary Baek jerks in surprise but Man Seok's expression does not change. His black eyes flick across my shift poking from beneath my jacket but I ignore him, not caring whether he thinks it is inappropriate to be in public dressed as I am. I step toward the table. "What are you reading?"

Secretary Baek pushes quickly to his feet. "Damo Dan Ji. I hope you can forgive me. I do not ... I have no experience with a case such as this one, and it is true I did not complete my work ... thoroughly ... yet I hope you can understand that I meant no..."

Man Seok waves his hand for silence and Secretary Baek immediately obeys, the words dying on his lips. I watch curiously as Man Seok nods toward the doors, effectively dismissing the older man without another word.

Secretary Baek scuttles past me as quickly as he can, visibly relieved to escape, candlelight shimmering across his sweat covered forehead.

I frown as the shutters close behind him. "What did you do to Secretary Baek?"

Man Seok says nothing, scowling at the annals beneath his hands, turning pages furiously. After a moment I drift around the table to settle beside him.

I study him in the candlelight, the new growth of an unshaven beard dusting his cheeks, the dark shadows beneath his black eyes. Sharp angles of his jaw. His mouth is drawn tight and I begin to see him as others do, a fierce and driven man not afraid to push and push and push to gain the answers he seeks.

I settle back, drawing my knees in and wrapping my arms around my legs, huddling beneath my padded jacket and layered skirts, watching.

"Man Seok. What are you looking at? Are they police records?"

He lifts his hand to his temple, rubbing his face.

He is exhausted.

"That son of a dog Secretary Baek never truly checked the valley's records when I asked. Do you remember, he told us there were no similar cases? He was lying through his teeth."

I sit straighter, unable to stop myself grasping hold of the bound annals from beneath Man Seok's hands, flicking through the pages. He stands and moves to my side, leaning over to point. "Here, this entry here. Eight years ago, a young woman goes missing from down the valley. They never found her." He reaches across me to drag over another record book, opening it to a different entry. "And that same year in winter, another girl. Never found."

"How many?" I breathe. The jumble in my head

begins to swirl again, the yellow dust storm building in force, scraping at my insides. "How many girls?"

"Going back twelve years ... at least four of them. Up and down the valley."

"Four?"

He nods. "Yet look here, there are also entries of reported runaways."

I read the statement he points to. Five years ago. A *gisaeng* disappears into the night and is never seen again. And in another record book, a servant girl disappears, a suspected runaway. A bitter laugh escapes my mouth. Such disappearances would barely be worth recording, except these women all belonged to someone, all of them servants or slaves or *gisaeng*. It is bad for the careful balance of the world if slaves think they can run, so records were dutifully made and investigations launched, albeit short and half-hearted.

Man Seok shifts closer, drawing my attention to a newer book, dropping it heavily on the existing pile. "And this woman, just last year. It is reported in the records as a suicide. A drowning."

"I remember Secretary Baek mentioning it."

"Well, there was no body. They could not have known for certain."

I stare up at him. "There were no bodies for ... any of them?"

"None," Man Seok confirms. He pushes the annals away as if he is tired of them. One teeters on the edge of the table and falls with a loud thump to the floor. He doesn't bother picking it up, instead he just returns to his seat.

"What are you thinking, Man Seok?"

"I don't know."

"Are there similarities between them? The women?"

"All of them were young. Yet all had reached puberty."

"Then none were children. What else?"

Man Seok flexes his fingers, moving them to keep the blood flowing. "All came from destitute families. Poor villagers. Merchants or innkeepers. Servants and entertainment troupes. Or they had no families at all." He glances across at me. "None had an influential father like Song Seorim."

Silence creeps as this information sinks in, until Man Seok breaks it once more.

"No money from their remaining family members equals no pressure on the police for a resolution. Investigations lasted only days. If that."

I see blank glassy eyes, staring at the night sky. Cold claw hands, blue, nails caked with dirt.

"No one even searched for them," I whisper.

Man Seok says nothing.

"How did Magistrate Hong not know of this?"

Again, Man Seok does not answer.

"Well, what about the guards? Or even the villagers, surely everyone in the valley must know. Surely there would be rumours, people would remember, they would…" The words die on my lips.

Man Seok's attention flicks to my face. "What is it?"

I almost laugh, bitterness searing through the swirl of threads inside my head, stopping everything dead. "I *did* hear about it. At the *gibang*. They talked about a human ghost on the north face of the mountain. They said it steals little girls. I thought it was … a tale."

Man Seok watches me steadily and I smile a little, barely lifting the corner of my mouth, just enough to hide how I feel. It is a failing. A mistake. The north face of the mountain. A human ghost. I should have sent the magistrate there sooner, and if I had, perhaps…

Clawed hands, stiff body half buried in dirt and snow.

I will make up for it. I will do better.

"We need to go up there," I tell Man Seok. "To that mountain. If there is something to see, I want to be there."

He nods. "I agree, I will organise it. But Dan Ji, you know Magistrate Hong has found Jeok Gong Hwa's son. It must be dealt with first."

"The dead girl's brother? Already? No. I did not know."

Man Seok's brow furrows. "I asked the magistrate to tell you."

I say nothing, only shrug. He should not expect Magistrate Hong to pass on news to a lowly *damo* like some kind of messenger boy. It's obvious the magistrate would not comply. I shrug off my disappointment, unbidden and unwanted.

"It does not matter," Man Seok says finally. "The magistrate's men are bringing the boy, Shin Yonggae, back from the next valley. I am told the party will arrive by dawn."

I pause, letting this new information soak in, letting it merge with the roaring storm. "And where has this brother been?"

"They found him at a *gibang*. The headmistress there says he has been staying for some time, drinking himself to death and spending all his money."

I frown. "He did not get very far. His mother was so certain he would be long gone by now. She said her son had travelled south, away toward Hanseong. Does he know about what happened to his sister?"

"I am not sure. We haven't told him."

I hesitate. "Jeok Gong Hwa, his mother. When I visited her house, she was ... she seemed..."

I falter, for I am uncertain suddenly what it is I mean to

say. Man Seok remains quiet, sitting with his arms folded across his chest, staring at me steadily. He says nothing and the flame light dances across his skin.

"I do not know." I shake my head. "Seeing that girl up there..." I smile at him, cheeks hot, self-conscious. "I hardly feel like myself, Man Seok."

He does not move, black eyes held on mine. "You are always yourself, Dan Ji *ssi*. Whether you are pretending to be someone else or not. You are the same."

I blink and then after a moment drop my gaze, cheeks still flushed.

It's good if he thinks so. I do not want to change too much.

Yet I feel these stories we unravel take little pieces of me away with them, and I become smaller and smaller. Less like myself with each passing day.

When I glance back at Man Seok he still watches me, and I wonder if that's how he felt when the corruption case ended. I wonder if he lost himself inside that place, during those six months he was there with me. And before that? I do not know. There were other cases. Other people he pretended to be. Other months, and, sometimes I suspect, even years when he was not himself.

Perhaps that is why he did what he did back then.

But I do not ask him.

And later that night after Man Seok has sent me back to my quarters, finally I do sleep. Yet I dream only of clawed hands and ginger taffee in the snow. Of little pieces of myself floating away into the mountains, drifting on winds that carry the howls of wolves.

12

To Interrogate

MAGISTRATE HONG and Secretary Baek hover within the doorway as Man Seok prepares to question Jeok Gong Hwa's son, the brother of the frozen girl from the mountain. I stand inside the prison building, leaning against the wall with my arms folded across my chest for warmth—keeping out of Magistrate Hong's way.

It is almost midday now, and I am frustrated it took so long to bring the young man here, for the later we finish interrogating him the later our party leaves for the north face of the mountain. And slowly, the day is wearing on.

Man Seok settles across from our prisoner on a thick wooden slab of tree trunk. Each time he shifts, the rushes beneath his boots waft damp and mouldy from the rising wet on the prison floor.

The young man is not inside a cell. Not yet. As far as we know he has done nothing worse than become utterly intoxicated and spend every last coin to his name on *gisaeng* and rice wine. All while his younger sister lay dead and half-buried on a mountain side in his home town.

"Shin Yonggae. That is your name, correct?" Man

Seok's voice is quiet and steady. "You are Jeok Gong Hwa's son?"

The young man nods, clouded with confusion and the thick after effects of alcohol, only now beginning to wear off. He looks terrible—skin pale, mouth drawn back in fear. One of his eyes is bulging and swollen black. Courtesy of Magistrate Hong's men, I am sure.

"I need to ask you some questions, Shin Yonggae *ssi*, and if you answer me truthfully and immediately, this will be a better experience for you. Do you understand me?"

The young man nods again. For a moment it seems as if he will retch. Instead he glances behind his shoulder to the cell. I cannot see from where I am standing, as only Man Seok's back is visible, but I'm sure some threat has passed between them.

"I understand … sir." The prisoner's voice shakes and Man Seok nods, satisfied.

"Tell me how you know Song Seorim," he orders. At the door the rest of us watch and wait, a collective held breath, a change in our bodies. Tension.

"Song Seorim?" The confusion returns and Shin Yonggae's face is flooded with emotion. "I know her from the marketplace. I sell things to her."

"Did you ever give her anything? Gifts perhaps?"

Shin Yonggae is taken aback. "Why? Why would I give her anything?"

Man Seok is silent, waiting. He shifts on the wooden block, dragging it closer to the prisoner, making his body bigger, more intimidating.

The young man flinches, lowering his head to protect his swollen face. "Yes, yes I did. I gave Song Seorim gifts. Do you work for her father? For Lord Song? What will you do to me?"

"Why would you suspect that I work for Lord Song?"

"I ... I do not know."

Man Seok gestures behind him to Magistrate Hong. "I operate on behalf of the *podocheong*, and on behalf of the district magistrate."

"Then why am I here? What do you want?"

"What did you do to Song Seorim?"

"Do to her?"

Magistrate Hong steps into the building, shadow covering half his face in the dark space. It doesn't hide his anger. "You fool! You killed her! You killed Song Seorim and buried her to hide your crime! Where is she? Where did you hide her?"

The prisoner falls back, eyes wide, mouth wide too. His skin is bloodshot and red. "K ... kill her? What do you...? I never ... even touched her. Why are you asking me this?"

Silence.

"Please," Shin Yonggae whimpers. "Please tell me, why would you ask such a thing?"

For a moment I think Magistrate Hong will explode and scream at the younger man, but the seconds pass and he bites his tongue, a look passing between him and Man Seok.

I see Guard Yu was right. The magistrate does indeed trust Lieutenant Jo to solve this problem for him. The older man turns and stalks from the building, striding away across the yard outside, his boots crunching on the gravel. Secretary Baek quickly follows at his heel.

When they are gone, Man Seok leans closer to the prisoner. "The magistrate suggests we torture you until you confess. He believes you have killed Song Seorim and buried her body in the mountains."

"No, no, please. Song Seorim? Why would I ever do that, please, I never did that."

Shin Yonggae is sobbing now, tears and sweat mixing

on his cheeks. He tries to wipe the mess yet only smears it further into his skin. "Please … believe me, I would never hurt her."

"Tell me why you would never hurt her."

Shin Yonggae is silent and then finally he whispers, "Because I love her."

Man Seok nods. "And tell me why you are so afraid of Lord Song."

"I … I thought he must have known what we were planning." Shin Yonggae's skin is pale and slick with sweat. "Lord Song must have known. That's why Song Seorim never arrived, is it not?" He almost smiles now, hope dawning. "I thought Seorim changed her mind, I thought it was impossible she would really come with me. But he stopped her, didn't he? That is what happened." He keeps mumbling to himself, until Man Seok finally holds up his hand for silence.

"No. That is not what happened. We believe Song Seorim did plan to meet you. She stole village clothes from her kitchen maids. She and her nurse disappeared in the dead of night. Presumably to meet with you."

Shin Yonggae's eyes widen. "But … but she did not meet with me."

"No. She has been missing for nearly a moon."

"Missing?" Shin Yonggae tries to push himself to his feet but he has been marching throughout the night and morning. His knees give out, his body collapsing onto the dirty river rushes strewn across the floor, gasping. "Where is she then?"

"That is what we are trying to find out, Shin Yonggae *ssi*." Man Seok remains calm, unmoved by the younger man's display of emotion.

"And Lord Song? Her father?" Shin Yonggae turns

paler. And rightly so. Men have died for less than he has attempted.

"If Lord Song is aware his daughter wished to run away with a commoner, he has told the police nothing of it," answers Man Seok. "Yet if he does know, you can rest easy he is not aware of your identity."

"How ... how can you be so certain?"

Man Seok leans closer. "Because if he knew, you would surely be dead."

Shin Yonggae cowers, crying again with dirt streaking his cheeks. I turn away, watching the outside world, the dim grey light that shines across the courtyard, the guards going about their business. Their steps crunch heavy as they avoid the patches of mud. Behind me in the dark, Man Seok compels our prisoner to tell him everything, to relive every event leading up to and beyond the night of Song Seorim's disappearance. But there is nothing new. He loved her. She loved him. They planned a future, chose a meeting place. And Shin Yonggae waited.

And Song Seorim never came.

Finally, I hear Man Seok's voice again, quiet and grim. "Shin Yonggae, tell me, how long since you have seen your younger sister?"

"My sister?" The young man blinks. "Awhile. Since before all this. She is at home, with my mother." He sways, seeming as if he might drop where he kneels, exhaustion dragging his body down toward the mouldy river rushes.

Man Seok must see it too, for he orders Shin Yonggae to rest before standing and taking me aside, leading me through the prison doors out into the dim daylight. Dark clouds hang low and heavy overhead. He readjusts the leather straps running across his chest, sliding his sword case in against his back. "What do you make of him?"

I answer without hesitation. "I think he speaks the

truth. I don't believe he knows what happened to Song Seorim. And if he did, I think he would tell us."

After all, he's already admitted to a serious crime. I shake my head. Shin Yonggae was a fool to let it go so far. The world we live in is filled with such familiar grooves, like channels of water carved into a farming field. It is impossible to lift from the pathways our birth sets out for us. Noble daughter or commoner, king or *damo*, we are born to be what we are.

It seems Shin Yonggae didn't know this simple rule.

Yet against my better judgement, there is still a small part of me that can almost see them together, almost wish it might've been true. Shin Yonggae and Seorim. Imagine if they'd made it across those mountains to the ocean, if they'd managed to flee Joseon over the sea.

Man Seok is oblivious to my wild imaginings. "I agree. Shin Yonggae does not know anything."

I am silent, trying to tie the threads together. "What do you suppose happened that night?"

"It is too much of a coincidence not to be connected. Shin Yonggae's sister. Shin Yonggae's lover. Do you not agree?"

I nod. "My guess is that Shin Yonggae's sister followed him that night, when he was going to meet Song Seorim. We know she wished to leave the valley with him when it was time for him to go, but perhaps she worried Shin Yonggae wouldn't allow her to accompany him, so she followed secretly. And I think somehow the two girls met each other on the roadside, long before either of them ever reached Shin Yonggae. And when they met … something happened."

Here I falter, for I cannot guess the rest of the events of that night. I sigh. "Also, I keep wondering about Seorim's nurse. Shin Yonggae barely seems to know anything about her; he never even spoke to her directly."

Man Seok rubs his jaw. "What do you want to do with Shin Yonggae after Secretary Baek records his statement?"

I hesitate. "Can we not let him go home?"

I predict Man Seok will protest but he does not, surprising me. Instead he nods. "We can. For now. But, this is a small valley, people will talk. And you know Lord Song has his ear close to the ground."

"We could still try." I feel as if I'm pleading with him. I don't even know why. "Perhaps Shin Yonggae could leave the valley … for a short while."

Man Seok shrugs. "Perhaps. If he's willing to leave his mother behind."

I bite my lip, lost in thought. There's not much we can do for the young man, to let him go is inadvisable, but I can't bear to lock him away or sentence him to lashes.

Man Seok sighs, hand rubbing his eyes. "Wait for me outside the front gate. I've organised for Guard Kim to take us up the mountain this afternoon."

I blink at the sky, thick grey clouds gathering across the valley. "But it's getting late. It will be dark before we return."

"Do you prefer to wait?" Man Seok raises his brows at me, challenging, and I glare back at him. He knows how to make anyone do exactly what he wants.

"No," I admit. "I don't want to wait."

"Good. Because Guard Kim led a team to search the north face and they found a deserted shack up there. The other men are too afraid to go back, but he's agreed to take us."

"They are afraid? Why?"

"They say the place is bad. Filled with rot. They heard a ghost lives there, a man without a face."

"A man without … a face?" I repeat the words slowly, a chill stealing across my skin. I glance back at the dark sky. "Alright. I'll wait at the front gates. What will you do?"

"I'm going back inside to tell Shin Yonggae what happened to his sister."

I nod, not envying Man Seok such a terrible task, thinking back to Shin Yonggae's mother, crumpled and alone inside her dark damp house.

I turn to leave, for I will return to my room and find every piece of winter clothing I can for this journey up the mountain. The snow is heavier toward the peaks and I do not know how far we must travel through that deep icy forest.

I have already begun to walk away when he calls my name.

"Dan Ji *ssi*."

He is by my side already, his body blocking out the weak sun, covering me in shadow. "Here. For you. For the mountain." He pushes material into my hands, soft and silken beneath my chill fingers, and then he is gone, striding back toward the prison. I stare at his broad back and then down at the thing he has given me.

A winter hat. A *nambawi*.

Lined with soft rabbit fur, silk on the outside coloured black, shaped to sit low across a woman's forehead and drape over her ears and the back of her neck, fur against skin. An ornament is sewn to the front, tassels of deep red hanging low across the forehead.

I stare at it for a long time. It is beautiful, and not something for a lowly woman like me to wear, no matter how cold it becomes, no matter how deep north I have travelled. I stare at it and run my fingers through the soft fur.

I hesitate in the courtyard long after Man Seok is gone.

And then I creep closer to the prison building doorway, open like a gaping cave leading into shadow. I peer into the darkness. I cannot hear what Man Seok says to our prisoner, but I see him kneel in the dirty river reeds next to Shin Yonggae.

His hand is placed on the younger man's shoulder. Shin Yonggae sobs with his fingers clasped across his face and his head bowed low against the cold hard floor.

13

A Demon

GUARD KIM LEADS us into the mountains and I steadfastly ignore the faltering light, ignore the thick shadows cast across the forest by the peaks above. It is not the time of day to travel deep into the spaces between the ranges, the towering mountains lining the valley and hemming us in on all sides.

Yet we are here anyway.

Guard Kim is agitated and keeps glancing behind us from his position at the head of our party, focus flicking across bare trees and between the rock shadows running long and shifting along the black earth. Perhaps he is afraid of tigers. I've heard those beasts wander isolated mountains such as this, far more dangerous than a pack of hungry wolves. I shiver.

Three other men follow close behind, sent to bring us safely to our destination. Their hands clasp tightly around yet unlit torches, ready to ward off wandering wolves. The men whisper among themselves furiously and I catch the word *gwishin*, or ghost, often, feel the fear dripping from their mouths even as the steam of their breath rises ever upwards.

We struggle higher, the snow setting in. It creeps at the edges of large boulders and twisted shrubs, clinging to the winter trees. The landscape changes as we near the north face of the mountain, the snow deepening, turning crisp and white, clean like freshly pressed silk, not marred by the dirt and mud of the village far below.

I turn once, just before we cross the ridge to the north face, stand staring over the dark thin valley. My eyes follow the winding black river and the dirty grey smoke rising from a hundred *hanok* kitchen fires.

And then we are over to the other side.

I follow behind Man Seok without speaking, trudging through the snow, pressing my cold fingers beneath my arms to keep warm. He glances back at me often, his skin almost blue with cold, cheeks flushed and forehead slick with sweat despite the ice hanging in the air. A frown holds tight to his face, never letting go, hard mouth, hard fingers holding his lacquered sword scabbard in a fist. And whenever Lieutenant Jo Man Seok draws near the guards they quickly drop into silence, leaving only echoes of their whispered words drifting in the cold air.

Gwishin.

Demon.

I say nothing to anyone and follow quietly, enveloped in silence as we begin to move downward again, following the natural slope of the hills toward a new valley below. A hidden twisting space empty of humans and life. When I catch glimpses of the valley floor between the trees, no kitchen fires burn, no plumes of smoking grey clouds rise into the horizon. Only empty space and forest stretches out before us. We continue walking down and I am sure, just for a single moment, that I catch sight of something slate grey on the horizon.

The sea.

Vast and never-ending. Just beyond the farthest mountain, the valley below a winding road to reach its distant shores.

I have never seen the sea.

Until this day.

Guard Kim abruptly holds up an arm, effectively halting us. When I peer to the horizon again my glimpse of the water is long gone, replaced now by grey bare forest and dark sky, smatterings of green where the evergreen pines and junipers grow. I lean with one numb hand pressed against the bark of a tree, head bowed to let the air creep back inside my lungs, resting.

"You need to go onwards through there," announces Guard Kim, and when I follow his pointed hand a thick grove of bamboo rises ahead, a splash of evergreen against a bleak winter. Bright and glaring within the grey surrounding us.

"The hut is through that place?" The frown is carved deep into Man Seok's face, turning his expression fierce. I wonder if he uses it to hide his own fear, for the air feels strange in this part of the mountain.

I do not believe the stories of the man who lives up here, the man who is not a man. Yet I feel unsettled all the same.

I turn to Guard Kim. "You will not take us?" My voice almost cracks from underuse.

Guard Kim slowly shakes his head.

The other men will not make eye contact, suddenly examining the ground and the trees and the sky.

"Fine," snaps Man Seok. His temper is short now, his

patience gone. He turns to me and his expression softens. "Are you ready?"

I nod, forging ahead across the small clearing without another word. There is no time to waste as the afternoon wears on. As the sun slowly slips away.

Approaching the copse of bright green, I slide my body carefully between the thick hard stalks. No pathway unfolds here, only rising bamboo and snow. White frost catches in each groove of the plant, piling onto long thin leaves, a canopy of white cloud clinging to green far above. I push a stalk aside and shower myself with light snow. Ice creeps beneath my *jeogori* and down my neck, the damp slicking my clothes against my back. I shiver.

"Careful," Man Seok warns but it is too late. My footing is lost in the deep snow and my hands reach wildly for the bamboo to catch myself, fingers tight against the hard-cold stems. I swear loudly as Man Seok drags me upright, hand tight on my upper arm. And then he carefully readjusts the thick worn material wrapped across my head and tied beneath my chin, cold fingers slow as he dusts snow from the top. He doesn't ask why I do not wear the *nambawi* he gifted me. And I do not raise the topic of its absence. I turn away instead, the strangeness of this place seeping inside my body, Man Seok's hands causing my skin to tingle bright and hot.

Mist rises as we push deeper into the grove. It hangs thick and white in the air, a soft haze that blinds us and hems us in.

I move closer to Man Seok.

Here the bamboo is bent low beneath the weight of snow. I try not to press into the thick stalks lest I disturb it. Loud harsh bird cries break the silence, the caws of big blackbirds. I am sure I almost glimpse one through the mist. But when we draw closer it is no longer there. My heart staggers against my chest and I am thinking of the stories my father told me when I was a child, stories of creatures with the smooth featureless face of an egg, with no eyes, no nose, no mouth. He told me they were the spirits of long forgotten ghosts, those with no one left to mourn them.

If you see one, it means that you will die.

Ghosts without faces.

"Man Seok," I breathe. I press my head with numb hands, trying to calm myself. Foolish. Childish. I am a *damo* of the *podocheong*, not some frightened little girl.

Man Seok hesitates, his skin dusted with ice, black hair dripping strands across his face. "Are you alright?"

I take deep sucking breaths of the mist, set my mouth and nod firmly. "I am. Keep going. I think I see the edges of the grove ahead. It seems to open out."

And it does.

Into a circular clearing of mud and grime that houses a sloping dilapidated *hanok* structure in the middle, the black earth rising behind it to become thick winter forest again. Light snow falls steadily from above but the ground here is carved up fresh, chunks of frozen mud pushed into the shape of deep footprints.

"Man Seok."

I point with my chin at the footprints, keeping one eye on the rotting house ahead.

"Guard Kim was here early yesterday with his men." Man Seok's voice is low. "They could be his."

I shake my head slowly, crouching down to point deliberately at a thatch of twisted woven straw left half-submerged in a chunk of solid mud.

None of the magistrate's guards wear woven straw sandals.

The footprints belong to someone else.

Man Seok uses his hands to communicate now, like we were taught back at the *podocheong*, the special silent way that explains a tactical approach when raiding requires utter silence. He twists his fingers, pointing to me and then to the hut. I nod and am off, stepping quickly across the cold ground, leaping silently over sharp hard earth to gain higher ground. I circle the hut to approach from behind.

The aches of my body are forgotten, the cold gone. I am sharp and my movements quick and calculated, every footfall precisely as I mean it to be.

As I round the back of the *hanok* the smell of damp wood and rice straw fills my nose, thick and sour.

And something else. The smell of rot.

Animal or human, I cannot tell.

My fingers trail across the back wall of the building and the wood crumbles beneath my touch. Black wet splinters disintegrate onto the cold earth, soaking into the snow. I keep one eye on the wall and the other trained into the thick trees lining the slope. It rises up and up to eventually become the north face of the mountain far above. There is no door here. No window. No route for escape. But a rotted board is broken through where a kitchen might be, a space big enough for a person to push through.

I draw closer and the thick silence is broken by Man Seok's deep voice, cracking as he calls my name sharply. "Dan Ji *ssi*! Dan Ji!"

I spin to follow the sound of his voice, blood pounding in my ears, hammering inside my throat. Pressing against my windpipe.

And there is a face.

Peering from the trees above. Caught between the branches.

Eyes and a wide-open mouth.

Staring at me.

And then it is gone, leaving only the crackle of fleeing footsteps smashing into low lying branches, snapping from within the trees. I scream out to Man Seok.

I think I do.

But already I am gone up the hill in pursuit, hands pressed deep into hard mud to gain traction up the rise and then sprinting upright again, running through the forest. I twist and dodge to miss the trees.

A flash of colour ahead. The back of a dark blue *jeogori*. A man wearing a straw sedge hat dyed black, disappearing between the trees.

I follow and already I can see I'm faster than him. I will catch him despite his immense head start. I swipe viciously at my face, at the melt dripping down my forehead to blind me. The snow comes heavy now, wet like sleet, soaking my hair. Soon the ground will melt too, each step wetter than the last.

"Stop now!" I scream. "Stop!"

But he does not.

It means taking a terrible risk, the risk of losing the first real suspect we have come across, but I take it. I dart to the left into a thick copse of trees, away into the bracken to disappear low, still running fast. And I am right, for the man is veering left too, ever so slightly. I saw it. I run low and fast, my breath heaving, the air too sharp and cold. And then I hear him, crashing through the forest, breathing heavily, heavier than I am, his body clumsier. He is struggling. And he is just ahead.

Drawing my small *jangdo* dagger from beneath my padded clothes, I slip the blade from its small plain case. I twist the wooden hilt so it sits comfortable and loose between my practised fingers. And then I launch myself from the trees at the running man, slamming his body with all my strength so we both go flying. His flesh softens my fall, a bone-crunching crack as his chin hits the ground. When he flings himself onto his back, blood pours from between his lips.

We are a mess of lunging arms and furious grunts, rolling in the dirt and snow as I try to push back with my legs, to get a higher purchase. I catch a glimpse of wild brown eyes, matted hair. He is reaching desperately for a thick wooden staff, tossed to the ground in our struggles. Every time he draws near, I pull him back, until finally his blood-covered hands close around my throat instead. He begins to squeeze.

I am choking, gasping, lights popping behind my eyes. My dagger slashes wildly, missing my assailant every time, ineffectual. Useless. Except the man changes his grip, loosening just for the smallest of moments to reposition, to hold me down better. I am flat on my back now, the man straddling me, wet snow seeping into my clothes. And just for that moment when his hands grow loose, the world snaps into focus and I sink my small blade into his chest just above his breast, cutting deep and viciously twisting.

Screaming, the man tears himself away. My hand still holds the *jangdo* tight and the small blade rips from his body in a spray of red, like fine dust settling across my face. His hands scrapple in the loose dirt and close around his discarded staff, thrusting it brutally toward my face. I lunge beyond its reach, only to slam my jaw against a rock half hidden in the now muddy snow.

An explosion of pain.

I gasp. But still stagger to my feet, unsteady and clumsy now. I am forced to lean against a curling tree as I suck in air, eyes rolling as I search for where he is, for his next attack.

It does not come.

The man disappears into the trees, limping and trailing blood in the snow, a line of shocking red against the white. I mean to follow, I try to. Instead, I sink to my knees in the dirt, hands clasping the bruised flesh of my throat. Forehead to earth, I work hard on drawing the sharp air into my crushed throat, on blinking away the black spots dancing at the corners of my vision that threaten to drag me under.

The forest grows quiet. No sound except the wind rushing through the trees, the wet drip of snow.

Slowly I return to myself. The only sign our suspect was ever here are the traces of blood left behind. The mud churning the snow. Nothing else. He is long gone.

I curse as I push myself to my feet, begin to stagger back to Man Seok and the dilapidated hut. My memory now plays out the sound of his voice when he called me, urgent and tight.

He shouted my name.

I move more quickly as the worry begins to seep in, my body forgetting pain, locking it away for later when there is time to sit and think. I break into a run.

"Man Seok! Man Seok!" My voice cracks, windpipe crushed and sound only hissing from between my lips.

I burst from the line of bare branched hawthorn trees above the rotten *hanok*, tearing down the slope. Sliding in a storm of mud and wet sleet, I slam my hands against the rotting black wood of the back wall.

"Man Seok," I rasp, fear fully taken hold now. No sounds come from inside the *hanok*. Only silence. The man I fought was a distraction, the real battle took place here inside the *hanok* where I left my partner all alone. I shout his name again, voice scraping against my raw crushed throat as I stagger onto the rotting terrace, almost sinking my foot into the wood as it gives way.

"Man Seok!"

I crawl through the remnants of the rotting door, into the dark space within. The smell of damp and mould fills the space, thick and acrid. And then I stand panting and frozen at the sight of Man Seok's crouching form, huddled on the floor in the centre of the room. A black silhouette in the gloom.

He barely moves as I edge slowly around the corners of the space, angling myself to see what it is he holds so carefully.

A girl. A young woman.

He glances up at me, black eyes glittering in the dark.

The girl is dressed in the shredded threadbare clothes of a lowly commoner, her feet bare and weakly kicking against Man Seok's grip. Her movements are strange and clumsy, spittle sliding from her lips. And her eyes move too fast, focusing on the roof, on the floor, on the walls.

On nothing at all.

I cannot understand what I'm seeing. But then Man Seok lifts her arm and pulls the girl's sleeve back, showing me the birthmark staining the crook of her inner elbow, the tiny delicate shape of it.

"No," I rasp.

Man Seok nods, looking grim, looking beyond tired. Looking bone weary.

"Yes," is all he says.

14

Resolution

WE HAVE FOUND SONG SEORIM. Or whatever is left of her to find.

We sit outside the small rotting *hanok* in the open air. It is better than the smell inside the room where we have left Song Seorim covered in stinking blankets. Man Seok sits close beside me, the warmth of his body like fire against my side. His hair hangs wet and dripping across his eyes, hands folded beneath his arms to keep dry.

I do not care about the wet, and sit directly in the falling sleet on the damp rotting *maru*. Cold trickles icy pathways beneath my clothes, soaking into everything. I am frozen, my fingers and toes stiff with cold. My throat numbed. Losing pieces of myself to the snow.

I do not care.

I push at him gently with my shoulder, for his face is blank, eyes empty and flat. For a moment I imagine he is just the same as Song Seorim. His eyes are open, yet he does not see.

"She was alive." I rasp the words out loud to rouse him, for he is frightening me, the emptiness echoing from his body so unlike his normal self. "Man Seok, all this time, Song Seorim was alive." I glance at the wavering trees tops. It is growing dark. "I did not expect it."

Man Seok jerks, as if awakening from a dream, as if noticing me for the first time. His face fills with life once more. "Dan Ji *ssi*. Were you hurt?"

"No."

Man Seok reaches across to carefully touch my throat anyway, gently exploring my jawline, my hair, cold fingers dancing across my skin. I am swollen and raw, exhaustion tugging at my eyelids. His fingers come back from my hair stained wet with blood.

"It's not mine," I tell him before he can ask, for his face is changing.

He watches me a moment longer, expression blank once more. Controlled. "Good." He hesitates. "Guard Kim searched this building yesterday."

My voice is quiet. "Yet he didn't find her."

"It can only mean she wasn't here yesterday."

Questions and threads hum in my mind, thoughts dancing across my tongue. But I say nothing. And then it seems our small interlude is over. Man Seok stands up. "If the man you fought survives his wounds, he could come back with others. We must take Song Seorim and leave."

"And the scene? Someone needs to search through the house, check for anything left behind."

"There's no time. I'm going to try and calm her down, and you do what you can with the scene. And then we go. Five minutes."

I nod as he crouches to re-enter the dark house. Wiping the caked mud from my skirts I stand to walk slowly around the building, attention trained on the ground despite the gathering darkness. I creep inside the kitchen. It is filled with the scent of rot and I search until I find a decaying rat squeezed behind the hearth. There is nothing that could be important, only an empty broken room.

Inside the main living area where Song Seorim lies with Man Seok by her side, a thick woven rope sits in long winding lengths. It is not damp like everything else, still dry and strong. When I sniff it, it smells clean, like straw and storage and animals.

I leave it on the floor, coiled like a thick yellow snake in the darkness.

Blankets are piled in one corner, musty and damp, but not beyond use. And out the back I find the bones of birds, thin and hollow, half buried in the mud. I sink my fingers into the snowy sludge, trying to find anything else discarded there, searching until my hands are black with muck and dripping wet. My fingers touch something soft and I extricate a long sopping hair ribbon, wide and caked black with dirt. It used to be red. Bright red. I can see it beneath the grime.

It is the kind of ribbon a young girl might wear, folded at the bottom of her long single braid. The hairstyle of an unmarried woman. I turn it over in my hands, examining it closely, and then tuck it away beneath my *jeogori*.

"Dan Ji *ssi*." Man Seok's voice rises from the front of the *hanok*. "It is time."

I stand and take one last look around the old building, at the thick tree line of bare twisting hawthorns above. Nothing. I slip through to meet Man Seok, helping him heave the silent girl onto his back. Her head lolls to the side, drool wetting her already stained chin. She is completely lost within her own mind.

A true *gwishin*.

For a moment I imagine Song Seorim with Shin Yonggae, before all this.

In the marketplace. Hidden smiles.

As Man Seok walks slowly back toward the bamboo grove I move to take Song Seorim's flailing hand, holding it tightly in mine, my fingers squeezing. She does not seem to notice I am there.

The struggle through the copse of thick bamboo is exhausting, more so for Man Seok who carries Song Seorim on his back. I urge him to stop and rest but it is only when he nearly loses his footing in the snow that he relents, letting me help him lower the girl carefully to the ground. We place her head in my lap, and I run my fingers over her hair, smoothing the matted strands gently as she gazes at the darkening sky with an empty expression. There are no bird sounds this time, only silence. Only the thick white mist. And the sound of sleet turning into rain, pattering onto the leafy canopy to melt the snow cover. It drips down the thick green stalks. Melting everything.

"Man Seok?"

He is crouched at my side, head down between his knees. He looks up. "Mmmh?"

"What do you suppose they did to her in that place?" I reach to pull Song Seorim's sleeve back from her wrist, revealing raw flesh circled there, skin scraped red.

Yellow rope, coiled like a snake.

Man Seok rubs his face, bowing his head again and looking away. "Do you want to check?"

I nod. "Yes." I slide from beneath Song Seorim's head, circle around to kneel beside her feet. I hesitate, telling her quietly what I am about to do, as if asking for permission. She does not give it, but neither does her expression change. It is clear she has not heard my words. Perhaps she doesn't realise I am here at all. Quickly I check beneath her underclothes for marks on her thighs, higher. "Nothing. No signs."

I am relieved, feel it sinking inside my chest. Man Seok too lets out his breath. But all he says is, "Let's go."

And we do, lifting Song Seorim high onto Man Seok's back, trying to ignore the way her attention roams everywhere but never focusses. Her lips turn blue so I rip apart my mud-stained *chima* skirt, tear thick strips of material to wrap around her bare feet, around her hands, across her head to protect her ears. And then we trudge, twisting through the thick bamboo forest.

When I emerge into the clearing on the other side, the men waiting there stand quickly, faces white and mouths gaping. Slowly they back away. I do not blame them, caked as I am in dirt and blood with torn clothes. One of the guards even whispers *"gwishin,"* half turning as if to scuttle off into the trees. Except at that moment Man Seok appears behind me, Song Seorim lolling and lifeless on his back. Guard Kim at least is immediately at our side, helping to take the damaged young woman, helping to lower her to the ground so Man Seok can rest.

The whispers cling to Song Seorim now.

With every moment we linger in the clearing, the guards become louder, talking among themselves, whispering furiously. They are filled with superstition. Two of the men refuse to even touch her. Just as Man Seok steps shaking toward them, fists curled and jaw tight, Guard Kim orders the two men to travel quickly ahead of us, to carry a message to the magistrate that we are coming. They are happy to relent, relieved to be away.

I am given a thick blazing torch to light our way, the bright flames barely making a difference in the gathering darkness of twilight, only casting shadows. Night falls as we walk, deep and enveloping, swallowing us up. Our torches flicker and smoke in the rain, yellow light probing the night forest. The blackness becomes a barrier, as if every step forward is a raging battle against the winding twisting dark, as if the pathways we tread will never really end.

But eventually they do.

Abruptly we break through the forest onto the valley floor, and for a moment my head spins at the sight of wide-open spaces and a long low sky. The embers of fading light silhouette the mountain shapes rising steadily all around us, behemoths outlined in deep black and blue. After the thick claustrophobia of the mountain forest, the valley feels empty and huge. Firelight twinkles within the small *hanok* houses dotting the fields, scattered and carved deep into the valley floor.

Secretary Baek waits for us with Guard Yu and other uniformed men from the government office. Their faces are strained, deep shadows carved beneath their eyes. Everyone focuses only on the girl supported between Man Seok and Guard Kim, disbelief written across their faces.

Everyone believed she was dead.

As did I.

They have brought a cow and cart, the splintered wooden tray piled high with blankets and furs. A waiting bed. They lower Song Seorim inside and as her head is laid against the soft fur her eyes widen. She lifts her hands as if to touch the skins but her fingers are clumsy and slow. She only gropes air.

Before they wrap her up, Man Seok orders me into the cart beside her, his voice low and his hand already pushing at my back. I do not hesitate before obeying. He says she needs the warmth of a human body to heat the small space between the layers. I am the only woman present so it is my duty. But I catch the way his eyes linger on the bruised flesh of my throat. I have worried him. And he forgets I am a *damo* and do not need his protection.

Still I do not protest, ashamed at my weakness as I

crawl into the soft space beside Seorim's cold body, wrapping my numb limbs around her as the furs are lifted high over my head to plunge us both into darkness.

My breath turns hot and damp against my skin.

Seorim shifts constantly, agitated and slow. I whisper comfort into her ear though I know she cannot hear me, holding her tightly until our wet clothes become warm. It is raining hard now, the patter loud against the upturned animal skins. I lie still and listen, the weight of the cart shifting violently back and forth as we move over uneven village roads. My fingers and toes begin to ache and burn as the cold retreats.

When we finally reach the government office, I must leave our small heated haven. The courtyard turns to muddy pools beneath my feet, the rain steady.

Man Seok lifts the girl into his arms, furs and all, and then they are both led away by the guards to some other part of the office. A trail of men follows at their wake, all talking at once, shouting and ordering and filling my ears with noise.

I retreat through the rain back to the main building and the open courtyard, sitting down shivering on the wooden terrace, my aching feet perched on the first stone step. Secretary Baek appears from within the magistrate's office to place a heavy blanket across my shoulders. I nod gratefully until he too disappears into the darkness, leaving me alone.

My hands are shaking. The courtyard is quiet. Empty now. Rain trickles from the roof, running in thick rivers down the wooden pillars and clinging to the corners of the terrace. Pools of muddy water stretch across the courtyard and I kick off my boots, sliding back on the dry wood to find warmth. The quest for heat takes me inside the magistrate's empty office and I kneel on the floor, searching with tingling fingers for the heat that runs beneath the oiled paper. I trace the spots where hot clay and wide river stones lie, following the lines to find the best place, the warmest place. And when I find it, far in the corner of the long office, I press my cheek against the floor, spreading my fingers wide and my body flat. Still covered in my thick quilted blanket, I drink up the warmth.

I lie there for a long time, perhaps even doze a little, until a creak at the doorway startles me and I glance up as Magistrate Hong enters the room. I should stand, should lower my eyes respectfully, should do something, but I cannot. The most I can manage is to heave my aching body upright, wrapping the blanket tighter against my shoulder blades.

"Magistrate Hong," I rasp in greeting. My voice sounds strange to my ears. Thin and crackling and so different from how it should.

"We called a physician," he says. "He has them warming her up. He's worried about her feet. Her toes turn black."

"And her mind?"

The magistrate pauses. "Song Seorim is no longer herself. That is clear."

"She still will not speak?"

"No. Not a word."

I rub carefully at my jaw, twisting until I can lean my back against the wall. The magistrate comes closer, crouching down across from me. He looks at me now, directly, no longer pretending he cannot see. And there is fire within his eyes. "Damo Dan Ji, Lieutenant Jo said you fought a man in the mountains."

"I did." It feels like a lifetime ago. A dream. I touch my jaw, running my fingers over the bruised flesh. "Yes, there was a man watching the abandoned hut."

"Would you recognise this man, if you saw him again?"

I think for a moment. Thick lips. High cheekbones. Pale skin and a soft chinless face. Round eyes. I would remember.

"Yes. I am certain of it." My rasping voice catches in my throat and I cough.

Magistrate Hong though seems pleased at my answer. "And if I brought in an artist from the village, do you think you could describe the man's face to him?"

I nod.

"Good. I will bring someone at first light. We will create posters and send horsemen to carry them through the whole valley by nightfall. We will flush him out."

I see the fire blazing within his face so am nervous when I shake my head. "Magistrate Hong, I am sorry. I must see Damo Choon Shim at first light. It is our scheduled meeting."

"This is more important."

"Someone must be there to meet her," I say. "It is what we agreed."

He frowns at me but I refuse to turn away. I am grateful that he speaks with me now, that he will meet my eyes. More grateful than I should be, considering I am long grown used to being ignored, to being overlooked no matter how many times I prove my capabilities. Yet no matter how much I like this new attention from the magistrate, on this topic I will not bend.

The magistrate's expression turns thoughtful, surprising me. "Perhaps Guard Yu could go instead?" he asks.

I nod carefully, pleased that he would ask for my opinion. Pleased that he now seems to trust me enough to ask for my help with the wanted posters, instead of directing orders at me via Man Seok.

Magistrate Hong gets up to go.

"Wait, Magistrate Hong. Please…" I pause to cough again before continuing. "I think you must ask your men to check with every physician up and down the valley."

He stops and waits, and I am encouraged by his silence to continue.

"Tell your guards to ask the physicians if a man has visited. I cut him deep, from here to here." I show him on my own chest. "If he did not die on the way down the mountain, he will need medical attention. And he will need it soon."

"I will send them."

I push my luck. "And Magistrate Hong, ask your men to check *uinyeo* as well, if he was desperate enough, the criminal may have forced a medicine woman to stitch him instead of finding a physician. He might even think it was safer, that we wouldn't think to check with the *uinyeo* of the valley."

He hesitates but then nods. "I will organise it and send them out at first light."

Magistrate Hong's expression has changed. I can see it. He believes we are closing in, finally drawing closer to the truth.

I am not sure yet if I agree. The threads still wait just beyond my grasp. But tonight, I am too tired to examine them.

Once he is gone I lie back on the warm *ondol* floor, letting the rising heat relax my tight body, untwist and unwind. I lie still and listen to the sound of rain pattering on the roof. I have only just closed my eyes when the doors open again. A long moment passes where I cannot be bothered moving at all, until Man Seok calls my name sharply, his voice tight and strange. "Dan Ji *ssi*!"

I sit up quickly and he stops mid-stride, frozen halfway across the room toward me. Immediately he blinks back whatever was in his black eyes.

Though for a moment I think it might have been … fear.

That I was unwell? That I was injured?

I cannot be certain.

Yet his expression reminds me of the black silk *nambawi*, folded carefully atop the low table in my small room. I look away as he speaks.

"Why are you lying on the floor?"

I shrug beneath my blanket, hand lightly touching my throat, voice still cracking when I speak. "It's warm. What's going on out there?"

Man Seok hesitates, expelling his breath slowly before he answers. "It is Lord Song. The guards at the gate informed me he's just arrived at the end of the road. He will reach the office any moment."

Lord Song.

I pull myself to my feet agonisingly slowly, aches and stiffness set in deep now. "I'll come with you. I want to watch him arrive. I want to see his face."

"His face?"

I only shrug. Lord Song is a mystery to unravel. And I am interested.

I follow Man Seok outside. The rain is thundering down and I cannot bring myself to venture into the haze. Man Seok plants himself at the edge of the terrace, feet wide, arms folded across his chest. I step into place beside him, protected from the downpour by the awning overhead and by his body.

Man Seok is right, it only takes moments for Lord Song

to arrive. He enters the courtyard on the back of a tall beautiful horse, which stamps and snorts in the rain as he pulls the beast to a halt. He has retainers with him of course, and I recognise his right-hand man from the mountain, the one who checked the body of the frozen girl for a birthmark. This man must be Lord Song's head servant or, now I remember Choon Shim saying, the leader of his personal soldier force.

Lord Song almost falls from his saddle in his haste, wet and sodden through, not caring how his expensive leather shoes disappear deep into the muddy puddles of the yard. He doesn't even notice us. The winds pick up, blowing winter across the *maru* and I lean closer to Man Seok, using his body as a shield. Warmth creeps into my side where it presses against him. I peer around his shoulder as Lord Song hurries across the courtyard, ushered away through the rain by the magistrate and Secretary Baek. Guard Kim follows behind with his men.

"What do you think?" I rasp. "He seems so very distraught."

"I do not like him."

I nod. "He has been ... strangely difficult when it comes to the investigation, it is true, yet you cannot deny the expression on his face each time he's been faced with finding his daughter. He loves her. It is clear."

He makes a strange sound, deep within his throat. Almost a laugh but not quite. "If a man loves his child do you think that makes him a good man?"

I crane my neck to look at Man Seok's blank face. "It doesn't?"

"A man can be many things, Dan Ji *ssi*."

Wind rises in the courtyard, rain smashing against the tiled terrace roof. I think suddenly that Man Seok is like a dark deep well, and I cannot see the bottom. The bitterness behind his words. The scars on his knuckles. I want to understand, but he offers no more words and after a time I turn away and sigh. "Then you think Lord Song is involved in this somehow?"

Part of me wishes Lord Song was not. Part of me wishes he was simply a doting father hoping for his daughter back.

But it's not meant to be.

A *damo* disappeared from his house, never to be seen again. Too many threads around Lord Song make no sense.

"He wishes for his daughter to return home," relents Man Seok finally. "But he is still involved."

I nod, accepting his judgement. The magistrate and Lord Song appear again now through the rain, trailed by Lord Song's personal soldier, who carries a large heavy bundle of furs in his arms.

Song Seorim.

I lurch forward but Man Seok reaches for my arm to hold me back.

"It is too late," he says as the soldier waves more of Lord Song's men inside from beyond the gate. They come carrying an enclosed *gama* palanquin, the kind rich women use to travel safely and in comfort through the streets, confined, segregated. Unseen.

The bundle of furs which is Song Seorim is placed carefully within the litter while Magistrate Hong and Lord Song argue, raging at each other in a war of vicious words. I hear only scraps above the rain sounds.

"He came to take her home," says Man Seok. He lets go of my arm now. There is clearly nothing any of us can do.

"Will Lord Song still let us question her? Examine her?"

"I do not know," says Man Seok. He peers down at me. "But that's not our biggest problem."

I glance at him, threads curling just beyond my fingertips, dread sinking deep inside my chest. "What is it?"

Lord Song and his men climb back onto their horses, finally leaving through the heavy rain, taking Song Seorim with them.

Man Seok's gaze follows them, his expression darkening. "None of us told Lord Song that his daughter was here."

I grow still. I do not need to ask him what that means.

It seems Lord Song still keeps a spy among us.

15

The Past

THE FACE IS DRAWN with thick black brush strokes, eyes painted wide and deep. I hold the loose sheet of paper, soft and delicate between my fingers as I consider the likeness. It is not quite right. Not quite.

But it will have to do.

I sit alone on the wooden *maru* terrace outside the magistrate's office, legs folded beneath me and threadbare scarf pulled high over my mouth and nose. Beneath the soft material, my skin has grown damp from my breath, trapped in place. Staring at the poster in my hands in the low light of morning, I remember the man in the mountains. My father told me ghosts look just as people do. I angle the paper again, peering closer. A man.

Or a demon?

I think of Song Seorim. Her clutching hands and black feet.

A man who acts as a demon does.

Grasping fingers, weak and useless. Or curled frozen claws, unmoving and locked in place. And ginger taffee on an outstretched palm.

My head pounds.

I unwrap the scarf, suddenly claustrophobic despite the frost clinging overhead on the awning and the snow melting in the mud of the courtyard.

When Man Seok appears from the inner courtyard I'm investigating my throat with careful fingers, touching the bruises to discover where they begin and end. He lowers himself onto the *maru* beside me, placing his sword onto the polished wood as he leans across to peel my scarf from my skin.

"It looks worse," he says without emotion.

My voice rasps and I wince. "The bruising is coming through now."

"Did you sleep?"

I do not even bother answering. He knows I did not. An hour or two at best before the artist arrived to draw the face of Song Seorim's kidnapper. Before five posters were copied and given to horsemen to ride through the valley and marketplace to show the people. Before the yard was filled with bustling guards from the next town over, ready to help search for the criminal.

I glance at Man Seok, at the dark shadows on his skin and the lines of his mouth. I know he didn't sleep either.

I sigh and touch my throat again with a frown. "Was the magistrate able to secure permission to question Song Seorim?"

"Lord Song agreed. Sundown. Only you may see her."

I nod, satisfied. That condition was to be expected. "Good."

"What will you do until then?"

I hesitate. "Secretary Baek and Guard Yu are heading into the village to question a physician and a *uinyeo*."

"Let them go by themselves."

I shake my head, determined. "I want to speak with

someone learned about the wound I inflicted. Perhaps it's possible the man bled out in the mountains. I need to be there to hear it myself."

Man Seok says nothing yet doesn't move, planted in place on the terrace and blocking my way. He gazes out above the enclosure walls at the rising mountains, peaks shrouded in mist. The hills are quiet today, the wolves gone elsewhere. He shifts, peering down at his scarred hands as he asks, "Do you ever think about the gambling inn? About your time working undercover?"

My eyes flutter, flicking to him. "No." A lie.

"Six months is a long time."

"Thirteen months," I breathe, correcting him. "I was there thirteen months."

Man Seok looks sideways at me. "Thirteen months," he repeats. "I think about it sometimes. That case."

I stare at him. "What is it you think of?"

He does not answer, even though he must have known I would ask. His expression stays carefully blank, focused only on the rising mountain range. Eventually he asks, "What did you think of it? Your time there."

I admit, "Just that … it wasn't how I thought it would be."

He says nothing.

I take a deep shaking breath. "There was a man there, Man Seok. I watched him die in the snow."

"Did you kill him?"

I shake my head.

Man Seok shrugs. "Men die all the time."

I stare at him. "Do you regret it?"

"Regret what?"

I gather my courage. "What you did during the arrest. I sometimes wonder if you regret it."

He is silent a long time. I do not think he will answer me.

"You did not know for certain he would walk free," I push, for suddenly I want to understand. It is a loose thread I've never been able to connect, even after all this time. "Poong Yi, I mean. You did not know for certain Poong Yi would walk free, Man Seok."

"I did know."

"How could you have known?"

"It is the world we live in. It's the way things are. The way they've always been."

He lapses into silence and I watch him carefully, only the distant crunching of footsteps sounding as guards move about their business in the yard.

What happened back then, it is another mystery I wish to unravel. Yet it is different too, perhaps because it is Man Seok himself I want to solve. It burns a hole inside me, I want to know so badly. The way he looked that night is locked inside my memory; chest heaving, knuckles split, his black eyes wild and rolling—so unlike himself.

I shift closer across the *maru*, leaning inwards toward his body. "What did you see there, Man Seok? What did you see Poong Yi do?"

Man Seok's jaw tightens, eyes fluttering closed.

But he does not answer.

I knew he wouldn't.

Secretary Baek hurries by, breaking the spell as he walks quickly toward the main gates. He sees us sitting beside the office and bows respectfully toward Man Seok, offering a tight smile before scurrying away. It does not reach his eyes. He is afraid of Man Seok now.

Like so many others. Both here and back in the capital.

I climb to my feet to follow after him. Secretary Baek

will visit the physician who came to see Song Seorim, the very man whom I wish to meet.

"What will you do until sundown?" I ask Man Seok as I slide into my shoes.

He stands, reaching for his sword. "Magistrate Hong has asked me to oversee the guards. He wants to create search parties to look for the wounded suspect."

I nod as Guard Yu and Guard Kim come past, both heading toward the main exit gates.

"Sundown then," I tell Man Seok before stepping away to follow after Secretary Baek.

Man Seok calls my name. His mouth is tight and black eyes hard.

"Dan Ji *ssi*. Go with Guard Yu and Kim," he tells me.

"Why?"

He says nothing, just turns to stride back into the inner yard where the guards are gathering.

I watch him go.

Outside the compound the day has grown crisp. Sunlight streams onto muddy pathways, slipping between clouds of shrouded mist clinging to mountains overhead. I follow along the main road, avoiding the sludge as best I can. Finally, I catch up with Secretary Baek and the two guards at the very edge of the village, where the big trees grow. They have already parted ways, Secretary Baek following the winding pathway leading through the bare oak trees and the two younger men striding away toward the heart of the village. I hesitate a long moment before choosing to heed Man Seok's instructions, following behind the two guards and calling out for them to wait.

"Are you visiting a *uinyeo*?" I ask breathlessly when I finally catch up.

"We are," answers Guard Yu. "Did you wish to speak with her?"

132

I nod, falling into step beside the two men and wishing Guard Kim was elsewhere so I could speak openly with Guard Yu about his visit with Choon Shim in the early morning. He must sense my frustration because he says almost too pointedly, "There was no news from anyone this morning. I went to see my grandmother in the marketplace as arranged but she never showed up."

I glance at him sharply.

Guard Kim seems interested, too, so Guard Yu quickly deflects him, "I had hoped Song Seorim's reappearance would explain what happened, and if anyone was talking in the village my grandmother would tell me what the rumours are. But it seems not."

My chest grows tight, skin prickling. If Choon Shim did not appear at the appointed meeting place, does it mean she was discovered? Is she in danger? My breath turns sharp and shallow.

After a long moment of silent walking, in which my mind continues to rage through every possibility leading to Choon Shim's absence, Guard Yu suddenly speaks in a different, softer voice.

"Damo Dan Ji … is it true? Guard Kim informed me that Song Seorim will not speak."

I clear my throat, blinking. "It is true. She cannot it seems."

We enter the busy marketplace, squeezing by a stall with tiny rice cakes frying in sizzling oil on a black flat pan. I focus on the scent to drown out thoughts of Choon Shim, saying, "Song Seorim has … I do not know if she will become well again. I am to see her this evening."

My gaze locks momentarily with Guard Kim's and I know we are both picturing the same scenes from that dark mountain.

Song Seorim's flesh turning black on her feet, her head

lolling to the side as we heaved her onto Man Seok's back. Her fluttering grasping hands.

I turn away.

"Did you hear about Shin Yonggae?" It is Guard Yu who speaks, addressing both myself and Guard Kim.

I shake my head as Guard Kim asks, "Shin Yonggae? Is he not the commoner who attempted to run away with Song Seorim?"

"Indeed. He received thirty lashes late yesterday."

I stop walking, causing the woman behind me, large with her black hair knotted thick and tight, to sidestep. She glares as she passes.

My hands clench. "Did Shin Yonggae survive it?"

Guard Yu nods and I feel slightly less sick, the nausea sinking.

"He was punished then," I say, walking again. "Man Seok and I had hoped..."

"Hoped what?" Guard Yu turns to me. "You know Shin Yonggae reached far beyond his place. At least, that's what Magistrate Hong said when he charged him."

"Magistrate Hong ordered his punishment?"

Guard Yu nods. My feet become unsteady on the uneven road, thoughts filled with images of my father. Flesh torn and blood seeping from broken skin. I blink quickly. The sun here is almost too harsh now, a sharp glare from the clouds above. My head begins to pound again. "Yet he survived it," I breathe.

My father did not.

"Shin Yonggae was lucky," Guard Yu agrees quietly. "Lord Song sent a message to the government office, right after your party left for the north mountain. He ordered the magistrate to inflict a much harsher punishment. Yet I believe Magistrate Hong is sick of bowing to Lord Song's every whim. Hence, he gave Shin Yonggae only thirty lashes."

I think again of the spy among us who carries news like the wind, always toward Lord Song's ears. I peer carefully across at Guard Yu and Kim as we walk, the smell of the marketplace less enticing now, my stomach queasy.

"Lucky indeed," I mutter as Guard Yu continues to chatter, telling me far more than I wish to know. It makes me think now of Shin Yonggae's mother, her body curled inwards, bent and aching within that dark crumbling *hanok* she calls her home.

For a moment I almost imagine visiting her to offer ... something, but I know I will not. I will not go to that place again, especially not after what has happened to Shin Yonggae. Not when that damp kitchen will be filled with the sour smell of blood, clinging thick in the air around the hearth. I shake my head to clear it, placing my hands against my eyes and pressing hard. Forcing myself to focus.

"Down here." Guard Kim's voice interrupts my thoughts. We follow him along the winding pathway, leading us through a curved tunnel of bracken. Twisted wood and reaching branches grasp my hair and skirts as we pass. The way is steep and my feet slide through mud as we descend.

Glimpses of the pathway curl ahead through the thick undergrowth that leads down to the black water, to the banks of the river where it lies around the village. Where the mud becomes sand on the river bank, crowded with yellow weed.

A small house appears nestled among the trees, hidden behind a crumbling stone wall strangled with twisted vine —bare, with not a leaf to be seen. We enter the yard and Guard Kim calls loudly until finally a woman emerges from behind the shuttered doors. She frowns down at us from her *maru* of rough wood.

"Who are you?" Her gaze slides over the two guards, across their uniforms and then comes to rest on me. I am still dressed in commoner clothes, dressed like a villager. She raises her eyebrows, questioning, and I step forward.

"Are you a medicine woman?" I ask.

She frowns. "Among other things."

"May I speak with you?"

She hesitates but gestures for me to come inside. Guard Yu follows after me without being invited but Guard Kim lingers outside near the gates.

Inside we sit as shown on the *uinyeo*'s floor across from her. My belly begins to settle, for her house could not be more different from Shin Yonggae's, poverty here clearly kept at bay. The tiny space is filled with hanging plants, dried and crackling, and various earthenware pots covered with cloth sit against the wall. Wooden boxes lie half open, revealing dried herbs and leaves spilling from their depths. I breathe deeply. The air is dry and sweet.

It is Guard Yu who speaks first. "Have you seen a wounded man come through here since last night? Seeking your attention, perhaps?"

The woman shakes her head, and Guard Yu's shoulders visibly slump.

"Never mind," I say. "You may still help me. We search for a wounded man, he's been cut in his chest. It was only a small knife, but the cut ran deep." I lean closer. "I wish to know if it's possible for a man of average height and build to survive such a wound? Do you believe he could return from high on the mountainside without losing too much blood? Without falling unconscious?"

The medicine woman blinks. "Please, show me where the man was cut."

I indicate on my own chest, from mid centre curving up to stop just beneath my left arm.

The *uinyeo* is silent, face drained of colour. Finally, she clears her throat. "I have seen that wound before."

Guard Yu stiffens. "When?"

"Early this morning, in the pre-dawn. Someone came to me for treatment."

I begin to stand, unable to control my movements, my body alive again. The threads of discovery untwist and move, curling outwards. "You said no one had come to you!"

The medicine woman slowly shakes her head. "No. I said no man had come."

Guard Yu stares. "No man?"

I place my hands over my eyes, listen as she says, "During the darkness a young woman came. She told me her husband attacked her with a knife. She asked for my help. And I helped her."

16

A Pathway

WE FIND blood-soaked men's clothes behind the *uinyeo*'s house, hidden deep within the yellow river rushes, half floating in the black water.

Not hidden well enough.

When we ask the villagers in the surrounding homes, we find that two sets of women's clothes are missing, commoner clothes stolen from within *hanok* women's quarters. It makes my head pound, and I keep picturing the face I saw in the mountains. Round and chinless. Soft. Thick lips. I had not guessed, not for a moment. Had not noticed as we fought, as we rolled over each other in the mud and snow. It makes me clench my fists.

Another mistake.

A mistake which costs us greatly, for as soon as I return to the government office I pull Man Seok aside to explain that the wanted posters our horsemen have displayed up and down the valley are entirely useless. They will not help us apprehend a woman.

Magistrate Hong is drinking in his office when Man Seok tells him the news. I stand behind Man Seok's broad body and so am sheltered when the magistrate flings his cup across the room. It smashes against the book shelves and rains searing tea onto the floor in jagged pieces, each porcelain shard tinkling like a chime. The artist is recalled from the village and half a day is wasted as he copies his former drawing, now adding a married woman's hairstyle of a thick bun rolled tight at the base of the neck.

I sit with the artist as the afternoon wanes, chewing my fingernails to the skin as I think of Choon Shim, locked away inside Lord Song's residence with no way to reach us. No way to contact us beyond our scheduled meetings. I imagine every possibility and feel sicker and sicker as the day wears on. I even refuse to eat when the bustling cook comes to press a soupy mixture of rice and bitter greens on me.

"THE SONG RESIDENCE IS IN UPHEAVAL," says Man Seok. It is later, almost sundown, and we walk the long way round to Lord Song's home, keeping to the winding hidden pathways that entwine the mountain edges. He places a warm solid hand against my shoulder. "Song Seorim returned late last night and the servants will be busy. Damo Choon Shim would have no opportunity for meetings today. It means nothing, Dan Ji ssi."

I nod, biting my nails harder, unable to stop.

When we near the Song compound, we loiter around the edges of the high stone walls. I peer carefully beyond our sheltered place among the trees toward the main gates of the residence. Men stand outside, long shadows from the mountains falling directly across them. They have swords in hand, standing alert and ready before the secure doorway.

"Lord Song is afraid of something," I whisper to Man Seok and he leans close beside me, body pressing against mine as he moves to see for himself.

"He is involved deeply in this case I think."

"He cannot be," I mutter. "I saw his face when we found his daughter. He could not have anything to do with her disappearance. It is not possible."

"Then explain why he is terrified for his life. Enough to post guards at his gates day and night." Man Seok gestures around us at the winter valley. "Here, in this quiet place."

"True," I admit. "Then he must have an enemy. And that enemy is surely connected to the disappearance of his daughter. Magistrate Hong said there never used to be guards here, not before Song Seorim went missing."

Man Seok nods, straightening up. He walks past me into full view of the two guards, causing them to grip their weapons tighter. Man Seok turns back, gaze locking onto mine as he mutters, "Lord Song knows who took her."

I am left behind, caught in place as Man Seok strides toward the gates.

Lord Song knows?

When I catch up it is too late to speak, both of Lord Song's soldiers greeting us roughly at the door. One holds his sword to block Man Seok's way, blade still covered with a hard-polished scabbard.

"Only the *damo* can enter." When Man Seok bristles the guard adds with a shrug, "It is Lord Song's order."

"It's fine," I say quickly, ready to defuse the tension, though in truth I am just as annoyed. Lord Song excels at making every part of our investigation more difficult than it should be and I grow tired of his interference.

Man Seok's jaw tightens but all he says is, "I will wait."

I am ushered inside the heavy wooden gates by one guard. The other remains outside with Man Seok who stands with his feet planted wide and weapon held like a warning. I catch his eye as the heavy doors swing closed behind me, until he is lost from view.

Inside I am faced with a wide-open courtyard of stony yellow earth. A long building lies ahead with stone stairs leading to a partially open *maru* and wide-covered veranda, which offers a clear view across the yard. The guard hands my care over to a maidservant, an older woman who is impeccably dressed with not a hair out of place. Her face is hard, years of service worn as lines that crease her skin. Something about the way she holds her body makes me think she would break in half before ever bending. She only speaks to tell me to follow, and I guess she must be Lord Song's head maidservant, head of the inner staff of the house, in charge of all domestic matters.

"May I also speak with Lord Song?" I ask as we walk.

The woman's hard mouth creeps down before she turns away. "No one is permitted to speak with Lord Song without an appointment. You have none."

Her back is rigid as she leads me further into the enclosure's interior, twisting and turning along pathways and inner courtyards. Soon we reach a vast garden hidden behind what I can only guess is the women's quarters of the vast house.

Here the garden is lusher than anything I have seen in my time spent within the valley. Evergreen pine trees rise like colossal pillars, wider than the wooden beams holding up the intricately painted roof of the pavilion that sits ahead. The structure is built so it half hangs out across a small black pond. After last night's rain the water has thawed, choked thick with reeds and lilies, their green pads twisted and half-submerged. Chunks of frost cling to the plants. None are in bloom.

The light above is soft blue, the sun now set behind the

mountains. And sitting on the balcony is a girl, her back to us.

When I step onto the polished dark wood of the pavilion, the girl is drawing—a set of black brushes laid out carefully upon the floor before her. She does not look up as I sink to a crouch across from her.

Song Seorim is wearing silk, an embroidered vest lined with white fur fitted across her chest. Her long thick braid spills from beneath a padded *nambawi* silk hat. It is tasselled with a red ornament and filled with warm soft rabbit fur. I reach to touch my own bare head before I can stop myself, thinking of Man Seok, of his black eyes when he pressed his gift into my hands.

Yet my head remains cold and bare.

It is too much to think of, too sudden, the look in his eye too deep. I push it all down and close it away, the threads to be examined another time.

The head maid clears her throat, calling my attention back to her face as she gestures toward Song Seorim, who still has not acknowledged my presence. "Ask your questions." The maidservant's voice is crisp. "You cannot stay."

I nod, forcing my features into a grateful mask for receiving this chance at all. Turning my attention back to Song Seorim, I reach across to take one of her hands in mine. She still does not know I'm here, painting now with her other hand instead. Her fingers ceaselessly move, nonsense scribbles spreading wet across the paper. She looks well enough, though thin and gaunt and sallow, but it seems her feet were not as frostbitten as I worried and her toes remain where they should.

"Mistress Seorim," I try gently. "Do you remember me?"

The girl only pulls her hand free from my grasp,

returning to her work, brows furrowed in concentration. Black drops of ink spill across her skirt and slowly the liquid moves outward, the black stain growing larger and larger.

Song Seorim does not notice.

"She is better than she was last night," offers the older woman beside me suddenly. Her voice sounds far away, attention locked on her charge. Face filled with pity. "I watched her grow up. Just a little girl, she was."

"Then … she still has not spoken?"

The woman shakes her head, reaching out a hand to touch Song Seorim's face.

Tenderly.

My gaze drops to the polished floor. I had thought the head maidservant was only cold and rigid, thought I knew who she was. I am shamed by my quick judgement.

"She will not speak," the older woman says. Slowly her eyes refocus on me. "Were you the one who found her? Up there in the mountains?"

I nod. "I was."

"And … and she was with a man? A stranger?" Her voice shakes and I do not answer.

It is not my place to tell her that the man within the mountains was no man. But finally, I do relent in some small way. "She was not … harmed by a man … in that way you are imagining." It is all I can give her. Small comfort. A meaningless gift.

Together we watch Song Seorim continue her messy painting until finally the head maid whispers, "Her mind is gone."

Images of Song Seorim rush through my head, of her and Shin Yonggae together somewhere beyond the mountains, the life they might have had. Happy and quiet.

Yet bitterness swells, for I know a life like that is not

real. It is a fancy, the kind of story a *gisaeng* might enjoy, something to give her hope she could escape her dreary days.

The real world ends with a young man's flesh torn apart by a whipping and the girl he loved gone away inside her own head, emptied out and silent.

"Song Seorim," I whisper. "What did you see?"

There is no answer.

The head maid has tears on her cheeks now and I stand and shift away to give her space.

A flicker moves at the edge of the garden. A figure. Half hidden in the evergreen. She is gesturing wildly at me. It grows darker now, the blue light of deep twilight gathering close. But I can still see.

It is Choon Shim.

My heart leaps, sudden blood pumping throughout my limbs. I mutter something about needing to relieve myself. The head maid takes a moment to process my statement before pointing to an arched gateway leading back the way we have come. It seems another maidservant waits there to escort me. I thank her softly and step from the open *maru* onto a crunching garden pathway, walking steadily toward the specified gate in the gathering twilight.

And if the head maidservant is distracted enough in her grief not to notice I never reach the gate, then I am glad of it. I veer into the garden trees. Perhaps I may steal five minutes of time before she realises her mistake.

I tread quickly through the wild garden, doubling back until I reach Choon Shim, clasping her shoulders, so glad, so glad, so *relieved* to see her well. Yet immediately she pulls me deeper behind the evergreen thicket, breathlessly clutching my arm. Sweat shines across her forehead as she hisses, "Quickly, follow me!" She strides away with her heavy basket of linen held before her, giving her an uneven gait. "Come quickly!"

I follow where she leads, numb with happiness but now slowly filling also with dread. Where does she take me? What does she risk her hidden identity for? Yet I am so glad to see her alive and well.

Choon Shim leads me deeper into the garden to another stone wall, ancient and crumbling. We creep along its length, hidden in the blue shadows. Choon Shim stops only long enough to untangle her washing from the reaching branches. She presses a finger against her lips in warning. Heart pounding, I follow behind her, already lost in whatever is coming next, my mind darting ahead to the small painted gates we are approaching.

"Through there," she whispers, pointing to the closed gates. "Follow the path to the back of the garden. As fast as you can. Lord Song ordered you never to be left alone, someone will come searching any moment. *Unni* ... I can't stay. If I'm missed..."

I nod and when Choon Shim pushes me toward the doors, I pull one side open, the rusty hinges shrill and creaking. The sound makes Choon Shim's breath come sharp and fast, her attention flicking back toward the main house, hair slicked to her forehead with sweat. I move through the open space and immediately she closes the gate behind me. Without a word. Without even a last look.

And I am alone.

As she said, a pathway winds away from the main house in the direction of the forest, though still within the walled structure of Lord Song's estate. Tall thick stalks of green bamboo close in tight on either side. I follow the way carefully, glancing over my shoulder once. Yet it is only the sound of wind rustling through the swaying bamboo. I am alone among the whispering trees and darkness. There is no one here. The place is empty. And cold.

At the end of the winding pathway lies a small building, half hidden in the shadows of the mountains. Gloom hangs thick and heavy in the dusk. It is not grand like the rest of Lord Song's house, the roof is thatched not made from tiles, the doors bolted tight with a rusty metal hanging lock. I creep closer through the pressing darkness, stepping carefully toward the bolted door, growing still when a light flickers to life inside.

A candle burns in there, visible through the smallest gap between the doors.

I lean closer, holding my breath steady as I press my hands carefully against the wall on either side of the opening. Slowly, I lower my face to the space between, to peer into the darkness that pools within.

An eye stares back at me.

17

Ghosts

I STUMBLE BACK onto the dirt, flinging my body away from the gap and the eye inside. My hands clutch withered weeds and rocks, heart slamming against my ribcage and breath coming hard and fast. Until a rasping voice wafts from within the building, "Who are you?"

A woman's voice, strained and worn.

A human. No ghost.

"I am Dan Ji," I stammer. I stand quickly, drawing my body tall, back straight. "I am a *damo* sent from the government office." And I am no little girl, to cower in the dirt.

"Why are you here?"

I pause. "Because ... because ... a girl went missing."

"Song Seorim."

I nod, stepping closer again, trying to see the eye behind the door, finding it impossible to focus in the dark of falling night. "Yes." I lower my face to the gap again, whisper, "Tell me who you are."

A long pause, sounds of someone moving within the

gloom of the thatched building. I can see nothing despite the dim flickering candle within.

The voice whispers in the dark. "I looked after her since birth. I fed her from my breast while my own child went hungry. I did all that she asked of me." The voice cracks with grief. "Is she dead?"

I shake my head, my mind slow and thick. "Then … you are Song Seorim's nurse. You both disappeared on the same night."

The woman laughs, the sound echoing through her small prison. "I came back."

I remember suddenly the story Choon Shim told me, of the servant who saw a wailing ghost on Lord Song's doorstep. The night after Song Seorim disappeared. I peer into the darkness again, at the ghost that dwells within.

"Is she dead?" the nurse asks again.

I shake my head. "No. Song Seorim has returned home." I hesitate but force myself to tell the truth. "Yet she is ... she is no longer herself."

Heavy breathing grows heavier, strained and distressed within the closed room. But I do not give the woman time to answer.

"Please nurse, can you tell me what happened that night? I do not know how long I can stay here. Please."

There is silence so I ask it again, this time my voice rises with the wind rushing through the bamboo high overhead.

"I told her..." the woman whispers finally "...I said I would help her meet her young man."

I nod, impatient. "Yet neither of you were at the meeting spot. Song Seorim never arrived to meet him. Tell me what went wrong."

"We waited there. Down beside the river. I began to think she had the place wrong, that the young mistress had misheard him. But a girl approached us, even younger than the young mistress, a village girl. I did not know her. But she seemed to know that we were waiting to meet with someone. Only a little girl. The young mistress didn't know her either."

Curled ice fingers turned blue from mountain snow.

A dead girl buried beneath the frosted dirt.

I shake my head to clear it, whispering, "What happened next?"

"Next? Next..." The woman shudders. Her voice is thick. "Next a man came through the forest, dressed in black. He came following the young girl, came bursting out of the trees. I thought it was Seorim's young man ... except it wasn't. This man, he was ... surprised, I think, to see us. But he took the little girl, tried to take her away and Seorim ... I told her not to. I told her. But she wanted to stop him. The little girl was screaming, you see?" The woman begins to cry. "Seorim. My Seorim. Such a foolish girl."

"A kind girl," I breathe, trying to ease her pain. "A young woman with a good heart. A brave girl." I picture Song Seorim as she is now, an empty shell. All her kindness, all her wanting and hope for the future, poured out of her and left behind in that small rotting hut on the north face of the mountain.

"A foolish girl," corrects the woman. The dim candle inside her building is snuffed out abruptly. Only blackness seeps from between the doors. "The man didn't want *me*. Thought he killed me. Took the young girl and the young mistress. He left me behind. I tried to follow them into the mountains, but there was no trail, no way to know where they had gone..."

I finish for her. "So, you returned here to tell Lord Song what had happened."

"Yes," she breathes. "The next evening, I returned home. In the dark I came."

A ghost glimpsed on the doorstep. A weeping woman.

My hands clench tight.

Lord Song has known all along exactly what happened to his daughter. He knew she had a lover. He knew she was abducted and forced into the mountains. Yet he told Magistrate Hong none of it.

Instead, he sent a letter to the capital to request more men for search parties, asked the magistrate to send everyone he had into the mountains.

Why?

Why not simply reveal the truth?

Lord Song knows who took her.

Man Seok's words. It is what Man Seok believes.

Lord Song knows the one who took his daughter. So, he used the police force to apply pressure on the man who was not a man, the one who took Song Seorim. To force her out of the mountains.

Why?

Because he was afraid to do it himself.

Why?

Lord Song is afraid of the kidnapper.

He protects the man's identity. Yet he is afraid.

Why?

Why?

I cannot make sense of the threads, they tangle and knot and do not fit together. I shake my head, press my hand over my face. "He has locked you up like this," I whisper. "Since you returned home? All this time."

A sudden hand closes hard over my shoulder from behind, yanking me from where I crouch beside the bolted doors. I stumble onto my knees, coughing and spluttering, earth in my mouth.

The looming silhouette of a man hangs over me and I yell as he reaches to grasp the front of my *jeogori*, dragging me painfully to my feet.

"You are not permitted in this place." The man's voice is barely controlled. "How dare you wander the master's house."

The leader of Lord Song's private soldiers. The man always by Lord Song's side. A sword is tightly gripped between his clenched fingers. Yet he does not draw his blade. "Get up! On your feet!"

I rip my body from his grip. "Why is this woman locked in here?"

The head soldier steps closer, holding his body big and menacing. "It is not your place to question the master!" He grasps my elbow and sharply yanks me from the building, back down the black bamboo pathway toward the gate and main house. "Lord Song has requested you leave, you are no longer welcome in this house."

There is only silence from the little building as I am dragged away.

I struggle and dig my heels into the stony earth but my feet slide and drag across the dirt. This man is a mountain who pulls me where he will. Glancing behind, I glimpse the building one last time before it is gone within the bamboo forest, hidden in the black. A lonely prison for a ghost. I dig my fingers into the head soldier's upper arm. "Will he let her out? He cannot keep her there!"

The man glares at me, face hard and sharp. He says nothing at all and I am propelled through the gardens, back through the warren of pathways and gates. We emerge into the main entrance courtyard, wide and spacious in the night. Flames lick the darkness near the gate, fire glow emanating from torches placed on either side of the heavy doors. The gates are opened by servants as we approach.

I am thrown from the compound, left stumbling onto the road outside where Man Seok waits with arms crossed over his chest. He steps forward to help me but I'm already back on my feet, stalking past the two gateway guards to yell at the head servant. "He cannot lock her away like that! The magistrate will force you to free her!" One of the guards grips my arms to pull me back from the steps.

As the doors are pushed shut the head soldier stares from within, face alight in orange fire glow. "That woman belongs to Lord Song," he says. "She's done him wrong and he can do with her what he likes."

The doors close and abruptly he is gone.

I shake the guards loose who still hold me, flicking their hands from my body and glaring before turning on my heel to stalk away. Yet I am stopped immediately by Man Seok, his hand tight on my shoulder, black eyes hard. I shake him off too. I am burning up with fury.

For Lord Song's head soldier is right.

The nurse is but a slave, and her body belongs to Lord Song. Like mine belongs to the *podocheong*. Like a *gisaeng* belongs to her gibang.

Like my father and I both belonged to the house where I was born.

A rich nobleman like Lord Song will face no repercussions for his actions. He has the right to punish this woman who supported his daughter's escape. And even if he didn't, it's illegal for a slave to raise allegations against their owner. The nurse could not testify.

Her fate is out of our hands. She will rot within that dark building, or she will not, depending on Lord Song's whim.

My body burns, feet moving fast through the night, away, away. I don't care where.

"Dan Ji! Dan Ji, stop!" Man Seok's voice is sharp. The voice of a man who expects to be obeyed.

I ignore him, too furious to care, striding through the darkness toward the black river, ignoring the winds rushing from the mountains now night has fallen. Ignoring the chill in the air. I take deep breaths and calm my pounding heart, clutching at the yellow river grasses, dragging the plants from their roots and discarding them on the winding river pathway. Man Seok stays behind me. I hear his crunching footsteps in the darkness.

Walking more slowly now, I follow the trail carefully as it threads back up the dark hillside toward the government office. Soon Man Seok walks by my side, and we climb the hill together in silence.

It is happening again.

Like it did when I investigated the taxation corruption case. The threads begin to sink beneath my skin, pulling outwards and outwards until I must solve the mystery or leave parts of myself behind.

I have always been like that. I cannot let things go, cannot step back and let things be.

I cannot get that woman's voice out of my mind. The sound of it, cracking with grief.

The corruption taxation case, too, had victims. Yet back then they were poor farmers who suffered beyond my reach, poverty-stricken commoners and villagers who I never met. Faces I never saw. And even when the tangled mess of threads and pieces was resolved, it is images of hands in the snow and ginger taffee that haunts me, not the fates of those farmers. In my mind the victims of that crime become tangled and twisted. Until I almost believe the one who suffered most could be a simple father who tried to make something more from his world for his daughter. Just a mercenary who was used up and spat out in a war between corrupt noblemen and the police. A man who was no one. Who died in front of me and whose name I don't even remember.

I stop suddenly in the darkness, reaching between the river reeds for Man Seok's sleeve, clutching the rough material tightly between my numb fingers.

His walking ceases, his body growing still.

"Man Seok. It's different this time, do you not think? Here it's too late to save anyone already."

I peer up at him, wanting … *something*, for I am thinking again of frozen hands buried in the dirt and an empty shell of a girl, all the life within her snuffed out.

"You will give up?" he breathes. His voice tangles with the wind on the river.

He misunderstands me. I shake my head. "I want to find the truth. I want to know why she did it, the woman who dresses as a man. Why did she abduct those girls? I want to know."

Man Seok is silent, just staring down at me. Close now. Finally, he says, "You may not like the answer."

"I do not care."

He nods, seeming satisfied. "I too want to know what Lord Song is so afraid of." The corners of his mouth curl, an almost-smile in the darkness. As if we are together in this.

It makes me stare.

I have never seen him smile.

My fingers drop abruptly from Man Seok's sleeve and I resume walking, wrapping my arms tight around my body against the chill in the air, my head humming and my cheeks flush with cold.

After a moment I hear Man Seok's footsteps follow behind.

The government office is ablaze when we arrive. Metal bowls filled with flaming oil are scattered throughout the main courtyard on stands, fires sparking embers into the black sky. A crowd of men gather in the yard. The police officers that came to help from down the valley mill about in the mud dressed in full uniform, clutching staffs and weapons, waiting.

Man Seok and I hesitate at the gates, watching from the shadows as the magistrate himself steps from his office with Secretary Baek at his side, positioned on the highest stone step to address the men. His voice booms across the yard.

"Our office thanks you for the aid you have provided us in locating the missing noblewoman, Song Seorim. Now that she has been returned to her home safely there is no longer need of your presence here. I authorise you to travel back to your homes. Our office is grateful this case has been resolved."

I glance sharply at Man Seok but his attention is trained on Magistrate Hong. The older man motions for Secretary Baek to take over, his right-hand man walking down the stairs to speak further with small clusters of guards. He and the large woman servant, the office cook, begin to hand out small wrapped parcels.

"Supplies," I say in disbelief. "For their journey home."

Immediately my anger returns, bubbling and popping. I stalk across the courtyard, pushing through the dispersing guards to reach the main building.

"Magistrate Hong," I call out sharply, catching him just before he disappears again inside his office. "You are sending the guards home? Now? When we finally know what the criminal looks like? That she is a woman who is deeply wounded? We are drawing closer to the truth!"

Magistrate Hong's dark eyes flash and for a moment I think he will berate me for my lack of respect, for my bold questions. Yet he does not, though the anger stays etched into his face. It takes me a moment longer to realise his fury is not directed at me. When he speaks it's through clenched teeth, as if he must struggle to say the words.

"A messenger has come with a letter from Hanseong. Direct from the head of the *podocheong*."

I shake my head. "What did it say?"

"As of the moment we received the letter, this case has been closed."

18

The Ribbon

I SIT inside the magistrate's office, nursing a cup of steaming roasted barley tea the cook has served us, wrapping my fingers tightly around the burning porcelain.

"This cannot be," I say again. Man Seok sits across from me, Secretary Baek standing at the magistrate's shoulder. Everyone looks as grim as I feel. "Please, Magistrate Hong, I do not understand how this can be."

"The case is closed," the magistrate answers sharply. He is defensive, for it was on his order that the last of the guards slipped from the courtyard, filtering out of the main gates. The government office is now desolate and empty, despite the blazing fires still lighting the yard.

"It is Lord Song," he adds quietly, his words a rush now, escaping like steam. "He sent another message through his uncle to the prince, requesting the case be closed as a favour. He does not care to discover the culprit, he only cares that his daughter had been returned to him safe and sound."

Secretary Baek shakes his head and says in a whisper,

"It makes no sense. Does he not wish to know who did this to his daughter?" His face is shiny with sweat despite the cold, the sleepless nights taking their toll.

"No. It is the timing that makes no sense," Man Seok interjects, his voice without emotion.

He stares at the surface of his tea, ripples moving outwards. "If Lord Song contacted his uncle in Hanseong, it took time. It took time again for the message to be relayed to the prince and the order to come back to us through the *podocheong*." He looks over at me. "Lord Song requested the case be closed because his daughter was located."

I laugh suddenly, filled with disbelief. "Yet he initiated that request long before we ever found Song Seorim. Which means ... what? Lord Song knew she would be found?"

The magistrate slams his hands hard against the table, tea cups and porcelain dishes rattling loudly. "He manipulates us! We've been used by him over and over!"

I smile, though there's no humour in it. I tell Magistrate Hong and Secretary Baek about the nurse I found locked in Lord Song's residence. Lord Song knew his daughter was abducted into the mountains long ago, yet he chose not to share any of this information with the police.

"He has played us for a fool," spits Magistrate Hong. His skin is flushed and he keeps running his fingers through his beard, over and over again. "He used the royal family to manipulate me, to tie my hands!"

Secretary Baek ventures, "Magistrate Hong, it's true this turn is devastating, yet I do point out that our rescue of Lord Song's daughter will be seen by the *podocheong* as a successful outcome of this case. And if Lord Song himself has withdrawn his request for investigation, there can be no question as to your right to continue on as magistrate in this district. It is ... as successful an outcome as we could have hoped."

Magistrate Hong glares at his right-hand man, as do I. The only difference is the magistrate seems to relent after a long-charged moment, while the injustice of our situation builds up and up within my chest.

"So that's it?" I snap. "You will just give up? You will let Lord Song walk all over you without repercussion?"

Magistrate Hong's voice drops low. "Watch your tongue, *damo*. You go too far. How dare you speak to me thus?"

I glare at him for choosing this moment to begin caring about rank and etiquette. "I dare," I challenge. "What about the girl we found buried in the mountain? She was *murdered*! Will you leave her killer uncharged? Will you not even try?"

The magistrate stands, knocking his chair back so it crashes to the ground. "You speak out of turn," he roars at me. "I've been ordered by the head of the *podocheong* to close this case. By the actual prince himself! You think I should defy them? You think I should place my head on the line for a dead villager who tripped and broke her neck in the mountains?" His chest is heaving, face flushed with blood. "Know your place! This case is closed. You and Lieutenant Jo will return to the capital as ordered and you, lowly *damo*, will know your place."

I surge to my feet, ready to scream back at him except Man Seok grips my wrist hard and forces me to sit.

"Damo Dan Ji," he says sharply, his voice warning.

I flash my eyes at him too, at the magistrate, at Secretary Baek. And then I rip myself from Man Seok's grip and stomp to the door. I fling the shutters open and leave them battering loudly against the building as I launch myself away across the cold empty courtyard.

Inside my room I throw my blanket against the wall, kick at the low wooden table that sits unused beside the door. I almost scream at the flood of pain that tears through my foot, at my jaw where the criminal hurt me. At my heart whose threads still extend out into the valley all around me. Threads that will never come back home, only be ripped apart and left here long after I leave for Hanseong.

Even Man Seok will do nothing.

Even after what happened during the mass arrest for the taxation corruption case. Even after what he did. He will still comply and do nothing. With one little girl lying dead and the other an empty shell. I find the silk *nambawi* tangled among my blanket and I fling that hard against the wall too.

I turn my back to it and sink to the floor, breathing heavily.

It is a long time before I have calmed, before I finally begin fixing the things I have destroyed. Folding my blanket neatly and turning the table upright.

I light a single candle. The *nambawi* winter hat remains where it fell, hidden in the corner of the dark room where the light from my single flame cannot reach. It stays there, coiled and soft like a live thing, and I try not to think of it.

Instead, I think of the dead girl buried in the snow. And I think of her killer who we allow to keep eating and sleeping and breathing, to keep living, when that small broken girl cannot. And then I think of her older brother Shin Yonggae and the ravaged skin of his back, the torn flesh that I can see so vividly in my mind. Though when I picture it, it's my father lying there in that hot stifling room, thick with the smell of blood and death.

He promised me that night, that I would be born as his daughter again in the next life. He said we would never scatter. Me. My mother. Him.

The room where he lay then was so unlike this one right now. It was filled with people, other servants of that great house, and it was humid, thick with the smell of blood. Moisture in the air. Sweat. Fire from the furnace. He promised me. He said our next life together would be easier.

He promised.

I sigh, calm now, anger gone from my body until I only feel cold, alone in my quiet empty room. I am a fool to get so upset over things I cannot control. Life is as it is.

Yet sometimes I do not want to wait. I do not want to wait for my next life.

I climb to my feet slowly, stepping to retrieve the *nambawi* Man Seok gave me, replacing it carefully on the little table beside my candle.

Flickering flame-light shines bright across the black silk. I touch the winter hat softly with my fingertips, stroking the smooth surface, staying like that for a long time before finally blowing out the candle. I force myself instead to think of Choon Shim, who will surely be glad to withdraw from Lord Song's service. I picture her hands, chapped and raw from the washing water, as I attempt to sleep. I try to focus on how good it will be to see her again, for all of us to return together to Hanseong. I try to let it all go. The threads. I try to sleep.

I cannot.

A ribbon. Red beneath the stain of dirt, half buried in the snow on the north face of the mountain. It did not belong to Song Seorim, hers was still tied within her hair when we located her, embroidered with her name.

So, it belonged to someone else. Yet the material was not old, rot had not yet set in.

A red ribbon, buried in the snow.

A thread.

19

Threads

I SIT WAITING outside Man Seok's room in the men's quarters. The area is quiet now after the guards have returned home. Even the local men have gone back into the village, with only a few unlucky guards left behind to watch the main gates.

I play with the hair ribbon in my hands, the colour of it bright against the dark night, against the close heavy sky. The material flutters in the quiet wind as wolves begin to howl, the sound louder than ever before, closer. It makes me glad of the high stone walls that keep the forest out. I imagine for a moment that the walls are the only barrier stopping the mountains from swallowing the offices, from taking back this small valley from the community that have made it their home.

I sigh, my breath a thick white mist and still I wait, rubbing my hands together for warmth.

I am angry when he comes, unreasonable. I snap, "Where have you been?"

Man Seok hesitates in the courtyard, darkness clinging to him, making it difficult to see his face.

"I've been making arrangements for us to leave tomorrow, for Choon Shim to be extracted."

I stay where I am, sitting huddled on the low wooden *maru*. "Tomorrow?" My voice shakes like I will cry and I cannot stand the sound of it. I am a *damo* of the *podocheong*, not some emotional little girl. I cannot bear for Man Seok to see me this way, yet I cannot help the desperate words spilling from my mouth.

"We cannot leave, Man Seok. This ribbon, do you remember it? I found it in the mountains, at that hut on the north face, buried in the ground. It belongs to Shin Yonggae's dead sister, don't you see?"

Man Seok says nothing.

"It means she was murdered! For certainty. The girl did not simply slip and fall as Magistrate Hong has recorded in his annals. She was in that place with Song Seorim! Perhaps she died right there, at the hut, or maybe she escaped and was killed and buried further down the mountain. But whatever happened, Man Seok, it means that the woman who abducted Seorim, she is a killer. She has murdered a little girl and no one will do anything about it! I went to see the dead girl's mother, and she recognised the ribbon. Shin Yonggae had given it to his little sister, a treasure from the big city. It proves she was there."

I pause, breathless, waiting for him to understand, waiting for him to launch into action.

Yet he says nothing.

"Man Seok *ssi*, what do you think? What should we do?"

"I think you should let it go."

I stare at him. At the darkness that covers the place where he stands.

"No, you do not really think that, I know you don't."

"I do. It is as Magistrate Hong has said. We cannot go against the orders we've been given. You must let it go."

I shake my head. "How can you say that to me? After what you did on the night Poong Yi was arrested?"

He shifts in the darkness. A flinch? Gravel crunches beneath his boots.

"Please," I whisper. "Man Seok *ssi*. Help me."

His voice is soft. Gentle. "It is done. Tomorrow we return to Hanseong. It's over."

My body tenses, fills with winding threads all clamouring for my attention. Images of curling hands gone blue with cold, dirt beneath fingernails, like claws in the snow. I hang my head, touch my hands to my temples. I don't want to let it go.

Yet tomorrow, the wanted posters will be filed away and a killer will walk free.

And I will leave this valley.

Man Seok draws closer now in the quiet night, positioning himself carefully on the wooden *maru* beside me. Close but not touching. "Do you remember what I told you at the gambling inn?"

I glance at him, startled by the abrupt shift. I shake my head.

"My uncle has asked me to join him beside the ocean. Do you remember?"

"He has a business there," I say slowly, beginning to remember his words. So long ago. Another world. "He wants you to help him run it."

Man Seok faces the thick stone walls, the night where the mountains rise. There is nothing out there but black. Yet still he looks. "Yes, a small guesthouse. My uncle has no children. He grows old." Man Seok turns to me, steady black eyes holding mine. "You told me you've never seen the ocean."

I feel strange, like the darkness has grown warmer, pressing in from all sides. I stumble over my words, "You said that you would go after the taxation corruption case was finished. You said you would leave the *podocheong* and go."

He stares at me. "Yet I did not go."

I cannot meet his eyes. "And when we return to Hanseong? What will you do then, will you go?"

My question hangs in the air as Man Seok climbs to his feet, steps away across the crunching gravel into the building shadows, standing with his back to me.

"I will follow you, Dan Ji *ssi*," he says quietly. "I will go where you go."

My mind grows still and quiet, my body locked into place where I sit. The wolves sound again in the mountains, far away now, and I say nothing. Silence draws out between us.

Man Seok comes back. Stands before me. Mist rises from his mouth, his body warm and alive in this deep winter. His heavy boots crunch against the gravel, then on the stone steps as he moves into a low crouch, his knee meeting cold rock just below my folded legs. When his fingers touch my jaw, my neck, they are made from ice but I do not flinch away. They travel across my skin and I stare into Man Seok's black eyes.

There is no expression on his face. It is his way. Always. To keep himself to himself. And yet, his hands are different. They tell a story. His mouth too, tells a different story. On mine, with hands against my jaw, my throat, a kiss so deep it presses breath and skin, filled with life and living. And wanting. Pushing me back.

He breaks away. Stands again. Waiting. Breathing heavy.

Still I say nothing. My thoughts are not my own and I

cannot control them. So, I bite my lips and we both wait in silence, until finally Man Seok steps past me onto the terrace, kicking off his boots and leaving them on the stone steps.

"Good night, Dan Ji *ssi*," is all he says. And his voice sounds like it always does. I cannot read his thoughts within the sound of it.

Yet when Man Seok opens the small shutters of his room and enters that dark space, he does not close them again. He leaves the doors open to the cold night, gaping black and wide.

An invitation.

Abruptly I stand, walking away across the crunching courtyard, breathing hard and almost stumbling. I am so fast, direct and certain of my destination. And yet I do not make it to the gates, hesitating in the shadows.

His doors remain open.

I go back.

Slip inside that black space, stand in darkness before Man Seok who seems half surprised to see me, his breath suddenly gone. Slowly he reaches beyond me to close the doors at my back and I lean into him, pressing my mouth to his, my hands to his face, sharp bones and bristled skin. I am brave in the darkness. Beneath his clothes his skin runs smooth and strange beneath my fingertips, layered and folded from the edges of his throat down across his chest. Fire. Long since healed. His body marred by it. Another secret part of him I do not know. I would ask him of it, yet his mouth is on mine and there is no time left for words.

The night closes in and one by one the threads extending from my chest into the valley, slowly come back home.

20

The Village

IN THE BLUE light of morning I wake, night still clinging to the dark corners of Man Seok's small room. We lie pressed together beneath padded blankets, skin to skin. He sleeps deeply, face clear and untroubled. Yet I am different. The walls close in and the small space becomes smaller still. I am suffocating, flushed with confusion.

Dragging my body from the blankets I stumble into my clothes, cold in the early morning after so long lying warm beside his body.

For a moment I hesitate beside the closed door with my heart beating fast, hand hovering over the iron ring. The blanket is pulled back, Man Seok's shoulder exposed to the winter, and just for a moment I'm thinking of his hands in my hair, his mouth on mine, how it felt to lie beneath him.

Outside. I burst into the dim light of dawn and breathe deep. Cold air, sharp and clear. I take it into my lungs as I walk quickly across the courtyard, out of the men's quarters before anyone can see me here.

In my own room with the doors shut I sink to the floor,

press my hands against my face, trying to focus again on what comes next. A trip back to Hanseong? A journey.

And then?

A choice.

I don't know what I have done. It was unexpected. A new experience I did not foresee or plan for, a new curling idea I have long since avoided.

I am not yet ready to become some man's wife. To give up all I've worked so hard to become. Yet my head hums heavy with confusion, my skin tingles where Man Seok's hands and his mouth…

I wash and dress and soon am outside the enclosure gates, striding down the winding road toward the village. I am to meet Choon Shim this morning and I focus on the sun as it slides from behind misty peaks overhead. Focus on the clouds that cling to the evergreen pines and drip down into the valley. It turns the sky heavy as the morning dawns.

Again, I think of Man Seok's sleeping face flushed in blue light.

And I think of how he looked standing in the gambling inn courtyard surrounded by police officers, with his hands smeared red with streaking blood.

Choon Shim is beside the black river. Standing hidden among the high reeds, which are yellow and swaying. Her cheeks are pink and her lips chapped and red, yet she smiles when she sees me. The curve of her mouth changes to a frown as I draw closer, trudging across the river bank toward her.

I attempt to smooth over my expression, but already it is too late.

"Dan Ji *Unni*, what has happened?"

"Nothing," I answer quickly. "Of course, nothing has

happened. Today is your last day at Lord Song's residence, we will leave this valley by midday. Have you been told?" I force myself to smile. For there is truly nothing wrong. Except I must leave this place before I am ready, beside a man who has asked me for something I cannot quite understand with the touch of his hands and mouth.

Choon Shim nods, relieved. She bends to the water, standing on piled flat stones placed beside the bank to combat the mud and grass rot. She presses one hand to her mouth, suppressing her dry coughs as she fills a large earthenware pot. Cold water gurgles into its depths, small slivers of ice sucked in as well. When it is full, I help her drag it from the water onto the rocks beside us.

"I am glad we are going," Choon Shim tells me as I help lift the heavy clay pot onto her head. It rests atop a small rolled piece of cloth, which is worn like a crown to protect her skull. "It is too cold here. It gets inside me. Like ice." She shivers and coughs again. I hate myself for what I am about to do.

"Choon Shim, I need to ask you a favour. Please, will you help me? One last thing before you leave Lord Song's house."

She frowns. "What favour? I thought we were done? I thought we were leaving?"

I want to scream at her that she didn't see what I did, those girls in the mountain, one dead and the other a living ghost. Instead I force myself to look at her tired eyes, at her raw hands and the way her body bends under the weight of the water pot. And I tell myself she will do these same chores when we return to Hanseong, her life will not change. This existence is not so very different from our home. What I ask of her will not be so very difficult. Not really.

I lie to myself.

I take a deep shuddering breath. "Do you think you can get inside Lord Song's room?"

Choon Shim stares at me, heaves the pot back onto the ground where the water spills over the edges.

"*Please*, Choon Shim," I say. "You told me he's barely left his residence since you arrived there?"

She is uncertain. And afraid. It's in the way her focus flicks to the surface of the black river and back again, always moving but never seeing. "Yes … that's right. The only times he left home was when he went to the government office. After you found his daughter. And when you found the body in the mountains. The rest of the time he stays within the house. I told you, he is afraid to leave."

I nod, taking her raw hands into mine. "Lord Song has been communicating with the person who abducted his daughter. Somehow. He *knew* his daughter was coming back home. He knew long before we found her, of this we are certain. Yet he never leaves his residence. So how are they communicating?"

"Lord Song's head soldier … he leaves the house often. He must be carrying messages."

"Exactly," I breathe. "Messages. Written messages. There must be letters in Lord Song's private rooms, communication between him and the killer. If we could find them, we would have evidence that Lord Song is involved. It would be enough to reopen the case, for it is only because of his word that it has closed."

Choon Shim's dark eyes dart across my face, her fingers clutching onto mine. "What if they passed messages using only words? What if they do not write anything down?"

I ignore the desperate hope in her voice. Ignore it and

say firmly, "We need to know for certain. Choon Shim, you must do this. Today, do not show up at the spot where you are meant to be extracted. If you are not there, then none of us can leave the valley. Lieutenant Jo Man Seok and I will be forced to stay. Please. Please give me two more days."

"What will you do?"

"I will find a way to draw Lord Song from his house. It will give you a chance to search his private quarters."

Her fingers tighten on mine. Hard. Too hard. "And if there's nothing there? No evidence?"

"We will leave. I promise."

For a moment she seems just like a child. Small and vulnerable. She whispers, "*Unni*, did Lieutenant Jo send you here with these instructions?"

I flinch at the sound of Man Seok's name, hope she does not see what happened between us written across my face as her questions keep flowing.

"Is this what the *podocheong* and the magistrate wants? A way to circumvent the prince's orders?"

I hesitate. "Of course," I tell her soothingly, holding her hands tightly, reassuringly. "It is Lieutenant … Jo's direct orders. Why else would I come?" I smile at her, wide and open, the second thing I have done today that is so unlike myself.

Choon Shim nods unhappily, reaching down for her water pot. Her hands shake and she pauses there, fingers grasping onto the cold glazed earthenware. "*Unni*," she whispers. "What if I cannot get into his rooms? Even if he is gone, Lord Song has many servants. The house will not be unattended."

Placing my hand against her back, I crouch beside Choon Shim among the yellow reeds. Slowly I point at the mountain shrouded in mist behind us, rising up and up against the grey skies. "I found her body up there, Choon Shim." My voice is low, thin like a reed. "She was small and thin, and her hands were curled like this." I show Choon Shim on her own hands, pulling her fingers back and curling them until they appear as claws. "Frozen like that, in place. She was only a child, yet someone murdered her up there. They broke her neck, and then they dug a shallow hole and covered her with dirt and snow. They left her like that. All alone on the mountainside. By herself in a dark hole."

I reach for Choon Shim's face, force her to look into my eyes. "We carried her body down the mountain to the office. And it was only when she was lying on a table in a room with torches burning that she began to thaw. Her face was blue and her skin turned black when she melted. That little girl's mouth was filled with dirt. Someone *did* that to her. They *murdered* her. And Lord Song is protecting them. He is protecting a killer. But we can do something about it. You. And me."

I let go of her face, her chin red where my grip has hardened, leaving pink marks that fade slowly. She peers into the sky and blinks rapidly and I know my words have infected her, just as they have infected me.

"Thank you, Choon Shim," I whisper, touching her shoulder again, softly now. "Thank you. Thank you."

I help her with the heavy pot, press my fingers against the glazed belly of it to steady her load as we walk back through the river weeds to the main path. The river bank is silent this early, empty of all signs of life. Only the mountains rise on either side, the treetops clear of snow after the thick rains. Mist descends from the peaks to lie close across the crowded *hanok* houses and market stalls of the sprawling village.

I am slow to return to the government offices after what I have done.

Slow to return and face Man Seok.

I cannot face him.

I linger in the village, gazing at the stalls and keeping my mind blank. I run my fingers over the pretty things, over the cotton and silk and the bright coloured hair ribbons, until a merchant yells at me to back away if I will not buy. I sit for a long time on a table outside a small restaurant, where I order light frothy stew. And then I linger even longer, ordering fermented cabbage and a jug of sour *makgeolli*, the white cloudy liquid burning my stomach and filling me with heat. Yet my body does not warm, the pit of my belly remains like ice.

When I finally return to the government offices in the late afternoon, the yards are in chaos. Men in the magistrate guard uniform scurry past and shouts erupt at the back of the compound, men with weapons running toward the enclosure's prison building. I follow the sounds, find Secretary Baek standing outside the prison speaking with Guards Kim and Yu. Magistrate Hong emerges from the hidden depths of the building, his face flushing red with fury when he sees me. "Where have you been?"

"What happened?" My mind is slow from the alcohol I have drunk. Much too much. It has numbed my thoughts, like I am dreaming, seeing the world through a haze of cloud. I step closer, trying to appear steady on my feet, ignoring the exhaustion the liquor has released inside my chest and bones.

"The woman has been arrested," snaps the magistrate.

I blink at him. "The woman?"

"She has arrived just now. Are you ready? She must be interrogated."

I don't move, seeing from beyond a sheet of water, of

ice. The images and voices flood outwards across the smooth surface, bleeding into each other.

"Damo Dan Ji!" The magistrate's eyes flash. "This is what you wanted, was it not? The case to remain open? So do your job! Come!"

I step forward, just as someone else appears from behind, hovering at my side.

Man Seok.

He peers down at me, deep and dark, questioning. He reaches to touch me, fingers hesitant against my arm, and my mind snaps back into focus. I shake him off. It's too much, those images of him sleeping in the blue dawn. I cannot bring myself to examine what they mean to me, cannot, so I turn away.

"Dan Ji *ssi*," he breathes. He takes my arm again to hold me still, for I attempt to walk now toward the prison. His eyes are wounded. Black.

I wrench away, unable to look again, my mind filled with pictures of blue morning light and the terrible thing I have done to Choon Shim.

He says my name again. The same voice he used when he spoke to me of the ocean. Of a quiet house. When he said he would follow where I go.

"Please … don't touch me," I breathe, backing away, into the open gaping mouth of the prison. Blood roars inside my ears. I am no longer myself. I am no longer sure of who I want to be. I do not turn back. I do not want to see the hurt in his eyes.

Inside the prison, the ground turns to rotting yellow river rushes. Even during the day torches burn, the building almost stuffy. In the last cell a figure crouches, curled in on itself, dressed all in white.

A woman, hair in a long-looped braid, the end of her plait tied at the base of her neck, tendrils coming loose around her face. A wide face. Thick lips. High cheekbones. Pale skin. A soft chinless jaw. The woman I fought in the mountains. The woman who abducted Song Seorim.

The woman Lord Song protects.

A killer.

21

A Suspect

"THE TRUE INTERROGATION has not yet begun," I tell the murderer quietly, crouched down beside her cell among the damp river rushes strewn across the floor.

She peers at me through thick wooden bars, impassive. Blood is smeared across her face. One of the guards must have struck her as they dragged her in.

Her white *jeogori* is stained rust red beneath her shoulder, blood from the wound I inflicted seeping into her clothes. Perhaps the stitches came undone in her violent struggle with the magistrate's men.

The woman was found further up the valley. Hidden in a small ramshackle inn at the edges of the wide forest, too exhausted and hurt to travel the long winding mountain road to escape the district. The innkeeper's wife tipped the government office off. She spied on the wounded woman who spent days and days suspiciously cloistered away within her room, only coming out when hunger drove her to.

The magistrate's men were already waiting by then, and the killer did not stand a chance.

She does not seem like much now, leaning her head against the dirty wall and watching me through half closed lids. She must be in pain yet she does not show it. Only the blood seeping wet into her prison clothes betrays her, the rest of her body remaining so motionless it's as if she's not really here at all.

I grow frustrated at her silence, at her refusal to answer my questions.

"Did you hear me?" I say. "If you do not tell me what you know, the magistrate will torture you until you speak. He will force you to explain your connection to Lord Song. We know you are working alongside him."

She says nothing and I try again.

"Lord Song has been protecting you, even though you stole his only daughter away. Why?"

The woman only blinks at me and I shift in the straw rushes. I am very aware of the men who stand behind me, who wait for me to draw some sort of confession from this killer. They expect it because I am a woman myself. As if somehow my words will sink deeper into this killer's mind than theirs ever could. As if we share some kind of secret similarity because of our womanhood.

Even though she is a murderer and I am not.

"Tell me," I snap, but she says nothing.

I turn toward the magistrate, waiting for his instruction, yet his attention is still locked onto the prisoner. I hear the sound of her shifting within her cell and turn to find she has struggled to her feet, her hand clasped tightly across her wounded shoulder. Blood oozes between her fingers. She staggers closer, barefoot despite the cold, walking until she stands right against the bars. I rise to meet her, face to face.

She is taller than me, broader, strong and muscular.

Her blood-stained fingers curl around the wooden bars, expression empty. She still does not speak, staring at me.

I move closer, completely ignoring Man Seok's warning from behind, standing so close now she could reach through the bars and touch me. Choke me. If she willed it.

She does not. There is no movement from within the cell.

"How long have you dressed as a man?" I ask, curious now despite myself, despite what she has done to the little girl in the mountain. Threads wrap around her, tight and winding. I want to unearth her secrets. "How long?"

"Since I was fourteen years."

I am taken aback. Truly I had not expected her to answer. There is an accent, though she speaks our Joseon language well. "Why?"

She smiles without humour. "Money."

"Money?"

"Why else do anything?"

I taste bile in the back of my throat. "So, you murdered that young girl in the mountains for money?"

The woman nods. "In a way."

"You were paid to assassinate her? That little girl? Why?"

She shrugs her broad shoulders, loosening the muscles, twisting her neck. "It was a mistake that she died. She was not meant to. But she fought me. And it is what happened."

"Then what were you paid to do?"

She only smiles, but there is something else in her expression now too. I step closer, studying her face in the flickering glow of the orange torches. Is it fear I see? I tilt my head, uncertain. "What are you afraid of?"

Her smile does not move. "I am not afraid."

I lean closer. "I think you are."

The prisoner does not answer and I almost glance behind me again, almost find Man Seok's eyes. But I cannot bring myself to do it, for all I wish to know what he is thinking. He has always been better with people than me, better at reading them.

Yet the way he looks at me now is different, for he has offered me a choice, and I do not know what the answer is, cannot see it in this gloomy place. So, I don't look.

I turn back to the murderer. "Who do you work for?"

Her smile is gone.

"I work alone."

"I don't believe you."

Secretary Baek's voice rises from where the men stand. "You think she works for someone else?"

I ignore him, though I hear harsh whispers from the magistrate, shushing him.

I clear my throat. "Why did you abduct Song Seorim?"

The prisoner leans her head closer, forehead touching the wooden bars. "If I tell you, what will you give me?"

Magistrate Hong grunts. "Nothing, fool. You will be executed for your crimes."

The woman's expression does not change. "Well then," she concedes, beginning to move back to her original place across the cell.

I reach out and grasp her sleeve to stop her. "Wait! You brought her back, didn't you? Song Seorim. You took her away and then you brought her back." I hesitate, threads slowly connecting. "We never rescued her, you were bringing her home. That night in the mountains, you were bringing Song Seorim home to her father. Am I right?"

The woman's gaze moves slowly across my face, assessing me. Then she smiles, cold and hard. "A truth," she agrees.

I nod. This is a game I can play.

"You never meant to abduct her, only the young village girl, except it went wrong. You ended up with both girls, and you couldn't manage it. One escaped from the hut, the little girl, and you struggled together. You killed her. And you buried her. Truth?"

The woman says nothing, but she does not deny it. I glance back at the magistrate behind me, satisfied I am right.

"Tell me," I repeat to the prisoner, "who do you work for?"

The woman does not speak. She shakes me from her arm and retreats to her corner, crouching against the wall and becoming small and helpless again, clutching the wound on her chest.

"If you will not tell me what I ask," I call. "You know what will happen next, do you not?"

She watches me with hard eyes.

She knows.

WHEN IT HAPPENS, I stand back beside Secretary Baek near the stone wall. Man Seok is closer, hovering near Magistrate Hong. None of us speak, silent and still as we witness the killer's interrogation.

Flickering torches burn in the courtyard, embers leaping into the dusk sky on the wind. Towering mountains loom blue and dark in the distance, only outlines of the valley now. And the wind rises, the prisoner's skirts fluttering and her hair torn from the single braid wound at her neck.

At first, she says nothing, refuses to answer the questions Magistrate Hong barks at her, her body bound to a wooden chair placed in the centre of the freezing courtyard. Her bare feet are blistered from cold and the wet gravel.

I clutch my hands into fists, nails biting into my palms when the screaming begins. And then the woman does not say much of anything, only begging the two guards who wield the thick wooden poles to stop. But they do not. The men, one on each side, press the poles against her legs and push down hard on her thighs until she screams with agony. Her legs slowly crush beneath the pressure, the poles twisting her bones and splitting her muscle.

She screams and the magistrate watches as overhead the sky turns black.

And she tells us nothing.

22

To Depart

"SHE IS A FOREIGNER," I say quietly to the men who share the table within the magistrate's private office. Guard Yu and Secretary Baek sit across from me, with Magistrate Hong placed at the head. "I can hear it in her voice."

"From Ming," says Man Seok and I glance at him. He sounds certain.

I look away, cheeks flushed.

"Why?" asks Secretary Baek. "Why on earth would a woman from Ming come to this valley and attempt to abduct two women?"

"More than two women," I say quietly. "Many more. If we count the records in the office annals."

"She told us nothing. Even under torture!" Magistrate Hong places his head in his hands, then snaps at his secretary, "Send a message to Hanseong. Tell them what has occurred, ask them ... ask them what we should do. Reopen the case?"

Man Seok peers at his hands. "They will order you to reopen it, Magistrate Hong. The prisoner must be charged with murder. Even the prince will not stand in the way of that."

"Interrogate her again," chimes in Guard Yu. "She cannot hold out much longer. Soon she will break. I am certain of it."

I shake my head. "She is afraid," I say. "Deathly afraid. Yet she will not speak. What does that tell you?"

Guard Yu peers at me blankly, and it is Man Seok who answers my question, making me flinch.

"It is not us that she fears."

"Lord Song?" guesses Magistrate Hong. "After all, this woman risked her life to bring Lord Song's daughter home. It must be Lord Song that she fears."

Man Seok shakes his head. "Lord Song no longer leaves his home. He too, is afraid."

A long silence stretches and my heart hums with a need for the truth, an utter craving for it, until Magistrate Hong breaks the quiet. "Someone else then. Someone else who stands behind them both."

The room lapses into silence.

Finally, I say, "Ming. It is so very far away. Another world."

"It is not so far."

I turn to Man Seok, meeting his black eyes for the second time since I watched him sleeping in the blue dawn. He stares back, clear and open, until I must look away.

Magistrate Hong nods thoughtfully. "Ming lies beyond the valley, across the mountains. There is a port there with ships that leave Joseon often. Once out in the wide sea, who knows where they travel to. Or who they trade with."

"It is time, I think," says Man Seok, "to visit Lord Song's chosen in-laws. Did you not say, Magistrate Hong, that the family was powerful? That they are situated in that same nearby port?"

"Why would we meet with them?" Secretary Baek asks, frowning. "The port is so far away, how could they be involved in this?"

Magistrate Hong is watching Man Seok. "It is not so very far," he says, echoing Man Seok's earlier statement. "Will you go, Lieutenant Jo?"

"I will."

"And Damo Dan Ji?"

I open my mouth to answer but Man Seok speaks for me. "Damo Dan Ji will stay in the valley."

I glance at him sharply, barely hearing as Guard Yu asks, "What do you think you will find there?"

"That I do not know," Man Seok answers. "Though now the case has reopened we must strive for the full truth. Nothing else will satisfy the prince." He rises to his feet, candlelight flickering across his hard face. "And from what I have heard of his nature, it is best that we offer him full satisfaction."

He does not look at me as Magistrate Hong discusses the logistics of the journey, naming trusted guards as part of his assigned travelling party, to keep Lieutenant Jo safe. I clench my hands and listen, furious now that Man Seok would speak for me so, yet still I remain silent, climbing slowly to my feet and leaving without another word to anyone.

Is that what it will feel like to become a wife? My choices stripped from me?

Yet my anger cools fast.

Perhaps he only wishes to give me time. I pleaded with him not to touch me. Perhaps Man Seok listened.

I do not know how I feel.

Later that night when I am tucked safely inside my small room, warm beneath my thick blanket, I hear movement outside in the women's quarters courtyard.

Boots crunching across the stony ground.

The wind whistles loudly through the rooftops and far away there are the sounds of wolves. I slip from beneath my warm covers and the cold dusts my skin, like the frozen top layer of the black river, frost and ice. I press my face against the smallest gap in the shutters, peering into the darkness of the night.

I am sure it is Man Seok, am certain it is the shape of him emerging from within the black. Yet he draws no closer, standing for a few moments in the dark only to move away again, back the same way he has come.

In the morning he has already gone, though I rise with the dawn.

I linger at the front gates anyway, gazing over the village road winding away across the valley, imagining the men riding through the mountains toward the sea. I curl my hands into fists and bring them to my mouth, blowing warm breath across the gaps between my fingers, clouds of mist escaping.

I tell myself it is better this way. Much better. For now, I will not have to see Man Seok's disbelieving face when he hears what I have asked Choon Shim to do on his order. It is so much better he has gone away.

I tell myself this and ignore the sickness creeping inside my belly.

I find Guard Kim near the men's quarters, crouched down beside the wall with two soft rice cakes in his hands. He is kind enough to pass one my way when I crouch beside him, and together we eat in silence. Even that makes my mind wander back to Man Seok, and I must shake my head to clear it.

We eat quietly for a time, until Guard Yu comes running across the yard with heaving chest, stopping abruptly only when he sees I am not alone. Guard Kim rolls his eyes at the younger man's pointed look, understanding he is not wanted. After stuffing the last of his rice cake between his teeth, he gathers his weapons and re-enters the men's quarters, leaving us be.

"Damo Dan Ji, I have been searching for you," Guard Yu whispers, crouching close beside me. "Lieutenant Jo left me orders to bring Damo Choon Shim away this morning, but she has not appeared at the extraction point." His mouth is tight with worry.

I stand. "Where were you to meet her?"

"Down beside the river. She draws water before dawn."

I hesitate. "Even with the case reopened, you will bring Damo Choon Shim out?"

Guard Yu nods. "Yes. Lieutenant Jo had arranged for her to stay in a village at the far end of the valley. It would be safe there. Did you not know?"

"I knew. Yet things have now changed."

I focus on the outlines of rising peaks appearing through the heavy clouds, forcing myself to say it. "If Damo Choon Shim stays within Lord Song's residence, perhaps she can still do some good there."

"What do you mean?"

I turn to Guard Yu and bite my lip. "I have a question to ask you. Will you help me?"

He nods uncertainly.

"Guard Yu. If I wanted to create a distraction big enough to force Lord Song from his home, how would I go about it?"

The young man hesitates, then says doubtfully, "Bribes. Or threats. There is no other way. Lord Song still refuses to meet with us."

"We have no money to bribe him with. So, threats it will have to be."

Guard Yu stares at me.

"I must speak with Magistrate Hong," I say. "I have an idea."

23

A Plot

I EMERGE from the dark prison, striding urgently through the courtyard with Guard Yu at my side.

"The prisoner has been speaking?" Guard Yu hisses. "She truly threatened Lord Song?"

I nod grimly. "She tells of an attack on his person. Tonight."

"Tell me what she said exactly."

We near the main courtyard, passing by a group of the magistrate's guards who glance at us in interest. The office cook is with them too, serving bowls of steaming tea.

"It is all she will admit to," I tell Guard Yu in a rushed whisper. "An attack on Lord Song's life. Tonight. His home is to be raided, with Lord Song himself the target. And something about the *gisaeng* house up the valley. I could not understand it, but we must investigate."

"We must inform the magistrate." Guard Yu says this just as we reach the main office building. We climb the stone stairs to the wooden *maru* terrace above. Kicking off my shoes urgently, I stride across the floorboards and wrench open the magistrate's office doors, Guard Yu following me into the dark quiet space within.

Magistrate Hong waits at the long table, sitting in silence with Guard Kim standing behind. When the door is shut Guard Yu and I hover a while behind it, listening to the yards outside.

"Will it work?"

I turn to Guard Yu and answer, "It will be enough to start rumours. Whether those rumours reach Lord Song's ears or not, I cannot say."

"It will have to be enough." Magistrate Hong stands, reaching for his wide-brimmed hat and adjusting the black ties beneath his chin. "I am leaving. I trust you will handle this situation well in my absence?"

Guard Yu nods and bows respectfully as Guard Kim and I lower our gaze. The magistrate strides by us onto the open *maru*. In the courtyard he gathers more men, readying them for the long journey up the valley to the *gisaeng* house. A pointless mission to investigate a fake thread of information.

Magistrate Hong's alibi.

The rest of the day is spent waiting. And watching. I linger in the main courtyard, attention trained on the entrance gates, wanting to see which of Magistrate Hong's men leave the enclosure. Who is the traitor who carries information straight to Lord Song's ears?

IT IS LATE AFTERNOON, two days after Man Seok has left us, growing dark enough now that the cook has begun to ignite the lanterns along the main building terrace. Light spills over the latticed wood of the private quarters. I sit and watch the sun disappear behind the rising mountains, watch as the sky blackens and the ranges become nothing but giants barely visible in the early night. And I wait. My body thick with tension, my fingernails biting into my palms until they draw blood.

Guard Yu steps from the office behind me with Secretary Baek.

"It is time."

I nod, trying not to think of what Man Seok would say about this rash idea. If he were here. Which he is not.

It is only later, when the night has deepened and turned black, that finally the screams begin. Blood-curdling cries of a young maidservant echo through the thick forest beyond Lord Song's residence. We stay hidden among the trees, myself and Guard Yu, listening to the sounds of panic wailing from within Lord Song's stone walls.

The fire burns hot and bright, crackling and popping as the roof of the abandoned shack left lonely in the forest finally caves in. The fire flames scorch the residence walls and sear the stone black. And the wind blows just the right way, perfectly.

Thick acrid smoke swells through the air, pouring into Lord Song's residence, sparks from the wood fire and the dry pine needles we have piled inside the shack rise into the black. Servants within Lord Song's enclosure scream and cry, lost in the thick smoke, so certain it is their own buildings that burn, chaos driving the panic higher.

Another of Magistrate Hong's guards appears between the trees to join us, followed by more men. They keep close and low beside the shelter of the enclosure's outer walls. The heat is unbearable, thick and smoking. One man waves to us, his voice low. "Guard Yu. Lord Song and his family have left the house, everyone is gathering out on the main road. It is working."

"Good. Where is Guard Kim?"

"He succeeded in hitting the target, sir."

Guard Yu smiles at me, a flash of teeth in darkness. Reckless and wild. Light from the fire is reflected in his eyes.

I follow behind the men as they pick their way through the dark forest, stepping over twisted roots and sidling around fallen trees. The smell of smoking pine needles hangs thick in the air.

It takes a while to find the right vantage point, hidden a short way up the mountain side near the front of Lord Song's residence. The roadside glows with bobbing lights, torches and lanterns and screaming servant children all certain their residence burns. The scene is marred by orange haze. Thick smoke swells inside Lord Song's enclosure and spills outwards onto the road, servants and soldiers alike doubled over and coughing.

I cannot see Choon Shim.

But I do see Lord Song. He is protected by his soldiers, they surround him holding torches to keep the darkness at bay, the head soldier shouting orders. The other mercenaries run back and forth like ants, into the house and out again, bringing more servants in their wake, the panic taking hold.

And I see Song Seorim.

It is far away so I cannot see her well. But once I realise it's her, I cannot seem to look away. She stands aside from the smoke and panic, outside of it. She does not realise there is danger. Instead, she peers up into the black mountains, her chin raised and her face blank. And beside her waits the head maidservant, the woman I met during my one visit to that house. The older woman holds Song Seorim's limp hand and stares into the darkness too, as if she wishes to see whatever it is Song Seorim can. But there is nothing there but black.

"Where is Guard Kim?" I whisper finally, and it is one of the magistrate's guards who answers.

"He returned to the government office, Damo Dan Ji. He did not wish to be seen carrying a bow."

"And where did he manage to strike?"

The guard grins. "He hit the main building with the arrow. Right beside the door. Right before one of Lord Song's soldiers. Frightened him good and proper."

I allow myself a small smile. "He is talented then."

Guard Yu nods. "He is a good shot. And it has served us well. See how panicked they are. The soldiers. An arrow striking within inches of their faces! They believe they are under attack."

Guard Yu catches my eye then, and I know what he is thinking. What he is hoping. That Choon Shim has understood the danger is not real. That this is her opportunity for action, while chaos engulfs the house, while Lord Song and his soldiers mill about on the roadside. A small window of time, uninterrupted. It is all I can give her.

I hope it is enough.

The others get up to leave. Guard Yu is assigned to follow the magistrate down the valley to inform him of our success, and another man will watch Lord Song's house throughout the night. The others return to the government office. Or to their beds. I stay crouched where I am, unmoving. I cannot tear my gaze from the house below engulfed in smoke, from the sight of Lord Song and Song Seorim, still visible through the darkness.

The men leave me behind.

And still I wait.

Just for a moment I let myself think of Magistrate Hong, of Lord Song himself, how their attention slides over me, barely focusing for longer than a moment. A lowly *damo*. Not to be feared or noticed.

They underestimate me.

My fingernails bite into my skin as I whisper over and over beneath my breath, praying for Choon Shim's success. I am wild with hoping.

The smoke begins to clear. Slowly. The haze shifts and the air loses the scent of smouldering pine. Soon Lord Song's men will discover the fire was started beyond their own enclosure, harmless in the forest. They will realise that the arrow embedded deep within their wall was nothing but an empty threat. And they will realise we know of their spy within the government office, and that we know how to use him, to stir panic within Lord Song's household.

Down below, the household staff begin to trail back inside their walls, leaving the roadside empty and barren once more. Song Seorim is ushered away, and soon Lord Song disappears back inside his home, his head held high, hand gripping a sword despite his age, despite his swollen belly. He is so certain of his power, so certain of his position here in his small valley. Certain that he will not topple, no matter how hard we push.

I feel a new hatred bubble within my chest, for his own daughter is returned to him, yet he cares not for the mother who sits in her rotting *hanok* in the village and mourns a daughter who will never come home.

When the road is empty and the household turned quiet, I slip away through the thick darkness, circling back to the remnants of the smoking shack. The place is empty now and silent, the ground around the burned-out fire churned up by boots.

Lord Song's men.

They are long gone now, the threat extinguished along with the flames. But the quiet makes me nervous. Surely by now they know about our ruse, so would they not send patrols walking throughout the night? Yet all is calm. Still.

Silent.

I drift by the shack in the black night and climb onto the fallen juniper tree at the back of Lord Song's garden wall. I huddle down, wrapping my arms around my body tightly, and for a moment, just a moment, I dream of wearing the *nambawi* that Man Seok gifted me. I imagine it closing over my numb ears, soft fur against raw skin.

He will be back soon, from the port. Soon. I close my eyes.

And I wait.

Yet Choon Shim does not come.

IN THE DEEPEST hours of the night I cannot wait any longer. No sounds come from inside Lord Song's residence and no lights either. All is quiet as if the household sleeps. My fingers are without feeling now, even when I blow hot air onto their tips. My back aches from crouching against the tree, my muscles strained and shaking.

I climb down slowly, carefully, for my legs do not work exactly like they should, as if they too are made from ice. The longer I wait here, in this place, in this valley, the more of myself I am losing to the winter. Pieces. Threads.

Falling away.

I trail back slowly through the village, which is quiet and still, walking up the hill where the only sound is the rushing wind through the river reeds and the bare oak trees. The mountains are filled with silence. There are no wolves out tonight. The quiet feels strange and heavy.

When I get back to the government office I am

surprised to find the front gates unguarded, the burning torches snuffed out.

The place is empty and desolate.

It's true that Guard Yu and his small group of men left during the night to follow Magistrate Hong away down the valley, yet still, the office should not be this quiet.

I tread slowly up the stone steps, one by one. The gates are already open. I only have to push against the wood for the door to swing inwards with a deep creaking, to open the way into the main courtyard unobstructed.

That, too, is empty.

Yet something dark is spilled across the stony ground. I crouch to touch the gravel. My hand comes back wet and smelling of metal.

Of blood.

Silently I rise to my feet, draw my *jangdo* from its sheath beneath my *jeogori*, the sharp blade glinting in the darkness. I tread slowly across the stony earth without a sound, careful of my footsteps. Careful to keep my movements slow and even, so I do not draw attention in the thick black of night.

I find the first body lying in a heap against the next gate.

It is a man, crumpled against the doorway leading to the inner courtyards of the government office compound. He is dressed in the magistrate's guard uniform, hat askew and clothes gone black with blood. I reach down and touch his skin. Still warm. But there is no breath. When I touch his chest, my hand comes back slick with blood. I cannot see his face.

It is only the first body.

There are many more after that.

By the time I reach the inner courtyards at the back of

the compound I am sweating, blood pounding in my ears. I hear a sound then and smell smoke.

Murmurs of speech from behind the men's quarters. I creep closer. Flames flicker there, a glow against the rooftops beyond the high stone wall. I run my fingers over the rising walls, touching rough surface, cold and sharp, and I pause at the next gate. A man lies at my feet. This time I do not repeat the process of checking his vitals. He is dead, as they all have been.

A loud smashing of wood reverberates from beyond the wall, splintering, cracking. I drop to the ground, using the dead man as cover, reaching across his chest to push my fingers against the wooden doors of the small gate. It is the prison gate I have come to. It leads into the prison courtyard, and then onwards to the building itself.

The sounds of men speaking come from this place, from inside the prison courtyard walls. It makes me pause, blood pounding in my ears. I peer through the small gap I have made.

Lights. Flickering across the yard. And the heavy stench of smoke.

The glow of fire falls across my face through the cracked doorway and I flinch away, but it has already passed me by. Yet for a moment light illuminates the face of the dead man I lean on.

Guard Kim.

Eyes open and staring at the black sky. Mouth wide, teeth bloody.

I stretch blood-smeared fingers over my mouth, hold back the sound I want to make. Ignoring the buzzing building within my head, I force my heart to slow. Yet my breath still comes hard and fast, a constant cloud of fine mist clinging to my lips.

So many men, dead. And Guard Kim. Gone.

Why?

I shiver against the stone wall, pressing my body against the cold rock. The sounds fade. The lights flare and then go out.

Black. Utterly black.

Who has come to kill and maim our guards? Is their aim assassination? To murder Magistrate Hong?

But no. The magistrate is not here. That information would be easy to source.

He is gone away. As have most of the government office guards, either to the port with Man Seok or to the *gibang* with the magistrate himself. The offices are staffed only by a skeleton crew. A few stragglers left behind to keep the place safe.

Someone knew.

Knew the office would be almost empty because … of me. Because of the plan I suggested. Because I wished to give Choon Shim more time.

The attack was particularly timed. And I paved an opportunity.

I did this.

Another mistake. An utter failing.

Men are dead.

My fault.

Yet there is nothing here of value.

I stand abruptly, clinging to my *jangdo*.

Except the woman from Ming.

I burst from the gateway with wild eyes, sprinting across the dark yard and hugging the high walls as I move quickly toward the prison. Light flares again as I draw near, bursting from within its windows. I skid to a stop across from the prison building.

It is on fire within.

Nearing the open gaping doorway, I peer inside the

burning walls, hands clutched to my mouth to protect from the choking smoke. Three men dressed all in black are silhouetted against yellow flames. Still inside the building. As if it does not burn.

They stand outside the prisoner's cell, their faces obstructed by black cloth. By flame and thick smoke. They do not see me, but I see them. I see the woman from Ming fall back between the wooden bars of her cell, her body hitting the steaming damp straw with a hard crack. Her skull slamming rock beneath the dirty river rushes.

It is not the fall that kills her.

A knife protrudes from her chest, sunk deep within her breast. Blood glitters in the fire-light, streaming into deep pools until her body is painted red. Her last gasping breath is dragged from smoke-filled lungs.

Flames crackle from the far wall and I stagger back, thick acrid smoke filling my mouth. The far end of the building is already burning.

The killer we caught is dead. Assassinated. Murdered by ... I don't know who. I am choking on the thick smoke, staggering outside into the cold courtyard. I stumble across the crunching ground in an attempt to flee before the men know I have witnessed what they have done.

It is snowing now, falling from the black sky. Flames burst from the wooden storage shed beside the prison, crackling as they engulf the structure. I am knocked back by the heat of it, the destruction. I trip over something, another body. A young man, his throat opened ear to ear, mouth slack.

I am almost physically sick, scrabbling at the gravel to find my feet, my hair soaked with melted snow that blinds me. I force myself back up. For I am a *damo* of the *podocheong*. Not some squeamish useless girl, and I have done this, I have caused it. I have killed these men, killed our only witness, the woman from Ming, our only connection to Lord Song's guilt.

I have caused this catastrophe with my clever plans.

The intruders emerge from the burning building before I can reach the far gate. They see me, their figures silhouetted by bright flame, black against red. The three men shimmer and twist and within seconds they are around me. They move the way a river does, their bodies flowing like water, calm and smooth despite the chaos they have caused. They are warriors. Trained in war and killing. But I am ready now, my knife held close. I lunge and stab.

Yet my side is suddenly searing hot, agony like fire rippling through my skin. Through muscle and sinew and bone. Flesh torn apart by a warrior's blade.

I am on the ground. Flat on my back. Breath gone from my insides.

Black sky above. And wisps of snow coming harder now, thicker. My mind skips and jumps, thought to thought, erratic and strange, until it settles on one idea. One awareness.

If I was wearing my *nambawi* it would be warmer.

There would be no snow seeping cold and wet into my hair if I had worn it, into my skin. It would have been better.

A black boot engulfs my vision, violent and fast, the heel aimed at my face.

I raise my hands but I do not. I roll aside but I do not.

I lie still and wait.

Something seeps from my side, wet and hot. Into the snow.

There is an explosion. Fire. I taste metal.

And then I do not.

24

Choices

VOICES.

My face is on fire. I whimper. Like a child. Like a useless child.

"It hurts."

I think I am crying.

"Your nose is broken." A deep voice. I hope it is Man Seok.

And I hope it is not.

I roll over. Away. Squeeze my eyes shut at the pain searing from my side. Gasp until I … drift.

WHEN I NEXT wake there is candlelight. Flames flickering across the walls. It is Man Seok sitting there, Secretary Baek too. Both of them sleeping, propped together against the wall.

I struggle up off the bedroll, tangled, frustrated at my agony, at how difficult it is to move. At how my broken body betrays me. I feel as if I cannot breathe. As if I am suffocating.

The walls close in and I need the heavy blanket off my body. I manage to push it away and then touch my hand to my searing face. Fingers carefully exploring. Hot skin. Swollen and tight. My brow. Split and scabbed. Unbearable pain. My nose.

I jerk my hand back from the agony that lances through my skull. My eyes drip water.

Broken bones. Crunched by a boot heel.

My side aches yet it is dull. A cut in my skin. Deep perhaps. Or not. I cannot tell. I inspect the wound beneath my clothes, examine the stitching threading through my red puffed flesh. I have had worse. Long ago when my father and I were still together. I have been beaten and had much worse. But my face aches deeply, my cheeks wet and my head pounding. And that is new.

I glance at Man Seok. His expression while he sleeps is easier to read. Exhaustion lines his brow and deep circles mar the skin across his cheekbones. He sleeps fitfully, hands twitching and jaw clenching. He dreams.

I watch him sleep and think again of my father's promise.

I cannot bear to wait for my next life. I do not want to die and start again. I am not ready. And when I look at Man Seok I am fiercely glad I am not dead.

Secretary Baek stirs, his head dropping suddenly from where it leans against the wall, the movement jerking him awake. This in turn rouses Man Seok and I must turn away from them both, unable to meet their eyes.

"Dan Ji *ssi*," Man Seok breathes. "Lie back down."

My voice is like sand, scratching and dry. "How long … have I been here?"

Secretary Baek clears his throat. "Only a day and a night. Dawn draws near."

"The prisoner from Ming … is dead," I say quietly,

though surely they know this already. My gaze stays locked on my hands and my split mouth hurts when I speak. "She was assassinated. Three men in masks. I could not identify them."

I feel sick, nausea welling within my chest. I bite down on my lips to taste pain, holding until it passes. I deserve to feel nauseated. I deserve to feel pain. I made the wrong choices. My actions have killed men.

I force myself to face Man Seok. "Without the suspect in our custody we cannot connect Lord Song to the crime. It is over."

"We know nothing for certain," Man Seok answers gently.

I stare at him and blink. It's unusual for his voice to sound that way. I fight back tears. I want to cry.

But I do not.

I do not deserve to.

I turn away. "Choon Shim? Have you seen her?"

Man Seok still watches me. "Not yet."

"We need to extract her. Will you send Guard Yu? I asked her to … to search his rooms." I bite my lip again. "That is why Magistrate Hong approved my…"

Man Seok interrupts by holding up his hands. "I know. Magistrate Hong has told me."

Silence draws out and I am thinking of Magistrate Hong, how I have proved him right, every doubt he had in me. I am incompetent. Worse. I am reckless.

If I had not interfered Choon Shim would be free of the Song household, safe in a faraway village. And the woman from Ming, she would live still.

Secretary Baek shifts uncomfortably. He coughs and then announces, "Lieutenant Jo has news from his visit to the port. Song Seorim's betrothed owns a trading company.

He is from a family of merchants. Self-made. But very rich."

I press my hands across my burning face, fingers cool against my flaming puffed skin. I cannot think clearly, clouds of smoke invading my mind. "How does that help us?"

"It seems his family's ships sometimes travel north to Ming," Man Seok answers quietly. "Or so the rumours say."

I watch him through the candlelight and say nothing.

Ming. So very far away.

Guard Yu enters through the doors then, the small room becoming crowded enough that Man Seok begins to frown. He stares at Secretary Baek until the older man excuses himself and leaves. And all the while the men shift and re-position themselves I am lost in thought, pictures of a little girl frozen in the forest drifting through my mind.

"Damo Dan Ji, are you well?"

I might ask Guard Yu the same question. He seems tired and worn thin, the expression clinging to his face reminding me suddenly of Guard Kim. Of a family somewhere down in that small village, of how drastically their lives will now change without him.

I do not know if Guard Kim had a wife, if he had children.

And now I do not dare to ask, only answering, "I am well." I hate myself for my cowardice. Lying back down carefully, I peer at the ceiling as Man Seok repeats the findings of his journey to Guard Yu.

"Lord Song's in-laws trade with Ming? What is it you think they trade?"

"Linen," answers Man Seok. "Joseon cloth. Or pottery. Perfumes."

I laugh bitterly.

"Little girls," I say into the silence that follows. "Prostitutes."

Man Seok says nothing. Yet his eyes are deep and dark. He already knew, I am certain that he did.

Yet he did not tell me. For he too is aware of what my reckless actions have cost us. The woman from Ming. The opportunity to connect Lord Song to people traffickers. The entire case.

The silence draws out between the three of us, long and heavy. Until finally Guard Yu breaks it, his voice wavering, "Perhaps Damo Choon Shim has already discovered evidence in Lord Song's rooms?" He sounds just like a child. Filled with hoping. "Perhaps we can still arrest Lord Song?"

And naivety.

I turn away from them, ignoring the pain that sears my side.

I squeeze my eyes shut as Man Seok says only, "Perhaps."

25

To Fall

MAGISTRATE HONG REFUSES to see me. I soon understand that whatever shreds are still left of this investigation, they will not include me.

I am no longer to be trusted.

If I ever was.

Now I am afraid to leave my room. Afraid to face the men out there, the guards who listened to my words only to see their colleagues cut down. Murdered. By ghosts. By men trained in war.

Men who did not belong to Lord Song's household.

That much is clear, for our guard was posted to watch Lord Song's residence that night after the distraction we created, to wait and see what Lord Song might do. And he did nothing. No one came or left his dark residence that long night through.

The men in black came from somewhere else.

I shift and wince on my bedroll, chewing over the events in my mind, again and again. Tearing my choices apart and then placing them back together again. Getting nowhere. Even Man Seok does not come back. Not after that first time.

I think of Guard Kim often but do not say his name when Guard Yu comes to visit, checking on me throughout the long slow days to ensure I am recovering well.

"Here," he offers, handing me a rough wooden bowl filled with steamed sweet potatoes. "You look terrible, Damo Dan Ji."

I struggle to sit, clutching at my side. "Do I?"

The knife that sliced my skin did not leave a deep cut, but it has pulled wide. Only the small stitches, sewn there by the government office cook who lives down in the village, hold my side in place. When I move the skin stretches, stitches tugging, threatening to reopen and split apart.

"Yes, you do," answers Guard Yu. "Just like a swollen rotting apple. All red and black and green."

I gape at him, taken aback, and Guard Yu's face splits wide into a grin, amused by my expression and his own daring joke.

I cannot help but smile, though the movement of my lips is small and weak.

"It's not so very bad," he continues in the same teasing way. "Your nose will surely heal crooked though. Perhaps you will become ugly now."

I touch the swollen mass gingerly. I do not care about my nose. "I will live."

He nods, sobering. "Though at first we were less sure. When we found you ... I do not know how long you'd been lying there, Damo Dan Ji. But it was snowing. Lieutenant Jo, he ... surely, he thought you were dead. That much was clear. I did wonder if he and you…"

His words abruptly stop, but the way he cocks his head to the side makes me uncomfortable, like he's grasping at threads of his own, trying to connect pathways and make a puzzle fit. Suddenly he smiles wide, as if he's found his answer, and quickly I squeeze my eyes shut, unable to listen, reaching to change the subject.

"What are your thoughts, Guard Yu, on this suggestion of people trafficking?"

He is startled by the abrupt change. "I … I cannot believe it to be true."

"Why is that?"

"I heard from a travelling merchant once that slavery is outlawed in Ming. Or at least they attempt to abolish it."

"There is always a market for illegal things," I say. "Here in Joseon and however far away you travel, there is always a black market."

He nods thoughtfully. "And you and Lieutenant Jo both believe Lord Song is at the centre of this organisation? That he collaborates with his in-laws to smuggle girls out of Joseon?"

I bite my lip, thinking of the soldiers Lord Song has posted at his gates. They stand there night and day, protecting him. And I think of the men in black, who came at night to kill the woman from Ming, a suspect in murder and now people trafficking. Threads. Unconnected. Yet connected.

"I am not sure," I say finally. "It does not explain everything."

"It is a difficult case," muses Guard Yu. "And we have hit a wall in our investigation. I do not know what the magistrate plans to do next. It looks bad. A suspect killed while in his custody and protection? I do not know how he will explain it to his superiors." He leans closer and breathes, "He will be culpable. He will lose his position."

A knock sounds on the shutters and a harsh voice calls

for Guard Yu from outside. Man Seok's voice. He does not come in to see me.

Guard Yu smiles apologetically. "I will return later and bring you news of Damo Choon Shim."

Man Seok's voice snaps from behind the door, ordering Guard Yu to quicken his pace. I flinch at the sharpness behind his words.

Guard Yu opens the shutters to my room quickly, yet still pauses to say, "It is not your fault, Damo Dan Ji. If Lord Song wanted to assassinate our suspect, he would have found a way."

"Yet I gave those men the opportunity."

"They would have created their own opportunity."

He smiles at me, and then he is gone. Shouting erupts outside in the yard. Movement and noise of men calling to each other. It has been that way since I first woke after my deep sleep. There was much to do after the attack, bodies to return to families, spilled blood and worse to scrub from stone. And a charred prison building to dismantle and rebuild.

During my deep sleep, when my injuries kept me drifting, endless wailing had invaded my mind. I had thought I was only dreaming, terrible fever dreams dredged from deep inside my head, yet they were not. It was only later I understood that relatives visited us, to identify and collect their dead, villagers bringing carts to take their men back home. Although I cannot stop thinking of it, I will not ask who was left behind to mourn Guard Kim.

There is no one to ask anyway. I am left alone.

BY MID-MORNING I realise there are guards posted beyond my door.

To keep me safe. To protect me.

Or to keep me inside where I can do no more damage.

I do not know.

And by midday, when sunlight filters into my dark room from between the shutters, I grow bored enough to struggle to my feet and creep beside the closed shutters to listen to their endless murmurs. Two men, grown frustrated by waiting. They talk and talk.

Yet I cannot believe what they say.

They speak of a young woman. Dead in the trees beside the black river.

They say she killed herself with a rope, that she was found hanging from the branches of a tall tree.

They say she was one of Lord Song's young maidservants.

26

Pine Trees

MY BODY MOVES as if within a dream, numb, as I struggle into my clothes, into my *damo* uniform for the first time since I arrived into this valley. I throw my commoner village girl clothes aside. They are stained dark with dried blood, crusting into the *jeogori* and disappearing into the worn folds of my *chima* skirts.

I drag my hair high into the bun I must wear with this uniform and tie it with my wide ribbon, not caring when loose strands escape to hang across my broken face. I tie the sash tight around my waist and do not feel it when the stitches on my side pull tight. Or at least I do not care.

It cannot be her.

I am the same as Lord Song, vile and selective. I do not care what family members this dead maidservant leaves behind to mourn her, as long as it is not me who is left. I cannot bear to mourn Choon Shim. Please let it be some other girl. Please.

Exploding from the doors, I startle both young guards outside. They jerk to their feet, bathed in light pouring from the mountains, crisp and cool from unusually clear blue skies. The courtyard and rooftops are thick with snow, glaringly white in the sunshine.

I have never seen the valley like this. So clean and clear. The snow still pure, not yet mixed with mud.

"Tell me what's happened," I demand. "Tell me what you were speaking of just now."

The men bristle and I bite down on my tongue before asking again, quietly this time, through grit teeth. "Please, I heard you speaking. A maidservant has been killed? From Lord Song's household?"

One man glances to the other, who shrugs.

"Not killed," he says finally. "Suicide. Or so they say."

"And who ... who was this girl?"

The guard hesitates. "No one seems to know. Though Magistrate Hong has made the inquiry a priority. He sent men down to the river to investigate."

I sink to my knees, hands clutching hard at the material of my uniform gathering at my chest, digging my fingers in. "Show me," I breathe.

They glance at each other again. "Secretary Baek ordered us to keep an eye on you. For your own safety. You are not well."

"Did he say I could not leave? Am I a prisoner?"

One of the men presses his lips into a white thin line. "No. We are here to protect you." He does not like me. It rolls off him in waves. He does not believe he's been given a worthy assignment.

"Protect me down at the river then," I snap.

"I do not think..."

I scream it at him. "Take me to the river!"

The man who dislikes me glares back. Rigid. But then he rolls his eyes. Clearly it is where he wishes to go as well. To where the action is.

"Go then," he relents. "If you fall and die on the way,

what is it to me? Not even Secretary Baek will truly care."
He shrugs and walks off, leaving the other guard to watch
over me. This man's hands flutter nervously after his
colleague in the sharp mountain breeze. But the other
guard is gone.

"Help me," I order the remaining man. I make him
hold my elbow steady as I drag my shoes onto my feet.
Make him help me down the stairs as I clutch my hand to
my injury, my footsteps sinking deep into the crunching
snow. And then I shake him off, leaving him to trail behind
as I stagger across the uneven snow, fingers pressed close
against my side. Tight against the straining stitches.

It is hard to breathe through my swollen face, my
nostrils closed tight. Soon my eyes are watering and my
skin burning, heat scorching my cheeks. My nose grows
tighter, as if my face is swelling, blood rushing through my
body from the effort of dragging my limbs beyond the
government office gates. I grunt from the pain but do not
stop. All the way down the river path I go, slipping and
sliding in the snow until the view is wide open and I see the
river.

It is different in the sunlight. It shimmers like the sky,
ice the colour of the opaque string of jewels I found so
long ago in the gambling den. The whole valley has
changed. The mountains white and crisp and the pine
trees heavy with hanging snow. Beautiful. Or it could be. If
I could breathe, if I wasn't blinded by streaming water. If
the maidservant is not her.

Men swarm like ants beside the river. Moving back and
forth from the reed-choked banks into a small copse of
evergreen pines growing thick and tall beside the last of the
village houses. I almost run down the hill, stumbling once
hard onto my knees, dragging myself up and onwards. By
the time I reach the copse of trees, emerging from the tall

river grasses with my guard still in tow, my side seeps wet and hot. When I take my hand from my waist sash it is coloured dark red, wet and glittering in the sun. I cannot find it in myself to care.

Marching into the copse of pine trees, my feet crunch across thick snow that smells of fresh pine needles. The guards milling between the tree trunks begin to watch me and murmur, but no one holds me back. The path opens into a small clearing, the ground churned from men's boots, their heels cutting deep into the earth.

"Damo Dan Ji!" Guard Yu appears before me. He looks afraid, so very afraid, his mouth set tight. "Why are you here? Go back, *damo*, go back."

"Tell me what has happened." My hands clutch at his uniform. Panic now. It cannot be real. "Is it Choon Shim? It is not!"

He says nothing, yet I see the truth already.

In his eyes.

And beneath the muddy white sheet placed clumsily across the body at the far end of the clearing. A hand hangs from beneath the stained material. The fingernails are caked with mud.

I cannot breathe. My face is too swollen. My airways close up tight. I gasp and double over. It is not her.

It is not her.

Please do not let it be her.

I cough into the mud at my feet, choking.

"Calm down," Guard Yu is saying urgently. His hand presses against my back. "Calm down, Damo Dan Ji. Be calm."

I stand, force myself to breathe, to slow my heart. "Is it her?" It cannot be her.

Yet he slowly nods.

Black spots crowd my vision. "But they … they said she killed herself?"

"Yes. A villager found her hanging from a tree." He points. "There. That branch."

I shake my head, thinking only of Choon Shim's smile, the sweetness in her eyes. I stare up at the tree. It is too high. Much too high.

"That is dog shit," I scream, ripping my aching body from Guard Yu's hands, my feet sliding wildly in the deep mud. "You know it is!"

Freeing myself, I turn away. I do not want to see her body. I do not want to see her face. "Lord Song," I mutter. "Lord Song cleans up loose ends."

Or Choon Shim was found searching his private quarters.

Like I told her to.

I dare not say those words aloud.

"Lord Song," I hiss. "That son of a bitch!" I swing away from Guard Yu, clumsily sliding in the mud, half my skirts stained wet with dirt. My hands too, they are covered in it. Scrambling, I burst out into the sunlight again, beyond of the copse of trees, light pouring onto my skin. I lift my ruined face to meet the sunshine and then I am away, limping with purpose toward the wide village road.

Fury courses through my veins, white hot and pulsing. And I lose myself inside it, drown myself good and proper, fan the flames of it. Anything is easier … anything is better than…

Men and women from the village gather on the road edge, watching the magistrate's men swarm the crime scene. I pass through the small crowd, take in wind-burnt faces and threadbare clothes, hair coming loose and wild in the valley winds. They are like flies to a carcass. Come to see whatever horror there is to see.

I push past the last villager roughly, almost shoving against him. Guard Yu is caught behind, lost in the crowd of people and though I hear him calling my name I do not stop. I do not stop when he shouts for Lieutenant Jo either. I stumble faster up the hill, until I've struggled the whole way into the marketplace.

Everyone stares at me just like they should. I am wild with hatred. Clutching my side with fingers that come back wet with blood. It makes me scream in frustration. My body will fail me. But I will not stop.

When I reach the gates to his house they are closed tight. The two private soldiers stand tall and strong to block my way, watching me with interest. And I scream and pound at them like it will make a difference, like they will change their minds and allow me inside.

I shout his name over and over again, until something miraculous happens. The heavy wooden doors swing inwards and Lord Song's head soldier appears at the top of the stone steps. "What is this commotion?" He does not look at me, attention only for his two men.

I will make him look at me.

"Where is Lord Song? Where is he?" I kick at the guard who holds me back but it does no damage. My body is weakened from injury and fever. Useless.

"Lord Song does not see just anybody, *damo*." The head soldier turns to his men and flicks his head to the side. A dismissal.

Immediately the heavy gates begin to close and I'm shrieking because I cannot bear it. Except then abruptly he is there, like I summoned him, he has appeared.

Lord Song.

Across the inner courtyard in the distance, I can see him. He emerges from the main building across the gravel yard, and at the sound of his voice the head soldier raises his hand to stop the gates.

"Who is making such noise?" Lord Song comes no closer. Only stands there so very far away, inside the gate, across the courtyard, up the stairs.

Far, far away.

I squint at him and no sound comes from my throat. It has closed over again, the guards' hands tightening on my shoulders.

"Release her."

At Lord Song's order I am dropped suddenly to the ground. I cannot see his expression clearly. He is much too far away.

My voice returns.

"What have you done?" At first my words are only a hiss of merest sound, yet my voice steadily rises like a storm raging, threads torn and tossed aside. All except for one. I am screaming. "You killed her! You murdered her, you bastard! I know. I know!"

Lord Song's head leans to the side. "Of whom are you referring to?"

I surge forward and scream the words at him, losing myself. "How dare you? We know what you did! We will prove you killed a *damo*. You cannot attack the *podocheong*. You will be arrested and charged with murder! You will be executed!"

I have stumbled up the stone steps now, panting and fighting viciously against Lord Song's head soldier who holds me from the main gates easily. And then I am on the ground. Pushed over like I am made of paper.

"You will pay!" I scream.

"A *damo*, you say?" Lord Song takes one step down from across the courtyard and then stops again, fingers threading through his grey course beard. "Then you admit Magistrate Hong placed an undercover agent within my household? Did the *podocheong* approve such an action? Was the prince aware?"

I gape across the yard at him.

And then I begin to laugh, heavy and cracking. Tears stream down my swollen face, salt in my split flesh.

Because the *podocheong* did approve it. Yet they will still cut us loose in the face of the prince's anger. Blame Magistrate Hong. Blame Lieutenant Jo.

Blame me.

And Lord Song knows it.

He knows the government far better than I, he knows what the *podocheong* will do even when I do not. Though I have dedicated my life to furthering justice on their behalf.

Lord Song calls out the name of his head soldier. "Heo Tae Hak, did you know of an agent placed illegally within my household?"

"No Master. Though I have heard our young laundry maidservant, Choon Shim, sir, has hanged herself beside the river." The head soldier bows his head low. "Forgive me for not informing you sooner, Master. I did not wish to bother you with such an ... insignificant detail."

Choon Shim.

They throw their actions in my face.

They play with me.

Fire surges through my flesh and I am on my feet screaming again, incoherent now. I do not even know what I say except that my voice rages on and on and I call them terrible names, enough to get myself whipped, enough to be severely punished by a nobleman if he wished to.

Yet Lord Song does not. He only flicks his head the smallest bit and the head soldier in front of me begins to close the gates. In my face. The doors swing shut and I throw myself at the heavy wood, still screaming rage at

Lord Song. I spit and smash my fist against the hard planks to force him to open it again, over and over pounding with my knuckle so he will face me.

But he does not.

Instead the two soldiers who guard his gates take hold of my writhing body and drag me further down the road, push me over the side into a wet drift of snow and grass, a tangle of plants and limbs. Yet the fire inside me still burns and I heave myself to my feet, staggering back to hurt them, to force them to listen, to do...

Something.

Except I cannot because Man Seok stands there and blocks my way.

Vast and unmoving.

"Stop, Dan Ji. Stop it."

But I cannot. I am crying now. I only know because my cheeks are wet and hot. Tears streaming. I do not want to stop. I want to rage for hours, for the rest of my life.

"Stop it!" He is yelling at me now, one hand closing tightly around my chin, forcing my head up to meet his. "*Calm. Down.*"

And then he has taken my wrist in a hard grip, and I realise for the first time that my hand is dripping blood, skin split open across the knuckles and embedded with thick dark splinters. My fingers curl uselessly just like the dead girl in the forest, and bright red spots fall to stain the snow at my feet. I begin to laugh and Man Seok drags me closer, until I am half pressed against his chest, my ruined hand held out before us so it touches nothing. He drags me away across the snow, bundled and held tight like I am within a vice, no escape. Away down the wide village road.

I am breathing hard by the time we emerge from the snowy forest into the marketplace, mist from my open mouth like a cloud to cover everything. My nose is blocked again and black spots swarm my vision.

My hand truly hurts now, the surge of rage finally abated. Now my head is clearing. Tears still smear my cheeks but I do not care.

Man Seok drags me through the huddle of stalls, past steaming snacks and sizzling wheat-flour cakes burning on wide metal dishes. Smoke rises into the clear sky. Everyone stares at us but I do not care.

I laugh again.

If Lord Song is a killer then so am I.

He did not touch Choon Shim with his own hand, as I did not.

Yet it is murder all the same.

27

The Spy

MAN SEOK STOPS our march abruptly, pushing me onto a wide wooden table at a ramshackle restaurant. We are in the heart of the market. Villagers mill past on either side, thick and busy in the sunshine. Man Seok calls loudly to the *ajumma* who runs the stall, ordering mung bean pancakes and *makgeolli*.

The fire is gone from inside me.

I am left exposed and vulnerable in this public place he has brought me. As I glance around, I attempt to wipe my tears away. Man Seok grabs my damaged hand before it touches my face. "Do not move," he tells me. "Don't do anything. Just sit here and drink. I am coming back."

By the time he returns I've downed three shallow bowls of sour cloudy liquor, my tongue fizzing and my head beginning to hum. I have not touched the food.

Man Seok sits at my side and takes my wrist carefully into his hand. A small cloth bag lies near his knee and he pulls the things he has bought from within its depths.

First a wet cloth for cleaning and then salve for after the splinters have been removed. I flinch and wince as he works, but neither of us speak. With my free hand I pour myself another bowl of *makgeolli*, and then after a moment of hesitation, I pour one for Man Seok too. He takes it and drinks, black eyes deep and dark, and then when it is gone he leans once more over my wounded hand, ignoring me.

I watch as he works. And I drink.

Man Seok does not look up. "Dan Ji *ssi*, why did you never wear the *nambawi*? It was a gift."

I blink.

"It did not fit me."

"Liar. It fits you." He spreads the salve thick over my knuckles where the skin has broken. The wound looks better now, cleaner, the blood and shards of wood gone.

"Can you bend your fingers?"

I comply, gasping at the sudden sharp pain.

"Good," Man Seok says. "Not broken."

And then he says nothing else, the silence broken only by the humming of the marketplace around us, until the feeling of not being able to breathe returns. Until the silence turns my chest tight and my face tighter, clogging my airways. I am abruptly angry again. I do not know why.

"Tell me," I demand, "what exactly do you expect will happen after you leave the *podocheong* and travel to your uncle's home beside the ocean?"

Man Seok meets my stare, steady and unwavering. "I expect I would take over my uncle's business and make a living. I expect I would take a wife, have children." He watches me. "Live quietly and well. Grow old. See my grandchildren grow."

"And you would just give all this up?" I am flushed with confusion, my voice snapping and sharp. "The *podocheong*, everything?"

"What? All this?" He gestures around us at the village

marketplace, down in the direction of the riverside. Back toward Lord Song's house.

I turn away, my face burning. I squeeze my injured hand away from his warm grip. His words hurt me, for it is my fault the investigation has become such a mess. He will not even pretend otherwise.

I say nothing and instead reach again for the jug of alcohol. Man Seok gets there first. He takes the pitcher and pours the cloudy liquid steadily into my waiting bowl. And I watch him. Watch him carefully. And realise that if I were just to ask, Man Seok will take me as his wife, will become the father of my children, live with me and work beside me until I am grown old. Until I die.

Man Seok holds the full bowl out to me, still staring.

All that, at my fingertips.

I take it and drink.

And I do not think about the night I chose to walk inside his room. I do not think about how, at that one moment, there was nothing else I wanted. Only him.

The alcohol wipes it all away, and I press my lips together when my bowl is empty. "I cannot leave," I say sharply. "You know I cannot. Look what I've done here. I've destroyed Magistrate Hong's case. I've derailed the entire investigation." I hesitate a moment before I say the last part, gathering my courage. "And I have … killed Choon Shim. How can I simply walk away?"

"Then what is it you will do instead?"

I say nothing for I do not know. I do not know what I want.

Except that I wish desperately not to feel as I do, as a killer and a failure.

I pour another bowl of *makgeolli*. And then after only a moment of hesitation, another for Man Seok too, and we drink together in silence as the day grows old. The shadows lengthen across the marketplace around us.

BY THE TIME Man Seok announces it is time to return to the office, it has grown dark and I'm unsteady on my feet. I am drunk enough to lean heavily on him as we walk, cradling my curled swollen hand to my chest, body leaning into his, steady and warm.

I imagine wolves as we walk. I imagine them slipping between the shadows, imagine shining yellow eyes staring from between the small village *hanok* houses, from behind the thick trees. They are stalking us.

My body tenses and Man Seok notices, his arm folded around my side, holding me upright. "What is it?"

"Nothing."

"Dan Ji *ssi* … it was not your fault," he says quietly. "Neither the attack on the office or what happened to Damo Choon Shim."

Even with my mind numbed by alcohol a surge of anger is reawakened. "Do not patronise me," I snap at him.

He only smiles, rare for him. And unexpected. It makes me stare and when I turn away, pressing back into him as he supports my walk, I feel his mouth press against my hair. A kiss, quiet and silent. And that is unexpected too, leaving my skin shivering in the dark.

We walk slowly through the thick snow in silence, back toward the office. Man Seok's hand presses steadily against my side, and I realise my wound no longer feels wet. Even with the bleeding ebbing I will need to ask the cook to examine the sliced skin again when we return to the government office.

If she will.

Perhaps one of the men killed within our enclosure was her son or her husband.

I grimace, thinking of Lord Song and Choon Shim and that killer from the mountains. Thinking of Song Seorim and her young lover. Pieces. That fit together or that don't.

Threads.

"Man Seok *ssi*," I say. "What did you find at the crime scene? Down by the river."

"What do you think I found?"

I grimace, lips curling bitter and cold. "I think you found that the branch Choon Shim hung from was too high for her to climb. She was strong and tall for a woman, but it was too high to reach alone."

"Yes. What else?"

"You probably checked her throat and found no signs of a struggle, no excessive bruising or cuts. If someone hangs themselves to death they usually struggle, unless the initial fall breaks their neck first."

"Her neck was not broken."

I nod. "It would be easier to ... to murder her first, then cover it by tying her to the tree. Easier than simply ... ending her life that way." I am struggling for breath again, panting softly in the darkness until our pace slows to a crawl.

"I agree," says Man Seok. "And the tree branch the rope was tied to, the bark was cracked only beneath the rope itself, nowhere else on either side of where it hung. There was no struggle. Once hung, the rope never moved."

Tears slide unbidden across my frozen cheeks. But my voice now when I speak is steady and strong, devoid of emotion. "Choon Shim died first then. If there were no signs of an obvious struggle marking her body, then she was most likely suffocated. Is that what you suspect?"

Man Seok hesitates and I do not like it.

"Do not keep it from me," I tell him. "It is not your right."

He relents. "We found a broken water pot beside the river. She must have gone down at dawn. And her face and hair were covered in crystals of ice. She was drowned. Her face held under."

I nod, taking deep breaths, slowing my heart rate. "Why did he kill her? Lord Song? I am certain it was him. He was not surprised to see me today."

We reach the government office gates, stop together in the thick darkness just beyond the torchlight. Flaming metal bowls burn beside the entrance and the wind picks up. Cold and sharp.

Man Seok peers at me curiously. "We are already well aware of why, are we not? Lord Song killed her because he has something to hide."

"Yes, but how did he know she was a *damo*? Choon Shim had been there so long. What changed? Why do it now?"

Man Seok says nothing and I know what he is thinking. I pull away from his warm body. I no longer need his help to stand. The alcohol has worn off, the cold wind clearing my head. Man Seok thinks Lord Song discovered Choon Shim breaking into his private quarters.

"Dan Ji *ssi*, come inside," is all he says. "It is cold tonight and you are not yet well." He moves as if to take my arm but I step back.

"*Listen* to me. If Choon Shim brought her heavy pot all the way down to the river at dawn, and it was broken in an unexpected struggle as she fought for her life, then she must not have known her identity was uncovered.

She did not know they had discovered who she worked for."

Man Seok stands still, waiting.

"Which means she either got away with searching his private quarters or never even had a chance to try. Don't you see, it means Lord Song found out her identity another way."

"Not necessarily. Perhaps someone witnessed Choon Shim exploring Lord Song's rooms and she never knew she had been seen."

I shake my head. "Unlikely. They witnessed her actions and then did nothing about it for three full days?"

I have his attention now. I can see the change in how he holds his body, taller and straighter as he considers my words. "What other way could they have known about Choon Shim then?" he asks slowly. "What is it you suspect?"

"Man Seok. We know someone within the government office has been leaking information. We have known a long time."

"But only Magistrate Hong and Guard Yu knew about Choon Shim," Man Seok breathes. His black eyes glitter in the darkness. "I trust them."

I press my hands against my face.

My fault again.

"And someone else," I whisper.

Man Seok stares. Waiting.

Always my fault.

"When I first woke up ... when I woke after the attack, I asked about her. I asked. Do you remember?"

Man Seok's eyes widen.

And then he is gone, sprinting into the government office, disappearing into the pool of warm light, leaving me alone outside in the night.

28

Wolves

SECRETARY BAEK SCREAMS as they drag him from his warm bed near the magistrate's inner quarters. Guards are on hand to arrest him, but it is not needed. He wears his sleeping clothes, and hair slips loose from the black *manggeon* band wrapped across his forehead. He is dishevelled and his eyes are wild, rolling in their sockets to show us the whites, visible even in the night.

I have never seen someone so afraid.

Except perhaps that small dead girl in the forest, fear etched onto her face for all of time, frozen in place. The image wipes my pity for Secretary Baek clean away.

The prison building is gone, destroyed by the fire and not yet rebuilt. Secretary Baek is taken screaming to a small storage shed near the men's quarters, a tiny structure made from stone and mud wall, built upon a frame of grass ropes and sticks.

I am not allowed to come close. Magistrate Hong storms through the courtyard, pacing back and forth until his face is shiny with sweat. When he sees me the expression on his face is enough to convey his feelings, yet his actions speak even louder. He waves across one of the few remaining guards to escort me outside the courtyard gates, beyond the men's quarters.

The government office is on lockdown.

The first thing Magistrate Hong did when Man Seok told him what we suspected was to dismiss half his men, sending them home into the village. The only men who remain are a trusted inner crew. Guard Yu and the four men he has vouched for.

They wish to keep this quiet; they wish to keep this news from Lord Song's ears.

I loiter in the darkness outside the gate, just beyond the wall. My swollen fingers press against the stone as I reach on tip toes to peer into the enclosure. The thick wall is too high, yet a small gap in the gate appears between the heavy metal hinges holding the planks together. I find that if I crouch, I can peer through the empty spaces.

Movement flickers across my view. The magistrate. Still pacing. And then I see Man Seok standing near the storage shed, arms folded across his chest, face fierce.

Secretary Baek will receive no sympathy tonight, not from these two men.

When they are finally ready to interrogate him, a thick wooden chair is carried into the centre of the yard and rope brought ready for binding. The magistrate's men drag the suspect from his small prison as he cries, face wet with tears and mouth drooling as he spews pleas for understanding. "Please, please! Magistrate Hong, please!"

No one listens.

Secretary Baek wails wordlessly as they bind him to the chair, and still the magistrate says nothing. I cannot see his face, but his pacing now has ended.

"I had no choice. Please, Magistrate Hong. I had no choice, Lord Song threatened me! He threatened me!"

It is Man Seok who speaks from his place in the corner. "And paid you as well, no doubt."

Secretary Baek's eyes bulge. "No! No, no, no. That is not why I did it, he made me. He forced me. I beg you, Magistrate Hong, you must believe me. I would never betray you!"

The magistrate remains silent and Secretary Baek sobs harder. The wailing from his mouth reminds me of wolves, calling to each other in the mountains, drifting on the wind. Yet so unlike the wolves as well. For Secretary Baek's voice is filled with fear, choked thick with it. He knows what will come next.

As do I.

Despite his screams, despite his promises of telling the truth, Secretary Baek is tortured using thick wooden poles to twist his legs. The anger in Magistrate Hong and Lieutenant Jo runs deep. They will not spare him, this betrayer, and soon Secretary Baek's screams fill the air, until the wolves in the mountains begin to howl in harmony.

I do not watch. But still I can hear, huddled and shivering with my back pressed against the gate. It draws on and on, until finally Secretary Baek's screams become whimpers and then there is nothing.

When I peer through the space between the hinges, Secretary Baek is doubled over, only the ropes that bind him holding his body in place and off the ground. Blood seeps through the cloth covering his legs, the skin broken from the twisting. He will be lucky if he walks again. Though even if he is lucky, I do not think the magistrate will ever let him walk away from this. He will surely die here. In this yard. Perhaps not tonight. But soon.

I am certain of it.

"Secretary Baek, tell me, how long?"

The magistrate still stands with his back to me, but finally it seems the real interrogation has begun. "How long have you betrayed us? Since this case began? Since I arrived for my term in this valley?"

Secretary Baek blinks heavily, spit hanging from his murmuring lips.

"If you do not speak, we will torture you again. Speak!"

"Since ... since I began working here, at the office. A long time..." Secretary Baek begins to cough, choke, but it soon passes. I lean nearer the cold gateway, pressing my face as close as I can to the small open gap.

"Before even I took up this position then," says Magistrate Hong. "And what was your role?"

"My ... my role, Magistrate Hong?"

"What were you paid to accomplish!"

"I was to ... to change the books. The records. The girls ... later, after the investigations came up empty, if they were investigated at all, I was to change the annals, change the entries to mark them as suicides, as runaways, before the reports were sent to the king."

Silence. Only the crackling of the flames still burning in the wide metal dishes, the howling of the wolves. Now they have started they will not stop.

"And what else," orders Magistrate Hong. "What else were you paid to do?"

"To ... to keep an eye on the magistrates throughout their term in office here, to ... to report back to Lord Song if there were any ... problems."

"What kind of problems?"

"Problems like this investigation ... sir. If you were getting too ... close." Secretary Baek crumples as if he would cry but seems to have no tears left. "Please, Magistrate Hong, it has always been this way. I never thought ... I never once thought ... and it was not what I wanted, but I had no choice. He offered me money or he said he would ... would cast me down, have me dismissed. My family, Magistrate Hong, who would feed them?"

The magistrate stands like the mountains that surround us, silent and unmoved by Secretary Baek's pleading. Through the flickering darkness I focus on Man Seok's face. His expression too is empty of emotion, but he steps forward now from the shadows, moves before the prisoner.

"What is Lord Song's involvement in this case?" he asks steadily. "He works alongside his prospective in-laws to sell young women into prostitution and slavery?"

"I did not know," gasps Secretary Baek. "I did not know."

Man Seok crouches close before him, until their faces are level. "You did know. Do not lie, Secretary Baek."

"I did not..."

Man Seok reaches out abruptly and viciously grasps the prisoner's chin, fingers digging in hard. Secretary Baek whimpers, tears leaking across his cheeks. Man Seok does not move, does not let go, his face impassive. "There is no point denying it, Secretary Baek. Admit the truth. You knew."

The prisoner's face changes, fear alive within his eyes, and then his expression crumples, whimpers coming hard and fast. "Yes ... yes, it is true." His words are so soft and raw I almost do not hear.

Man Seok lets the prisoner's face go.

"It was Lord Song's idea," hisses Secretary Baek. "His men take the girls and they are sent away to the port. He created this business himself, he is to blame for what has happened!"

"He built this business alone?" Man Seok asks quietly.

After a long moment of hesitation, Secretary Baek nods.

"Yet it seems such a large organisation for a provincial nobleman to run alone," presses Man Seok, "Do you not agree, Secretary Baek?"

"He runs it alone! Lord Song is the head of it!"

Man Seok leans closer, intimidating. "If that is indeed so, tell me then, the woman from Ming, who was she?"

"Just a woman ... she worked for Lord Song, too."

"Did she? And the assassins in black who broke into our prison and murdered her and our men, were they working for Lord Song too?"

"I … Of … course … yes, of course..."

Man Seok stands. "I see," is all he says.

Secretary Baek's eyes roll, focused on Man Seok as he moves away, showing the whites behind his lids.

Magistrate Hong clears his throat. "Perhaps, Secretary Baek, you are afraid you will meet the same fate as our past prisoner? Silenced by those you work for, before you can confess your crimes?" He walks over and bends low until his face is directly in his former secretary's line of vision.

The magistrate's voice is quiet but I still catch his words from across the yard. "I promise you, this will not happen. Secretary Baek, if you are to die, it will be on my orders. No one else's. This I can promise you. And will give you something to think about perhaps, as you wait alone in your cell."

Secretary Baek begins to sob again, and I think of the message he carried to Lord Song, knowing his words would mean a death, a young woman's death. Choon Shim's. Knowing it without a doubt. Yet making the choice to do so anyway.

It was he who informed Lord Song that the magistrate and most of his men would leave the prison unattended.

His colleagues died that night because of the words this man carried. Because of him, Choon Shim died.

My heart hardens and I do not turn away as the magistrate's guards begin to torture the prisoner once again. His screams ring out through the night and are lost on the wind.

And another piece of myself is lost along with them.

29

A Promise

MAGISTRATE HONG SITS at the head of his office table, flanked by two trusted guards.

"We know for certain that on the night of Song Seorim's disappearance, the woman from Ming was stalking the young village girl," he recites as Guard Yu writes down his words, creating a report. "Yet Song Seorim became involved, by chance. It seems the woman from Ming did not know the girl was Lord Song's daughter, dressed as she was, like a commoner."

Guard Yu nods in agreement as he writes. Man Seok does nothing except stare at his hands, folded on the table before him.

I am not invited to sit with them; instead, I stand just inside the doorway with my head lowered. It is late at night and frost creeps beneath the closed shutters, curling around my toes. My muddied *beoseon* socks are not enough to keep me warm.

"Both young women were abducted," Magistrate Hong continues. "Yet a struggle ensued whereby the village girl was killed. Secretary Baek has confessed that Lord Song used the local police to place pressure on the abductor, in order for his daughter to be returned home."

Guard Yu snorts, peering up from his report. "If that woman was working directly for Lord Song as Secretary Baek insists, there would be no need for such pressure. He lies."

"Secretary Baek is afraid," says Man Seok quietly. "Whomever stands behind Lord Song is powerful, and they will certainly attempt to kill our prisoner as soon as they realise we've taken him into custody."

Magistrate Hong's face flushes with anger. Red skin against his grey beard. He catches me looking and immediately I turn my gaze to the floor, flattening my stained uniform against my hips and smoothing my hair with my good hand. I do not want to be sent away again.

"Whatever trafficking organisation Lord Song is involved in," the magistrate continues, waving at Guard Yu to begin writing again. "…using the police to raid the mountains has worked. They sent his daughter back home to him. A husk of herself, but alive at least." He pauses while Guard Yu catches up with his words, and then continues, "Lord Song then wished the investigation to immediately cease in case he himself became implicated. Yet the most interesting aspect of all, is the way Lord Song has used the police and prince to achieve his goals, instead of directly dealing with the abductors himself. It makes me suspect that relations between him and this group he has partnered with are ... strained."

"I agree," says Man Seok. "He would not post soldiers by his gates each day and night if he were not worried of attack. Or assassination."

"Very well, it seems it is time to draw up a warrant for Lord Song's arrest."

As soon as the words have left Magistrate Hong's

mouth, Guard Yu is climbing to his feet, fire in his expression and the report long forgotten. The other two guards stride toward the door as well, and though I know I am not welcome, I cannot help but speak, my voice wavering.

"You cannot."

All movement ceases, all sound. All eyes on me.

Magistrate Hong glares, his gaze cold like the black river winding beside the village. "And why is that? Please, enlighten me, *damo*."

I hesitate. "It is only one testimony. Under torture. And Lord Song's connections in the capital run deep. He will get the arrest overturned."

The magistrate's expression is thunderous as slowly he rises to his feet. Quickly I stare at the floor, not daring to lift my head. I have killed Choon Shim through my careless actions. I created an opportunity for the assassination of a suspect. I know he does not wish to listen to my words.

Yet it is Man Seok who breaks the silence.

"Damo Dan Ji is right, Magistrate Hong."

"No, Lieutenant Jo," snaps the magistrate. "The *damo* is wrong. Again. I have a testimony and I will use it to end this farce of a case."

He glares at Man Seok over the table, hands spread wide across the wood. "And the *damo* is no longer welcome here! I told you this already."

Man Seok pulls himself to his feet as well, taller than the magistrate now. "Yet she is still right. The prince has used his influence to help Lord Song in the past. For us to mark Lord Song as a criminal and traitor to his country is to mark his uncle in Hanseong as the same, and Lord Song's uncle is *close* with the prince."

"What is it you are trying to say?" Guard Yu interjects.

His hands are curled into fists, his tense shoulders a mirror of the magistrate's own stance.

Man Seok does not back down. "A ruined reputation will taint the royal family. Do you truly imagine the prince will allow his own actions to come under question? Do you think the king will?"

"Then tell me, Lieutenant Jo," explodes Magistrate Hong. "What is your suggestion? What do you propose us to do? Allow Secretary Baek to walk free? Is that your plan?"

Man Seok bristles but does not answer, the two men fierce and unmoving until Guard Yu's wavering voice interjects, "What if we had *other* evidence of Lord Song's involvement? Something beyond the testimony of Secretary Baek?"

Man Seok nods without taking his eyes from the magistrate. "Indeed. With hard evidence of Lord Song's crimes, the prince could not protect him. The royal family would cast Lord Song aside immediately. Even his uncle if they must, no matter how close a friend that man is to the prince."

Guard Yu smiles. "They would sever the connection."

"Yet there *is* no other evidence," Magistrate Hong snaps. "This is all we have, now, our final chance to charge Lord Song for his crimes. The longer we wait the less likely we can keep Secretary Baek alive long enough to speak as a witness at Lord Song's trial."

In the silence that follows I cannot stop the words from spilling over, my voice rising with each sentence that escapes my lips.

"Magistrate Hong, have you not heard Lieutenant Jo's words? The testimony of a mere regional secretary can easily be undone. The royal family will bury our investigation to avoid scandal. And we will all be buried with it. You will lose your position. Or worse, be marked as incompetent and exiled to some island of rock in the sea."

I have gone too far. Much too far.

I blink at Magistrate Hong, breathing heavily, suddenly afraid. Always, I overstep my boundaries. Always, I cannot help but move beyond my place.

The magistrate's face is flushed with anger, his lips pressed thin and hard. Yet it is Man Seok he glares at, not me.

"Get her out of my office."

Man Seok does not move. "The *damo*'s words are true, Magistrate Hong."

The magistrate laughs suddenly. "I never thought to experience such disrespect from you, Lieutenant Jo. Yet I should have. Your reputation precedes you. And it seems you are what they say you are. Ruled by personal vendetta and passion. You cannot control your own subordinate. *You* are incompetent!"

The magistrate leans close to Man Seok across the table to spit out his next words, his voice rising like the wind outside the office, raging in the night.

"You think we do not know the truth? Because we are provincial officers? Because this valley is isolated? We know. You are a killer, Lieutenant Jo. You do not arrest your suspects, you beat them to death with your bare hands! Right in front of your superiors! Everyone here knows what you are. Everyone knows why you stand before me only as a lowly lieutenant!"

"You do *not* know," I yell into the shocked silence, my skin flushed and heart beating hard against my chest. "You were not there, Magistrate Hong! So you do not know!" My hands curl into fists and pain lances like a knife through my ruined fingers.

The magistrate turns on me, hissing. "You will leave my

office, *damo*! Do not make me say it again. You are no longer welcome here! You will go or be removed. Leave!"

And I do, rage burning my blood like fire, tearing through my chest. I slam against the office doors and storm outside into the rushing wind, feel it tearing at my muddy skirts and hair. I push my feet into my worn shoes and stomp through the snow into the yard, only stopping when I reach the far gate. I find shelter beneath a small awning, sinking to a crouch against the door. My body shakes. From anger or exhaustion, I do not know.

Crunching footsteps approach across the snow and Man Seok stops, standing just above me. He hesitates a moment before he speaks.

"Dan Ji *ssi*, I do not need you to protect me."

I look up. "No? You do not care what the magistrate thinks of you?"

"No. I do not."

I hesitate and then say, "I do."

"You should not. Magistrate Hong was not wrong. I did kill him. Poong Yi. I killed him."

"But you were..."

"There are no excuses for what I did."

Silence seeps between us and I remember how he looked that night, standing in the inn courtyard covered in another man's blood. The body at his feet lying there with the face caved in, firelight flickering across the wet that pooled beneath it. And Man Seok's face, alive with fury. With hatred that seemed to burn through his skin until it was all he was.

Poong Yi. A commoner. A nobody gangster. Yet a man with connections. A man with rich friends.

He would not have stayed in prison long. Freedom is a commodity it seems, another product to be bought and sold. And Poong Yi had money.

I peer up at Man Seok and wonder again what it was he saw Poong Yi do. All that time Man Seok spent undercover at Poong Yi's side, all those months. Pretending to be that criminal's bodyguard. Pretending to be Poong Yi's friend. And I heard the rumours. They flew like birds through the servant quarters of the gambling inn. I know what kind of man Poong Yi was.

Yet I do not know what Man Seok saw.

Something bad enough to drive him to that moment in the snow, his chest heaving and his hands smeared in Poong Yi's blood. A brutal murder instead of a sanctioned arrest.

One day I will ask him.

And I will tell him of the man who gave me the ginger taffee, the guard whose name I don't know. Yet whose kindness and bloody death live on inside me, breathing and simmering always. And I will ask Man Seok what it is that haunts *his* dreams.

But I do not ask him tonight.

I know why Man Seok did what he did. Sometimes I think I even understand it, my desperation to close this case sliding deep beneath my skin, threads taking sharp hold of my heart until I think they'll never let go.

But I still do not believe he was right.

"It is late," he says eventually, when we have been without speaking for too long. He nods his head at the gate, motioning for me to follow him through. Ice hangs in the chill air, snow lying thick in the darkness of the yard and clinging to the office rooftops and gates. We walk silently across the courtyard, our steps crunching loudly in the night.

The compound is mostly empty now. Magistrate Hong has lost much of his trust after what Secretary Baek has done. I do not blame him. Though Secretary Baek swears he was the last informant within these walls, it pays to be careful. The magistrate will not allow one of his own men to wound him so deeply again.

The winter air cools my anger and soon I am sorry for my careless words to Magistrate Hong. I should have handled it differently. Another mistake. I have alienated him further. He will not listen the next time I speak. Another foolish decision among many.

Man Seok leads me to the small kitchen at the back of Magistrate Hong's private quarters, pushing open the heavy wooden doors. Fire glows warm and orange from the furnace. It fills the room with thick humidity, thawing my fingers until my injured hand is throbbing, heavy and sore.

"Thank you for waiting," announces Man Seok, and at the sound of his voice the office cook appears from a small inner doorway.

"It's no trouble," she tells him. Her round face is strained, bone tired like the rest of us. She motions to me. "Please sit."

Man Seok ushers me toward a small wooden stool beside the furnace. "The cook will tend to your stitches. They have come undone."

I touch my side gently as Man Seok turns and exits the small warm space without another word, leaving me alone with the cook.

"Please sit," she says again. She motions for me to remove my uniform so she can probe the skin beneath. I do not resist, allowing her to help me from my clothes, untying my skirts so they can be pulled from their bindings at my chest to lie loose around my hips. The cook examines my wound and tells me to grit my teeth while she fixes the loose stitches, drawing them from my flesh only to begin all over again. The room is so humid and warm that it soaks deep inside my bones and a wave of exhaustion crashes over me. My eyes flutter shut.

"You should not have left your bed today," says the cook. "You are still not well. You were feverish for so long. I thought you might not wake."

I want to ask her whether she lost anyone during the attack on the office, but I cannot. I do not want to hear her answer.

My voice cracks as I admit, "My friend was murdered today. I had to go."

"The young woman at the river? I heard the guards talking." She hesitates. "I am sorry. I did not know she was your friend. I heard a rumour, that she was a *damo* like you?"

"She was. They have moved her body back to the office. When the case is over, she will be taken with us back to Hanseong."

"For her family."

I shrug uncomfortably. I do not know if Choon Shim had a family or not. We never spoke of such things. An idea creeps beneath my skin, that I barely knew this girl who gave her life following my instructions, who died because of my careless words in front of an informant.

"It was my fault," I whisper. It seems like the right kind of punishment to hear the words out loud.

The cook is silent, continuing to work on my torn side. I grunt with sudden pain as her needle sinks into my flesh. My words hang heavy in the air. I close my eyes again, hand to my face.

When the older woman finishes my side, she asks, "Do you want me to look at that hand too? I have salve from the physician somewhere here, he said it will reduce swelling."

I nod, waiting as she rummages through the pots and

bottles lining her shelves. The thick ointment is congealed and cold on my skin, yet it cools the burning in my fingers.

When we are finished the cook helps me clean up, running a wet cloth across my skin, scraping the dirt and blood from my body. She helps me dress in new fresh clothes, an old worn uniform that belonged to that other *damo*, the one I never met.

I feel hollow, like an impostor ghost, wearing the clothes of a girl who was wiped from this earth because of this same case that I have destroyed.

All these girls. And I did not protect anyone.

I think of kind hands, offering ginger taffee in the snow, and begin to cry, my fingers clutched to my mouth, curling inwards on myself, becoming smaller. The cook pulls me to her warm chest and I sink into her flesh, thinking this must be what it feels like to have a mother, soft in all the places a father is hard.

When I am finally dry of tears I pull away from the older woman's embrace, ashamed once again. Yet she is crying too, tears wetting her cheeks. She smiles at me and says, "Those are my daughter's clothes you wear."

It is all she says.

I lean forward and wrap my arms carefully around her neck, holding her tight for a long safe moment before I pull back into the cold.

At the door she calls my name and I hesitate there, my good hand pressed against the course wood, black icy night before me with fire and warmth at my back.

"If someone wanted to assassinate your prisoner from Ming," the cook says quietly, "they would have found a way. That night or another. Perhaps even more men would have died, if it was a different night, if the office was more heavily guarded. You do not know. No one knows."

I turn to her as she adds, "And your friend died

because Lord Song murdered her. As he stole my daughter. Two *damo* gone now."

I stare at her. Finally, I nod.

Outside the mountains are alive with howling, wind rising to meet the cries. The shapes of valley peaks rise within the night sky, covered with enough snow to make them visible, glowing soft and blue in the black.

I will not wait for my next life.

30

Treasure

"THINK, Guard Yu. The first *damo* to go missing in Lord Song's residence, what do you guess might have happened to her?"

I watch him carefully, waiting for an answer as Guard Yu shifts, warming his hands by blowing on them. It is early morning, the skies overhead heavy and grey. He's on guard duty at the front gates today, the other man he shares the job with gone round the corner to relieve himself, allowing me a small window of time alone with Guard Yu.

To convince him.

"I am not sure ... perhaps she was killed..." He hesitates abruptly, as if he does not wish to say the words *'like Choon Shim.'*

"Yes, except then where is her body?"

He looks at me and finally shrugs. "In the mountains?"

"Yes, possible. Yet your men searched those mountains and found nothing. Of course, it is possible her grave is buried deep, it is possible you missed her..."

"Yet you do not believe so."

"No," I agree. "If Lord Song wished to remove her, but we have not found a body, then perhaps the *damo* is not dead. Perhaps they smuggled her from Joseon."

"You think they have sold her?" Guard Yu seems sick. "If they did then she is lost. There is no way to find her."

"That is true," I concede. "She is lost. Though if the trafficking organisation did sell her, what is the one place we know for sure she must have passed through?"

Guard Yu's eyes widen. "The port."

"And who might we guess she may have been with?"

"The woman from Ming, perhaps?" He shakes his head. "What difference do these guesses make?"

"They are evidence, Guard Yu. Not much of it, but if we can place the missing *damo*, who disappeared while undercover at Lord Song's house, together with the trafficking suspect at a known location of people smuggling, it will help us build our case. It is a small piece, but everything will count if we truly wish to go against Lord Song and connect him to this case."

Guard Yu shakes his head. "Even if we can connect those pieces, Lord Song will surely plead it was illegal to place the *damo* within his house in the first place. He will turn it around on Magistrate Hong."

I nod. "A risk. But one that must be taken. If Magistrate Hong wishes to go against Lord Song, he risks all."

Guard Yu contemplates my words then suddenly smiles. "You came to me first because you do not want to ask the magistrate yourself. You wish me to do it for you."

I turn away as I admit, "Magistrate Hong will listen to you. Will you ask him?"

A pause. "I will. As you said, every piece counts. I know how much the magistrate wishes to indict Lord Song. I have never seen him this way before. Anything else?"

"Yes. Can you ask the magistrate for an artist? You will need to draw the *damo*'s likeness. Do you remember her face well enough?"

"I did not meet with her as she was new to the office. But our cook here is her mother, did you know? She will help us. I am sure of it."

"Good. And ... thank you, Guard Yu. I am grateful for your help."

I stand to walk away as the other guard returns from his unscheduled break, my footsteps pausing only when Guard Yu calls my name.

"Damo Dan Ji, you may not believe me, but Magistrate Hong is a good man. He cares about this case, just as you do."

I blink.

Finally, I nod, slipping back inside the enclosure. I return to Secretary Baek's empty office where I have spent the night trawling through his records, reading over the annals he kept on his shelves. I sink back into my seat and yawn heavily, rubbing at my temples.

Already I have learned that Lord Song's was not the only money that Secretary Baek enjoyed. He took bribes. Accepted gifts. It is not difficult to see where the entries have been altered, where the contents do not quite make sense. He would be called to settle a land dispute at the edges of the valley, and would rule in favour of one party over the other, with no understandable reason or logic. It can only mean he was receiving gifts.

A whole night of reading by candlelight has made my head spin, my mind thick and heavy from lack of sleep. The information I have found is...

Confusing.

One name, Heo Tae Hak, is written in the records over

and over again. A familiar name that I cannot quite grasp. It means something, I am sure.

But I am so very exhausted I cannot find the answers.

I step outside to clear my head, the cold biting my skin. I walk beneath the heavy grey sky. For a long time. Only circling the enclosure as I think, crunching across the courtyards, back and forth as I run over it all inside my head.

When I finally stop I am standing outside a long storage building, feet sinking into the snow. It is a place for keeping bodies. A morgue of sorts. Not like the ones back in Hanseong though, smaller, thinner, the roof low and the building squat.

It is where Choon Shim is now.

I stand still and cold, imagining her filling up the spaces within the shed. Her body. Lying there.

I enter quietly, the door unguarded. The shutters creak as I push them gently open.

A long thin room stretches before me, the walls lined heavily with books and jars. With shimmering sharp metal acupuncture needles. With boxes. And in the centre of the small space is a table with a figure lying motionless upon it, covered by a threadbare sheet. It is a long time before I find the courage to raise it.

Choon Shim is cold to the touch, her cheek smooth like polished stone. The colour flushing her skin is strange and cloudy. Almost blue. Her eyes are closed.

Someone has closed them. Man Seok. Or the magistrate perhaps.

I wonder about her family. If she had any. I wonder who it was Choon Shim was so determined to prove herself to. And I wonder if I will find out, when we return her body to Hanseong. Or if these parts of her life will forever remain a mystery.

I force myself to do it.

I run my fingers across her hands, checking beneath her nails. There is no evidence, nothing to indicate who murdered her. Only dirt.

I press my hands against her skull, running my fingers through her braided hair.

Nothing.

Force myself to check inside her mouth, behind her teeth. Under her swollen tongue.

Nothing.

Beneath her clothes, beneath her underthings. Nothing. I touch her feet, removing her sandals, the plaited straw old and untwisting. Running my hands beneath her heels, up across her ankles. I hear the faintest of rustling. Touching the material of one stained *beoseon*, I feel it. Eyes wide, I carefully pull the sock from her foot, feeling the crackling of stiff paper within. Something has been sewn into the lining of her *beoseon*. Underneath her foot. Where no one would expect to find it.

I am crying as I rip at the loose stitches Choon Shim has sewn, using my teeth to tear at the threads until they are frayed and broken.

Threads. Breaking apart.

Hidden between the layers there is an envelope marked with a seal I do not recognise, not the ones I've studied that belong to Lord Song. And inside the envelope, a letter. The paper is stained and crinkled, half soaked with mud.

Yet still legible.

I scan the words, gaze flicking across the scrawled writing contained inside. Yet the characters are blurred and I have sudden vivid imaginings of Choon Shim's drowning, of water dripping from her face and hair and sliding into her *beoseon* to stain her treasure. This letter she died for.

I sink to the floor, head in my hands.

The letter can still be deciphered. The water has not ruined it. But Choon Shim could not read the classical *hanja* characters that *yangban* noblemen use. She did not know the contents of the letter she stole, whether it would be useful or not. But I do, I learned the art of reading long ago in my master's house. A rare skill for someone as lowly as me.

The letter is not filled with secrets. Choon Shim must have taken only what she could. And Lord Song is a smart man.

He does not allow anyone to write his name.

31

A Letter

PIECES. Threads.

Shreds of evidence, but never enough to convict a man with powerful connections. Powerful in other ways too. Assets. Money.

I want to know where Lord Song's wealth is hidden.

"The letter can help us," Magistrate Hong says quietly, breaking into my thoughts. "Surely it is the people trafficking group who have sent it to Lord Song. Look, it confirms the return of his daughter is imminent, requests the removal of external pressures that place their group at risk. That must be us. It must have been written prior to Song Seorim's return, while my men still searched the mountains and valley. And look here, the writer of the letter threatens Lord Song with action if he does not immediately comply." The magistrate's eyes are shining with excitement. "It explains Lord Song's fear for his life."

"It is not enough," interrupts Man Seok. "There are no names. Nowhere in the letter have they identified themselves. They have not even named Lord Song. We cannot tie it to him."

Magistrate Hong shifts against the stone wall, his breath escaping his lips in clouds of mist. "It is something," he argues, yet his conviction is gone. "Along with a positive identification of our missing *damo* at the port, alongside a known suspect if we can get it, both of these things could make a difference to the case."

His anger seems to have cooled. He says nothing when I reach forward to take Choon Shim's letter back from Man Seok, again scanning the inky contents.

"What if we could tie the letter directly to Lord Song?" I ask.

Man Seok's brows draw close. "What do you mean?"

"Well, it seems Secretary Baek often made claims on land, transferred ownership of it, mostly on behalf of a man named Heo Tae Hak. It is a name that I have heard before." I turn to Magistrate Hong and ask, "Do you know him?"

He frowns and does not answer. Yet he does not tell me to stop speaking either and I am encouraged.

"There are multiple entries in your records, Magistrate Hong," I say. "People of all different names losing parcels of land to this Heo Tae Hak in games of chance, with Secretary Baek employed to manage the paperwork and records. It was his job to ensure the wealth of land changed hands as intended."

It is the piece of the puzzle that catches in my head every time I think of it.

Money.

Assets. Lord Song is rich. He has invested in his own force of personal soldiers. Yet where is the rest of his wealth?

"Dirty money must be hidden," I say quietly.

Magistrate Hong catches on. "Lord Song must be receiving a massive income from his involvement with the people trafficking group, or why would he risk his reputation and life on such treason? You suspect he received payment in land for his involvement?"

I nod.

Man Seok asks, "Heo Tae Hak, who is he?"

Magistrate Hong shifts, boots crunching in the snow. His face is hidden by shadow beneath the wide brim of his uniform hat. "Heo Tae Hak is the name of Lord Song's head soldier."

I crouch down in the snow. I heard Lord Song calling his name, but now Magistrate Hong has confirmed it.

And then I tell the men what I wish to do, the ideas that have been boiling away in my mind throughout the night.

Afterwards is only silence, until finally Magistrate Hong says, "It could be enough. If we can tie Lord Song to the gambled land parcels and to this letter, if we can source an eyewitness to the *damo*'s departure from that port, they can be added to Secretary Baek's testimony. We could charge Lord Song."

Man Seok shakes his head. "It will not be enough. The prince will not allow the charges to stick. And to set events in motion we must first arrest Heo Tae Hak. Yet we have no evidence against him. What can we arrest him for?"

I shift in my crouch, attention focused on the ground as my numb fingers drag a small twisted twig through the snow, making plough lines. Back and forth. "We can arrest him for Choon Shim's murder."

Magistrate Hong laughs. "We cannot. There is nothing to tie him to that event."

"But there could be," I say quietly, glancing up at him. "If you wanted it, there could be."

He pauses to consider, head tilted to one side. I do not look at Man Seok. I know how he will disapprove.

As I watch, a smile slowly spreads across Magistrate Hong's face and I realise that we are not so very different, he and I.

Neither of us is able to let this go. And unlike Man Seok, we still believe that justice is a possibility, that with evidence, our government will follow through and charge the criminals.

I smile. Small and crooked.

"I hope your hand is healing well, Damo Dan Ji," Magistrate Hong suddenly says. His eyes are shining. "I hope you have seen the woman who works in our kitchens. She will tend it for you."

A peace offering.

I stand, still refusing to face Man Seok. "Yes, Magistrate Hong. I have seen her. She tells me I am healing well."

"Good. That is good to hear." He half turns as if to move away, then makes a gesture for Man Seok to follow. "Come Lieutenant Jo, let us draft the message we must send to Hanseong."

I peer at my feet, ignoring the way Man Seok hesitates at my side. His voice lowers so only I can hear his quiet words. "You stand up for me, Dan Ji, but I know you don't like it."

I glance up at him, confused.

"What I did to Poong Yi, you don't like it." He leans closer. "Be careful. This is your first step. Planting evidence? It's the first step. Think about who you want to become."

I focus only on the snow until Magistrate Hong has drawn him away. Man Seok is wrong, his words are wrong. He doesn't know the difference between this and killing a man. He doesn't know what true justice is. I ignore him, bury his words deep.

And then I am gone from the enclosure, walking quickly down the village road to the old crumbling *hanok* that lies at the edge of the village.

It seems different in the thick snow. Cleaner. The yard less muddy and the awnings dripping with glistening ice crystals.

The inside though, is still the same. Filled with death and sadness.

Crouched beside the hearth, I whisper to the mother and son, weave them a story of a girl who was drowned beside a river. And the whole time I am speaking I feel the threads pulling closer around Lord Song, winding tighter and tighter.

32

The Arrest

TWO DAYS LATER, in the soft blue light of dawn, a village woman comes walking up the hill to the office, pounding on the front gates. I see her after they bring her inside, her small body weathered and hunched, curled in on herself against the relentless winter.

She stares at me as Guard Yu walks her across the yard to the magistrate's private office. Her eyes are wide and filled with tears.

Magistrate Hong stays inside his office with the village woman for a very long time. When he emerges onto the terrace, he calls for Lieutenant Jo and his remaining guards. He stands tall on the stone steps of his office and peers down where we have gathered.

Most of the remaining guards still in service have only just returned from days of hard travelling, scouting land parcels throughout the entire valley. This is because most of Heo Tae Hak's land is leased to free men, to poor villagers who use it for agriculture and farming—for scraping out a living in this harsh land. And they pay heavy taxes directly to Heo Tae Hak for the privilege.

Yet at the lip of the valley the guards found a house, a grand one, the land also owned by Heo Tae Hak. Heavily guarded yet lying apparently empty of family life. Isolated within the foothills of a deep forest.

A hiding place.

And I want to know what lies inside.

Magistrate Hong clears his throat and tells his men what they should do.

By the time we have arrived at Lord Song's compound the day has broken damp and wet, thick cloying mist rolling from the rising mountains to rest across the valley floor. My skin feels clammy and moist beneath my clothes. I pull my coat tighter across my chest, retying the worn material I wear wrapped over my head to protect my ears.

I still do not touch the *nambawi*, and Man Seok no longer asks me of it. Lately, he no longer asks me much at all.

Magistrate Hong argues with the soldiers who guard Lord Song's gates, their voices becoming louder and louder. Until finally the doors are forced open and our men pour inside, the mercenaries overcome. I slip after them and stand just within the inner courtyard wall, watching and waiting. The magistrate is positioned in the middle of the open space with a small remaining retinue, weapons raised against the residence soldiers, a stalemate of sorts. Man Seok has long since disappeared deep within the residence, leading his party of guards.

It is not long before Lord Song appears. At first it is only his voice, screaming about the loud noise, before suddenly he emerges from the doors of the main building before us. He stops abruptly, caught off guard before the magistrate and his men. He does not notice me.

Lord Song barks out a disbelieving laugh. "Have you come to arrest me, Magistrate Hong?" He spreads his arms wide and gestures about his residence. "Please, I have nothing to hide." He motions for his soldiers to step down, and the sound of swords being sheathed fills the grounds, metal sliding against wood.

Magistrate Hong smiles, thin lips curling as he shoots a pointed look at Guard Yu. The younger guard immediately pulls two men aside, murmuring to them in low voices.

"Thank you for your aid in this investigation," Magistrate Hong announces, never once bothering to meet Lord Song's eyes. This too, catches the nobleman off guard. "I will take your words as an invitation to thoroughly search your premises, Lord Song."

Magistrate Hong waves a hand at Guard Yu who boldly leads his men straight past Lord Song into the main building behind him. Immediately the crashes of ceramics and wood ring from within. Calculated in their loudness. Magistrate Hong orchestrates his own performance.

Lord Song does not move, but I am sure I see veins bulging from his throat. "You will find nothing, Magistrate Hong."

"I expect so, my Lord. Yet there is no harm in searching." Another loud crash reverberates from within Lord Song's house and the smile breaks wider across Magistrate Hong's face.

Lord Song's jaw tightens. He takes the first step down from the *maru* toward us. "Perhaps you should save yourself the trouble, Magistrate Hong. Just go ahead and arrest me." His mouth twists. A challenge. "Go ahead. See how long it lasts before I walk free."

There is silence in the courtyard, only the distant sounds of men yelling and furniture breaking still wafting from the house. I step from the shade and walk between the soldiers to stand beside the magistrate. His body is stiff and filled with tension, fingers white and bloodless clamped around his sword. Yet his face betrays nothing of his emotion.

"We have no intention of arresting you today, Lord Song," he says tightly. "Indeed, that is not why we are here."

Again, the nobleman is caught off guard. "Then … you are simply wasting my time."

"No. I do not believe so. Ahh, here they come now."

A man is thrown from a side gate onto the gravel, arms slung tight and high behind his back. With nothing to break his fall his shoulder and jaw hit the ground, and he grunts loudly, blood pouring from his mouth as if he's bitten his tongue.

Heo Tae Hak.

Man Seok is behind him, barking an order for his men to drag the prisoner back to his feet. Lord Song's head soldier struggles viciously, attempting to break loose, but his body is trussed up too tightly, the injuries to his face setting him off balance. Blood pours from his mouth onto his clothes, staining his robes dark red. Pushed and pulled, he is shoved until he's positioned directly behind Magistrate Hong. There he is forced roughly to his knees. Man Seok steps into place at my side.

"What is the meaning of this? You dare?!" Lord Song shouts his words, his careful composure collapsed, and I feel a tremor of excitement running through our guards, infecting them one by one. The smallest taste of success.

"We are arresting your head soldier, Heo Tae Hak," announces Magistrate Hong. "On the charge of murdering an undercover police officer."

Lord Song shakes his head in derision, mouth twisting into a sudden smile. "You cannot! There is no evidence … He was not *there*!"

My blood runs hot with crashing fury, my body starting

forward of its own accord. Yet Man Seok's hand closes over my forearm, gripping tight. He shakes his head, such a small movement I almost do not see it. He still does not look at me.

It is not my place.

Now it is only Magistrate Hong who has the floor. As it should be. I grit my teeth, forcing my body to relax as I listen to the magistrate speak.

"We have a witness, Lord Song, who places your man at the scene of the crime. He was seen committing the murder."

Heo Tae Hak behind us begins to struggle but his shouts are muffled by the men who hold him, by the blood that fills his mouth.

Lord Song protests and demands to see our witness. And slowly I sense the shift, the change between Magistrate Hong and his enemy. The balance flips. The magistrate climbs the steps to stand on the terrace beside the nobleman. He displays our arrest warrant within his hands, his voice calm and low as he orders Heo Tae Hak removed from the courtyard. And Lord Song … can do nothing.

He watches Magistrate Hong with burning eyes and does nothing.

As I follow the guards back out of the gates to the main road I turn back only once. Lord Song walks away without a word, back into the depths of his home, stepping over the wreckage we have left.

And for now, at least, he does nothing.

I am elated, filled with a humming energy that tingles my skin and burns my cheeks. And the feeling stays, as we walk back toward the government office, as I watch Magistrate Hong perched high on a horse at the head of our procession. The feeling stays right until Man Seok appears at my side and says, "Lord Song knew there was no witness."

"What are you trying to say?" I am irritated, the hum leaking from my body as his words crash through.

"Dan Ji, *think*. How could Lord Song be so utterly certain no witness saw Heo Tae Hak perform the murder?"

I refuse to speak and finally Man Seok must answer his own question. "He is certain no one saw Heo Tae Hak, because *Heo Tae Hak* did not commit this crime. It must have been another of Lord Song's men."

I glance up at him sharply. "Yet Heo Tae Hak will have done other things. He is not innocent."

"Perhaps. But he will die for this. Magistrate Hong will execute him immediately."

"I know that," I hiss.

Man Seok stares down at me longer, eyes dark. He does not believe I truly understand. Yet I do. I am aware of what will happen.

And my choices remain the same.

I have become cold and hard. Soon he will no longer recognise me at all.

Man Seok steps from my side, striding to join the head of our procession. I say nothing, but my chest hurts, like he has taken my insides and is twisting.

I follow after him, half-running to keep up until my side and face is throbbing in the sharp cold, until I am breathless. Magistrate Hong is still seated high on his horse, handing out orders to Guard Yu and Man Seok.

"Hit the closer plots of land first, rouse the villagers who live there, make noise. We want Lord Song to hear of it. Make sure you tell the people why the government is taking ownership. Make sure it is clear the owner has been charged with murder so they can relay the message."

Guard Yu nods. "And our men who watch the hidden house?"

"They will wait. We must give Lord Song time to become afraid. Did you station the others?"

"Yes, Magistrate. I've left two men to watch Lord Song's residence. If he moves we will know it."

Magistrate Hong turns to me then, from high on his swaying saddle. He inclines his head, ever so slightly, and does not break eye contact.

An acknowledgement.

My threads have woven into place.

I bite my lip and nod back at him. Then he has drawn ahead, kicking his horse to take the hill at the edge of the village faster, urging his beast onwards until he has gone from sight.

I stop walking, for my stomach and chest still ache where Man Seok has twisted me with his words. Abruptly the day feels less clear than it did only a moment before. Like the mountain mist has descended across the valley floor. Even the acknowledgement from Magistrate Hong only makes my chest churn harder.

The first step.

Who do I want to become?

Suddenly I do not want to hear Heo Tae Hak's screams as he is interrogated for this crime he did not commit.

I do not want to watch him die.

I am a coward.

Pushing my way through the huddle of guards, I glimpse our prisoner's bloody face as I stagger off the road into the snow-covered grasses. The day is dark and cold.

I slip and slide through the snow until I reach a place on the hilltop that has views over the village and river, a place that is hidden from the main roads. I stand in the long, wet grass and watch as the mountain's great shadow extends over the deep forest and creeps to the riverside. The darkness consumes the black water, sliding across the banks until the entire village is covered with mist.

I stay there a long time.

Until my hands are numb and my knees shake from standing. Until my body throbs.

And when I return to the office, creeping through the courtyards under the cover of night, I find myself outside Man Seok's room. I hesitate before knocking lightly on the door. I do not wish to disturb the other men whose quarters lie so nearby. But I need to see him. I do not wait for him to answer. Instead I push the shutters inwards, stepping through the slight gap I have made.

A single candle burns within the small space, flames flickering and light dancing across the walls, across Man Seok's unshaven face. The changing light carves deep shadows within his cheeks.

"Is he dead?" I whisper, settling against the far wall, across from him where we cannot touch.

Man Seok hesitates and then nods.

"Heo Tae Hak was not innocent," I say, and my words sound almost like a plea. "That man was a killer for hire, a mercenary for rich men."

Man Seok says nothing, silence drawing out long and deep between us.

Who do I want to become?

Finally, I ask, "Did he tell you anything? During the interrogation?"

"No."

I shift against the wall, cradling my bad hand near my chest. "It will be worth it when we charge Lord Song with treason."

I wait for him to agree but Man Seok only smiles, the barest curling of his mouth. Filled with bitterness.

"The charges will not stick," he says.

I blink at him.

"Men like Lord Song are untouchable, Dan Ji *ssi*."

"Why? Because he is rich? Because he is *yangban*? The prince will throw him away! He will be cast aside."

"Corruption runs deep. Have you not seen this yet?"

I say nothing and finally Man Seok's voice sounds once more in the low light.

"Do you know how many of the suspects of our gambling case still remain in prison?"

I open my mouth to answer, but Man Seok interrupts. "Not the poor commoner men, the other ones. The rich merchants and the noblemen. The government officials who took Poong Yi's bribes. Do you know how many?"

My voice is small. "No."

Man Seok only smiles at me, but the bitterness is gone. "Have you decided whether you still want to be a *damo* after we return to Hanseong?"

I stare at him, imagining a place far away near the ocean, a guesthouse beside the sea with waves breaking nearby and tables to be tended to. Yet the threads in my body have taken root in this valley. They cannot let go until the end. I cannot explain it to him.

I take too long to answer and Man Seok's gaze returns to his hands.

He does not ask again.

I sleep in Man Seok's room that night, but not in his bed.

TWO DAYS LATER, we receive an eye-witness statement positively identifying the missing *damo* as a girl who passed through the port during the beginning of winter. The dock worker who recognised her is adamant she boarded a ship accompanied by three other girls and two men. One of them whose face matched the wanted posters for the woman from Ming. Perhaps the dock worker received a few extra coins for his statement, perhaps not. I do not ask.

The day after that we receive reinforcements from the capital, a team of ten trained men led by an office inspector from the State Tribunal.

Arriving on Magistrate Hong's request.

And so it begins.

33

The Raid

CROUCHING IN THE DARKNESS, we wait.

Shadows move in the distance. Lord Song and his retinue, arriving on horseback, shapes shifting and sliding in the black. There is no moon tonight.

Man Seok turns to me, face close in the gloom, and makes gestures with his hands, signing that I should wait here until after the initial raid. I pretend not to understand and behind me, Guard Yu's breathing becomes shallow and fast.

Lord Song has soldiers already inside the hidden house, which is nestled deep within a side valley, an offshoot between mountains and thick winter forest. The snow here has long since turned to mud, despite the cold hanging heavy in the air. Tall twisted trees rise alongside the single access road, like solid walls of branches pushing inwards. The forest attempts to swallow the hidden house, which once belonged to the dead man, Heo Tae Hak.

It is one of the last of Heo Tae Hak's land parcels. The others have now been seized by the magistrate's men, the rights to ownership transferred over to the government one by one. Until only this last piece and some worthless fields at the mouth of the valley still remain.

And throughout those days, as Heo Tae Hak's land was forcibly taken by Magistrate Hong bit by bit, this one place stayed under guard, both day and night. Mercenaries milling about near the stone walls. Alert and watching.

Yet not aware that they in turn were being watched.

Now finally, Lord Song himself has made the long journey here under the cover of night. And I am certain I must be right.

Lord Song hides his wealth within this hidden house, a second stronghold that is off his books. A place the magistrate should never have been able to find. Yet a single thread in the government office annals has led us here.

And now we wait.

I think of Choon Shim as I crouch in the black. She was so desperate to prove herself on this case and I had been so certain I was different. Yet I am not. Like her I crave acknowledgement. From Magistrate Hong? The *podocheong*? Man Seok?

I do not know.

Yet pride burns in my chest, along with nausea. Pride because of what we have accomplished, and sickness because I am unable to let that part of myself go. The part that would feel pride for killing a man, for orchestrating fake evidence in his trial. They are not the actions of a true *damo*. Yet this is our last chance.

I will not let it pass us by.

Lord Song is not untouchable. He belongs now to Magistrate Hong.

And, he belongs to me.

Lord Song's soldiers melt from the shadows, dragging open the heavy gates to the hidden residence, clearing the way for the incoming procession commanded by their leader. My body tenses against the cold stone wall, fingers tucked over my chest for warmth. The crackle of paper beneath my *jeogori* assures me Choon Shim's letter is still in place.

Lord Song has brought so many men. They urge their horses inside the buildings, and from within light suddenly flares, torches lit as the gates slowly shut behind them.

We wait.

We must give Lord Song enough time to begin whatever plan he has for moving his belongings. He must be caught in the act, on this land that does not belong to him officially. It is the only way to tie him to this place.

It will be enough. I know it will be.

Magistrate Hong remains hidden within the thick trees, his guards spread within the forest all along the roadside. They circle behind the thick stone walls of Lord Song's hidden house.

And still we wait.

My body aches by the time we are given the signal. The sound of a wolf howling breaks through the silence, echoing from close by within the trees. It sounds strange. Not quite right. The voice of a man, rasping and shrill.

Man Seok is gone before I can even move, up and over the high wall immediately, using Guard Yu as a step. I bite my tongue and stay hidden in the shadows as Guard Yu follows behind. I am aware of my limits. To put the raid at risk, with my useless hand and my stitched-up side and swollen face, is something I would never do. Yet still I feel a surge of envy when they advance and I must remain behind. But there is reason for me to be here too, a role to play as a woman that they cannot accomplish. To move unnoticed and unsuspected through the house's halls.

The wall is high. Myself and the other guards all circle along the length of it quickly, my fingers trailing against the rough stone and sharp clay. Outside the closed gates, we stop and wait. Here the torches are snuffed out and the mercenaries on duty already lie dead across the wet grass.

Soon the gates open from within, torchlight like a raging fire gaping open to welcome us.

Man Seok does not emerge from the darkness. Instead other guards stand over the bodies of slain soldiers inside, silent in the shadows as the rest of the magistrate's men begin to move out from the shelter of the trees behind us. I do not enter with the guards, not even when Magistrate Hong strides by. He is an old man gone grey dressed in battle uniform and gripping tight to his sword. Instead I stay hidden outside the gates and he does not even see me, my injured hand curled against my chest and my side still weak from stitching. Pressing my body flat against the wall I wait, until the screaming begins from within the residence and I can wait no more.

As soon as I step inside the courtyard I am plunged into light, torches flaring and men lunging with swords dripping red with fresh blood. The air smells like burning and metal, thick with it. Like flesh split open, tart and sharp.

I stay close to the edges of the yard, away from the flickering torchlight. Away from the clash of metal on metal and the shouts of men, ringing out through the night. I am dressed as a village girl tonight, wrapped tight in layers to combat the snow. Magistrate Hong thought it would be easier for me to move within the buildings dressed like this, as any of Lord Song's soldiers who saw me might dismiss me as a servant. Yet as I step inside the first of the grand buildings I see no one else, no servants, no staff. No other women.

This place is abandoned, a storage shed only, built wide and grand like the home of a prince. Yet still it lies empty of people and life. Only soldiers outside screaming in the yard. Dying.

Darkness swells beyond the entrance. The torches remain unlit within the halls, no candlelight to guide me. I step over the body of a fallen man crashed through a screen of paper and lattice wood, his breathing weak and laboured. He does not wear the uniform of a magistrate guard, so I pay him no heed. He is dying. Slowly. Blood spreads beneath him, pooling across the floor. Only for a single moment do I think of blood on snow, of a taffee held out in kindness, but then the pictures are gone. The man who lies at my feet is dead. Unmoving. And I too, am unmoved.

I think this valley has infected me. I am changed. Just as the corruption case infected Man Seok, sinking deep beneath his skin.

I continue through the hallway, peering within the black rooms, searching with my fingers against the walls until I find a room filled with ... things. Shapes. Boxes that smell of clean cotton, rolls of covered black silk, tightly threaded squares cool against my fingers. The sharp smell of abalone and other strange things carrying the salty scent of the ocean. Boxes and boxes of it. Containers filled with a powder that slips through my fingers like sand. Others filled with grain. Ribbon. Piles of soft furs and trays of jade figurines, carved like smooth stones, cold to the touch.

Wealth. Mountains of it.

The price of little girls.

I tuck the letter beneath a tray of perfume oils, the ceramic pots clinking in the deep quiet of the house as I slip the paper between two rabbit hides.

I do not hide it very well.

And then I drift from the room.

34

An Ending

I SIT in my little room in the government office. It is quiet. No one shares the women's quarters with me anymore.

My belongings lie packed and ready in the centre of the small space, and I wait with my back against the wall. I could not sleep. Dreams of my father plaguing me again.

A sharp knock raps on the door and Man Seok's voice calls for me. "Are you ready, Dan Ji *ssi*?"

I peer about my small room, at the rolled blanket and low table. I do not know if I am ready. I think a part of me must surely stay behind, sunken too deep into this valley to ever truly tear itself away.

My shutters swing open and Man Seok fills the open space, cold mountain air creeping inside. "Come," is all he says.

And I do. Climbing to my feet, I hand Man Seok my small roll of belongings. His fingers press against mine as he takes them, his touch sending messages through my skin, whispers. I look away from his dark eyes, black filled to the brim with promises, and instead peer down at my small pile of belongings in his hands. Choon Shim's things are rolled into mine, her clothes, mine now I suppose, unless there is someone back home in Hanseong who wants them.

Man Seok asks again, "Are you ready?"

This time I have an answer. "Yes. I am ready."

He nods and leaves me be, stepping outside to crunch across the small courtyard to wait in the snow. I collect the last of my belongings and follow him outside, peering at the north facing mountain rising beyond the walls, covered with clinging mist.

I hesitate in the snow and carefully place the black silk *nambawi* over my braided hair. It fits well, settling low across my ears and neck, warm where the day is cold. Snow falls heavy from the sky. The thick rabbit fur is soft against my skin. I am suddenly unsure why I did not wear it long before.

Man Seok says nothing when I join him. He sees the *nambawi* but his expression does not change.

But that is his way.

Taking my pack, he walks ahead of me to the group of men and horses waiting in the main courtyard, securing my belongings to a cart. The other cart is overseen by the office inspector and his men, the group who arrived so recently from the capital on Magistrate Hong's request. Lord Song sits inside their cart, reduced to a caged animal. Still, his dignity has not been lost. He sits with his head held high despite the cold, despite the snow building on his shoulders and hair. His eyes still burn fire and fury.

Other prisoners are in our custody too of course, Secretary Baek and other mercenaries, but none so important as Lord Song. None that must make the journey with us to Hanseong. In the capital city he will be questioned by men far superior and of higher rank than anyone here in this isolated valley. Higher even than the office inspector.

Perhaps even the prince himself will attend the interrogation and trial.

Lord Song's soldiers fill the government office, captive wherever they will fit until the prison building is fully reconstructed. They will be tried and executed upon Magistrate Hong's return, if the result of the trial should be favourable to his indictment, as it surely must be. The evidence against him has mounted up, one of the office inspector's men discovering an incriminating letter within the hidden house during the raid. Just another thread among all the others to tie Lord Song to this crime. A pivotal one though, the strongest thread we have to bind the hidden house and all its treasures to the trafficking case.

Behind me someone clears his throat, and I turn to find Guard Yu standing there, smiling widely. He is dressed in new clothes today, newly promoted and filled with pride. *Secretary* Yu now. While Magistrate Hong travels to the capital to testify on this case, Secretary Yu will be left in charge of this place. A trusted man. And a loyal one.

Who was once the son of a servant.

I smile.

"Damo Dan Ji," he greets me. "I hope you will travel safely. And that you will return Damo Choon Shim well to her family."

I nod as Man Seok appears by my side to make his own farewells. Just as we turn to leave, after Magistrate Hong and the office inspector have already ridden from the office gates, Secretary Yu calls me back.

"I cannot help but be curious." He is breathless from hurrying after me. "Mistress Song Seorim, she remains at her father's home?"

"Yes," I answer. I watch him carefully, wondering if Song Seorim will be the ghost that haunts Secretary Yu. Like ginger taffee haunts me. As Poong Yi surely haunts Man Seok.

Secretary Yu shifts uncomfortably beneath my gaze. "What do you suppose will happen to her after her father is charged?"

A beautiful girl in the marketplace, glimpsed once by Guard Yu while he was walking with his old *halmeoni*.

I do not answer.

The family members of traitors are marked as traitors too. Secretary Yu knows this. It is the way of the world.

"It is only..." He clears his throat. "I ask because she cannot be cast down and made a servant. She cannot become a *gisaeng*. Her mind is gone." He pauses. "What happens to traitors who cannot work?"

I shake my head, wishing he had not asked, and I say nothing at all as I leave him behind and mount the horse that waits for me. Secretary Yu waves but I do not return it, my stomach churning.

Perhaps Song Seorim will haunt my dreams too.

We travel the length of the day, the wind rolling off the mountains like ice. The air burns my face, my skin half cold and half hot, cheeks flushed. My face still aches, though the swelling has gone down. Secretary Yu described it for me once, skin black and yellow with bruising, one eye smaller than the other and still puffed. The office inspector's men send glances my way as we travel, staring from over their shoulders and behind raised hands. I pretend not to see. I do not care what they think of me. Man Seok rides at my side, and he does not care either.

THE DAY GROWS LONG, shadows deep as we reach the end of the valley, exit over the far hills into the mountains beyond. For a while I ride alongside Lord Song's moving prison, but when I catch his eye he smiles at me.

As if he knows something I do not.

As if he knows exactly what awaits him in Hanseong.

I fall behind and watch his broad back as the cart carrying him pulls ahead, filled suddenly with deep unease.

Corruption runs deep, Dan Ji. Have you not seen this yet?

Man Seok's words, bitter and sharp.

But I cannot believe the prince would let Lord Song go. Not after all the crimes committed.

He couldn't.

Yet a sickness swells in my belly, sour and uncertain. And I no longer meet Lord Song's eye as we travel. Nor Man Seok's either.

When it becomes too dark to safely continue, the office inspector orders us to stop for the night in a small clearing among the trees. The snow is deep here beneath the pines and blood red *jumok*, their branches thick and reaching. Fires are lit to keep the winter at bay and soon the ground has turned to mush, churned by the many feet crossing our camp back and forth. Guards pull up tents for the officers. The rest of us lie on straw mats near the fires, men huddled in the darkness, wracked with shivers. Lord Song's wooden cage is covered with heavy canvas to keep the heat inside, and a rotating shift of guards is set to last the night.

I watch the bulky shadow of his cart in the flickering black. I am no fool. Even if Lord Song is executed after his trial, even if we manage to tie these crimes to his in-laws in the port town and indict them too … even then we've barely touched the organisation he worked for. We have not cut the head from the snake; we have barely nipped the merest tip of its tail.

I stare at the wide inky sky, my heart heavy with the truth.

In Joseon there will always be other valleys.

There will be other girls.

I sleep fitfully through the night, the stamping of horses invading my dreams, men complaining and shifting in the darkness. The cold creeps inside my bones, deep and needling.

I WAKE SUDDENLY TO SHOUTING.

Morning has dawned, light squeezing through the trees to fall on the forest floor. Pushing my body stiffly from my mat I try to focus, mind still thick with sleep.

Men huddle around one end of the clearing, pushing and shoving each other, their voices loud, ringing across the clearing.

I stand slowly, nausea rising in my throat.

The men surround Lord Song's small cage, the canvas used to cover him for the night pulled away and discarded, snow soaking the woven threads.

The prisoner lies on his side, the doors to his cage still locked.

I circle around until I see his face.

Skin blue.

Eyes wide.

Blood trickling from his ear.

Lord Song lies dead across his prison floor, one arm caught awkwardly beneath his heavy body.

"His heart gave out." It is Man Seok by my side.

His voice is low and steady, but mine when I answer shakes with disbelief.

"How could this happen? He was well. Only yesterday he was well! He was to face trial."

"He is old. And the night was cold."

I shake my head, it cannot be real. After everything that has happened. An ending like this. Snuffed out in the blink of an eye. Like a candle.

He has faced nothing. No justice has been forged. Lord Song's family name remains clear.

I blink at Man Seok, wanting him to tell me it is not real, that this is not the true ending of everything we have worked so hard for. That I have changed myself for.

It cannot be the ending Choon Shim has died for.

Man Seok simply shakes his head. "Lord Song was travelling to face interrogation in Hanseong. Fear is a killer. And he was an old man. His heart was weak."

Lord Song had not seemed weak. Yesterday as he smiled at me. As if he knew something I did not.

Tears sting my eyes and I turn so Man Seok cannot see, embarrassed how much it hurts me, this ending. How it suffocates me and fills my mind with images of Choon Shim who is dead for nothing.

A weak heart.

Because of a weak heart, Lord Song has escaped me.

I cannot stay in front of this ending a moment longer, cannot hold still. I think I must scream out loud. Biting down on my lips, I suppress the sounds building within me, clamp them tight.

Stumbling into the trees I leave the campsite behind, my feet sinking and sliding in the snow that covers the winding roots of the forest floor. I swipe my cold hands across my cheeks, knuckles hard against my bruises. I do not care. If he is dead I do not care. It is only that it is not right. It is not the right way for this to end.

I sink down beside a *jumok* tree. Hands deep in the wet snow.

And then stop crying. Instead grow utterly still.

It is unbelievable that I see it.

Inconceivable.

Yet I do.

Glinting in the morning sunlight that filters between the branches. Shimmering from within the snow. I lean over slowly, so very slowly, to pick it up between my swollen fingers, staring.

Staring.

Within moments I am on my feet, striding back toward the campsite filled with rage, filled with purpose and a storm that is brewing and building. It has not ended this way. It has not. I burst from the forest, catching sight first of the office inspector ordering his men back and forth. He points as they begin to dig a hole, deep and long within the dark frozen earth.

A grave.

I march toward him, though just before I reach the gravesite I find myself hesitating, my attention suddenly coming to rest on Magistrate Hong.

I cannot see his face. He stands alone at the edge of the road, hands folded neatly behind his back, gazing out into the forest.

Was it him? Did he do this?

I hesitate.

It could have been. And yet…

I glance across at the men gathering by the gravesite. Skin stained with dirt and sweat, official uniforms askew and travel-worn after the long night. Eyes cold and mouths hard.

I do not know who they are. Not really. These men wear

government uniforms and carry official weapons. And they hold their heads high and respond to their commander when he shouts for them to dig faster, harder. I watch them work and in my ears the sound of coins clink between palms, passing hand to hand, lining pockets of official uniforms.

Perhaps Lord Song's former friends do not wish their secrets spilled so easily.

My breathing turns shallow. Fast.

Then I see Man Seok.

He leans against Lord Song's empty wooden prison. Watching me, black eyes flickering across my fingers and the thing I hold there.

Waiting to see what I will do.

I stare back at him, locked in place. On the inside my body is raging, heart hammering, blood roaring. Outwardly I am utterly still.

Man Seok.

He's done it before.

I sway, head light. As I have, too.

For it was my own hands that twisted our case, my fingers that pointed and pressured and my words which convinced a woman to give false testimony. I was cold and detached.

And for what?

My fingers open and the needle drops from my hand onto the snow. Long and thin and shimmering in the sunlight.

An acupuncture needle. Stained with Lord Song's blood.

I stand on it with my boot heel, grinding it beneath the earth, digging down until it can no longer be seen at all.

And then I walk across to stand beside Lord Song's gravesite, watch numbly as the dead prisoner's body is dropped unceremoniously into the deep pit. He lands with a heavy thud, head twisted at an odd angle, in a way his neck could never have turned in life. His eyes still stare blankly, already crusted with fresh dirt. No one has bothered to close them.

Corruption runs deep, Dan Ji. Have you not seen this yet?

I ignore Man Seok's creeping words.

Lord Song's skin is pale like river stone but soon the earth covers that too. The drops of blood gathering at his ear are soaked away until it's as if they were never there at all.

When he disappears beneath the ground I am thinking of the sea. Slowly I pull the *nambawi* from my head and let it drop onto the mud at my feet.

Epilogue

I STAND with my head bowed before the police chief, eyes locked on the polished floor at my feet. The air in his office is cold, though already, not quite as cold as only days before.

The seasons are turning it seems. Soon it will be spring.

"You requested a transfer, Damo Dan Ji."

It is not a question. The police chief knows it to be true. Yet he raises his eyebrows and awaits my answer nonetheless.

"Yes sir. I heard of a need for experienced *damo* at the Tamnado office."

He leans back in his chair to study me. We are alone, candlelight flickering across the crowded shelves, darkness seeping from the ceiling.

"You like the idea of living in such an isolated place? An island so far from home?" This time he does not await my answer, instead clearing his throat as if already tired of this conversation. "You have found a taste for adventure, no doubt, after your time in the north. Perhaps Hanseong is small after all you have seen?"

"Hanseong is the largest city in the kingdom, sir."

The police chief's eyes flash and I bow my head lower, biting my tongue.

"You have not learned so very much during your time away, it seems." His voice now is cold and hard, chest swelling as he takes up all the space behind his desk. A large man. And powerful. Not one to be trifled with. "Despite your clear capacity to resolve complex cases, Damo Dan Ji, you are not indispensable to me. Nor will you be on Tamna Island. Despite your growing … reputation."

"Yes sir," I breathe. He has heard the rumours then. They swell and seep through the *damo* quarters, spill over into the official buildings and training grounds to rise high enough to reach even the police chief's ears. *Battle axe. Rebellious. Disobedient. Corrupt. Law breaker.*

Murderess.

They say many things about me these days. Most of them true.

It does not matter.

I have made my decision.

When the police chief applies his seal to my transfer papers I am thinking once again of the ocean, of a small guesthouse beside the waves and a life that will never be mine.

The first step.

The woman painted by those rumours is me. As I could be.

I've taken the first step already. I tell myself Heo Tae Hak was a bad man, a mercenary who worked for Lord Song and committed many cruel deeds.

And yet…

What is so very different between one mercenary and another? What is so different between Heo Tae Hak and that other man, long dead, with his hand outstretched to me in the snow, a gift of ginger taffee on his palm. Both men walked and breathed and *lived*. Both are now dead.

Both will haunt me.

As Choon Shim does.

The first step.

Who do I want to become?

Someone different.

Someone who will not bend. My first step will be my last. I will not stray again. I will not lose myself.

I tread from the police chief's office into the cool air of the yard, inky darkness dripping from the black tiles and curling awnings of the government buildings. There is no moon tonight. The sky is black, stretching overhead and pressing down, thick and heavy.

I have not walked far when a hulking shadow looms from an open archway as if waiting for me, lit from behind into silhouette by weak torchlight. My precious transfer papers are snatched from my outstretched fingers before I have a chance to hold them back.

Jo Man Seok turns his broad back to me as he reads my orders, angling the papers toward the flame-light of the sparking torch. I wait silently for him to finish. And I close my eyes, face angled at the sky, breathing deep.

I have not seen so very much of Man Seok since our return to Hanseong. At first it was because I brought Choon Shim's body home to her family. Afterwards though, my absence from his side was by my design. And he is aware of it. As the days stretched on and I did not speak with him, did not look him in the eye, he knew.

Yet here he stands, expression carefully blank, shoulders tight and fists clenched as he reads. Finally, he lifts his head, face half hidden by shadow as he hands the papers back, his voice low.

"You are leaving then."

I lift my chin. "Yes."

He says nothing, expression betraying nothing. Only his chest rises and falls faster than it should. Eventually he breaks the silence. "Why so far away?"

"It was the furthest I could find."

He hesitates. From within his uniform he pulls a shimmering black bundle and offers it to me, rabbit fur and silk. My *nambawi*. Stained with mountain mud from Lord Song's gravesite.

Man Seok's voice is steady and flat. No emotion creeps beneath his words. "You left this behind."

"I don't want it."

He says nothing, black eyes deep and dark, until his silence compels me to add, "It doesn't fit me."

"Liar." The ghost of a smile touches his mouth and my breath catches in my throat. He shifts closer, boots crunching. "You chose the furthest post from Hanseong you could find."

My voice is barely a whisper. "Yes."

"And it is the furthest post from me."

"Yes."

He flinches. Only a little. But his face does not change. His voice does, though, slight desperation creeping beneath his words. "You shouldn't leave Hanseong, Dan Ji *ssi*. Have you not heard? Envoys came from over the sea. The rumours say they wish to march armies through our lands."

"For what?"

"To attack beyond our borders to the north." Man Seok hesitates. "Diplomacy did not end well. It seems the king refused to receive their letters."

My heart thuds against my chest. "What does that matter?"

A bitter laugh escapes Man Seok's lips. "You are smarter than that. War stirs. Things will soon begin to change."

"They already have. They've changed." I fling the words at him, my voice vicious. For long moments afterwards I force myself to be silent, breathing heavily, fingers clenching into fists. Hands shaking. Until I can remain silent no more. "Did you do it, Man Seok? Was it you?"

He stares. Not even blinking. "Did I do what?"

It is a challenge. He wants me to say those words out loud, the ones that carve deep inside my chest, slicing flesh and burning bone, crunching and cutting. For a whole month I have carefully avoided those words. So carefully.

It could have been anyone. Anyone with access to the morgue where the needles were stored in the valley's government office. It could have been Magistrate Hong himself, he had every reason to wish for Lord Song's death. Or it could have been one of the men we travelled with, a man paid to silence a traitor of the organisation we had almost, *almost* begun to uncover.

Or it could have been Man Seok.

Seeking justice where he believed he would receive none.

As he has done before.

I clear my throat, which is suddenly thick and swollen, and Man Seok steps closer in the darkness. So close now I could reach out to touch him if I wished.

I don't.

"Do you have evidence?" His head is bowed low, angled toward mine.

"No." I cannot meet his eyes. Stare instead at the stony ground. At the shadows creeping across our boots. "Yet I did. In my hands." We are so close now but never touching, my face almost against his chest. I watch the swell of his breath beneath his uniform, staring at the mud-stained *nambawi* clutched so tightly between his fingers. "I held proof of murder."

"And yet?"

"I left it behind … in the mountains."

Silence blooms between us and I peer up into his face, half hidden in shadows. "Tell me it wasn't you."

Black eyes. Mouth tight. He says nothing. Only stares down at me, unmoving and carefully expressionless.

As is his way.

I step back, out of his reach.

One step.

Two.

My boots crunch across the stony ground.

We are alone in the vast courtyard. It is late now, flames flickering weakly against the high stone walls. I stand still. "You asked me once who I want to become."

"I asked you other things too." There is almost a plea in his voice now, and it makes me think of blue light in the morning, of the feel of his bare skin beneath my hands.

I take another step back. Away.

"And you warned me, too," I whisper. "Of what it means to be like you."

He doesn't move, frozen in place like a village *jangseung* totem, carved from wood with empty blank eyes. Eyes only for me.

"I do not wish to become a woman who murders criminals, Man Seok. Who doesn't believe in the world around me. Who makes decisions on behalf of others. It is not right."

He is so still I think he hasn't heard. Until finally he lifts his head. "You do not wish to become like me."

My breath catches in my throat. "Will you … will you

leave the police? Will you go to your uncle's guesthouse beside the sea?"

"Without you?"

I take deep breaths but do not answer.

Man Seok only stares through the dark, black eyes glittering in the flame-light, reflecting orange fire. His mouth twists into a bitter smile.

"I travel tomorrow," I announce to shake the feeling creeping over me. I am angry at Man Seok. Furious with him. Hurt by him. That is all I need to remember. The rest I will forget. The bitter smile and the fire in his eyes.

Blue light mornings and bare skin.

Wiped from my memory.

"Be well, Man Seok."

I wait for him to reply but he does not, his hands clutching the stained *nambawi*. And finally, I spin on my heel and stride through the courtyard toward the women's quarters. I pretend the ache in my chest is from the cold. And I do not look back.

In that isolated valley to the north I came so very close to losing myself, to scattering pieces of me across the winding black river, leaving them behind to feed the hungry wolves. So close.

Never again.

I walked that first step just as Man Seok warned.

But now I will carve my own path.

"Soon it will be spring," I murmur beneath my breath as I walk, boots crunching across the stony ground. I take deep breaths and prepare myself for this fresh start I have created. A new place, a new role. A new life.

There will be other cases.

Other threads.

And I am a *damo* of the *podocheong* and I will not stray.

Want more historical fiction?

Thank you for reading A SONG FOR LONELY WOLVES, the first instalment in the Joseon Detective series by Lee Evie. Keep an eye out for Dan Ji's return in book two and book three of this trilogy!

If you enjoyed this novel, please consider leaving a review, which helps greatly in sharing this work with other readers.

For more historical fiction set in old Korea, sign up to Lee Evie's bookclub for fiction updates and receive a FREE BOOK - *Barely Fields: A Joseon Love Stor*y - a gentle romance told in verse:

www.leeevie.com

PROMISE SEASON
PROMISE SERIES BOOK ONE

A slave girl.

A spy.

A promise.

JOSEON DYNASTY, KOREA.

A humid summer storm rages across the Pavilion, the greatest entertainment house in the sprawling city of Hanyang. Within its stifling walls a *gisaeng* slave girl hides a fugitive in her bed, unexpectedly saving the life of a young man who is not all he seems.

Immediately Seorin is thrust into a razor-edged world of conspiracy and spies, doomed rebellion and murky intrigue. For the first time in years, she glimpses an opportunity for change.

Yet it is not her freedom Seorin so desperately desires, but something far more precious. She will risk anything, even death, to gain it.

A dark and romantic historical adventure set in old Korea.

PROMISE SEASON is available now!

About Lee Evie

LEE EVIE is a historical fiction author.

She writes with a focus on Korean history and loves dark adventures with a heavy dose of danger and romance.

When she's not writing, Lee Evie can be found watching drama, which she will do for hours on end. She believes drama watching is the ultimate joy of life. Even when they make her cry.

An avid photography and travel lover, Lee Evie thinks stories are the most precious gift to the universe.

Visit her website at: www.leeevie.com

SIGN UP to Lee Evie's monthly free bookclub for all the latest news on her historical Korean fiction novels.

www.leeevie.com

Acknowledgments

Huge thank you as always to my family and friends who support me and my writing dreams every day. Special thank you for Gus, Rory, Margie, Jane for the epilogue, my wonderful writing group, Sue and Kristy, Kirsty, Nicole and all the rest!

An enormous special thank you to readers, listeners and new friends, such as Lizzie and everyone else! You guys are the best!

Thank you to Jenny for my gorgeous covers, and my Korean cultural editor Kim for your amazing help, and also to my past Korean language teacher and wonderful friend Lee, for introducing me to everything.

Printed in Great Britain
by Amazon